JOANNA TOYE

THE
VICTORY GIRLS

Complete and Unabridged

MAGNA
Leicester

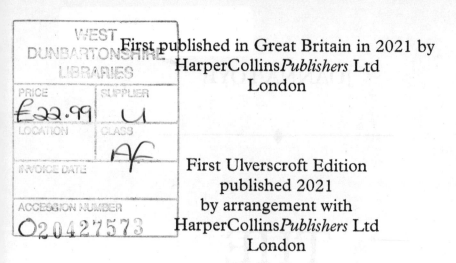

First published in Great Britain in 2021 by
HarperCollins*Publishers* Ltd
London

First Ulverscroft Edition
published 2021
by arrangement with
HarperCollins*Publishers* Ltd
London

A catalogue record for this book is available
from the British Library.

ISBN 978-0-7505-4916-5

Published by
Ulverscroft Limited
Anstey, Leicestershire

Printed and bound in Great Britain by
TJ Books Ltd., Padstow, Cornwall

This book is printed on acid-free paper

*To all shop workers, past and present —
you are much appreciated.*

1

It seemed as if the whole world was on the move and had chosen this particular day and this particular time to do it. The platform was seething with people.

'Mind your backs!' bawled the porters. They were women doing a man's job, thanks to the war, and they were good at it too, as they snaked through the crowd wheeling luggage.

Khaki, navy, and Air Force blue mingled with tweed or cloth coats and the occasional fur; forage caps vied with Homburgs, trilbies, and the velvet, felt, and feathers of women's headwear. Cigarettes and jutting elbows were a constant hazard as people craned their necks and waved at travelling companions.

Lily Collins gasped as she tripped over a suitcase and fell against a middle-aged man.

'Excuse me!' he said sarcastically.

Alongside Lily, Jim Goodridge gave him a glare and took her arm.

'So much for the age of chivalry! Are you all right?'

'Yes, thanks.' Lily righted her hat on her blonde curls. 'Can you see them?'

They were looking for their friends, Gladys and Bill. He was one of the many servicemen and women returning to duty, and in Bill's case, who knew for how long, depending on where his ship was sent. He might even be away till the end of the war, whenever that might be.

'No,' said Jim, frustrated. 'I thought they'd be easy to spot. I wasn't expecting it to be so busy. We should have met them outside.'

'Aye, aye!'

He wheeled around to see Bill behind him, his kit-bag over his shoulder, his ginger-blond hair peeking out from under his sailor's cap.

'There you are!' cried Lily. 'We thought we'd never find you!'

'With Gladys the size she is?' grinned Bill. Their first baby was due in June. 'I've parked her on a couple of crates. With all this crush, she came over a bit funny.'

He was putting a brave face on things; he had to. But Lily knew how concerned he was about Gladys having the baby without him around. On their wedding day last year he'd asked Lily, as her best friend, to look after Gladys when he wasn't there — and if he never came back.

Bill was a wireless operator on a cruiser, escorting convoys and under daily threat from U-boats and air attack, but he and Lily had never before spoken seriously about the danger he was in. Most serving men on leave didn't talk about it; her own brothers didn't. Bill's words had brought Lily up short and made her feel slightly sick — and that was before there was a baby on the way.

Bill had hardly got the words out when the empty train came clanking in under the blacked-out roof. It banged against the buffers with a screech of brakes and a theatrical puff of steam.

'Funny isn't it,' said Bill. 'When you start your leave, the train's always at least an hour late. But when it comes to going back, it's bang on time.'

2

'Hello!' Gladys joined them. She was trying to sound cheerful, but it was about as convincing as the bacon substitute 'macon' — made with mutton — that the Government had briefly tried to promote. Apart from two spots of rouge, her round face was pale, except around the eyes, which were already suspiciously pink.

Bill put his arm round her protectively.

'I'll let everyone else pile on first,' he said. 'It's not worth trying to get a seat.'

Lily nodded and they stood there, the four of them, no one really having anything to say, buffeted by people pushing past and around them. Lily hated goodbyes — didn't everyone? But Gladys would be in bits afterwards, and Lily didn't want her having to walk home on her own. It was lucky that Bill's departure was on their half-day from Marlow's. The two of them had been friends since Lily's very first day at the town's big store. They'd seen each other through several ups and downs and Lily wasn't about to fail Gladys in this one.

The crowd gradually thinned and with the press of people dispersed, Lily could see the stained slabs, littered with cigarette ends, under her feet. The WVS tea bar, in which her mother, Dora, often served, was doing a brisk trade as people stocked up on something for the journey. The train already looked crammed.

'Bill,' said Lily tentatively, 'hadn't you better . . . ?'

Jim took the initiative, shaking him by the hand.

'Good luck,' he said. 'And don't worry about Gladys. We'll take good care of her.'

'Thanks, mate.' The way Bill was gripping Jim's hand spoke for the emotion he couldn't express any other way. He leant and kissed Lily's cheek. 'You take care of yourself too, Lily, no getting into trouble. I

3

know what you're like!'

'I'll be good, promise!'

'Right then. We'll leave you to it.'

Jim put his hand under Lily's elbow and they moved a few feet off, through other couples spinning out the time till the last possible moment — husbands and wives, boyfriends and girlfriends, sisters and brothers, friends, parents, daughters and sons. A lot of eyes were being dabbed, a lot of last-minute instructions issued about not forgetting to write, and there was a lot of desperate clinging.

At the newsstand, Jim looked at the small selection of paperbacks on offer, but Lily watched as Bill took Gladys in his arms — he could just about get them round her — and rocked her gently in a hug. Gladys had hidden her face in his naval greatcoat and Bill was cradling her head and saying something — 'You know I love you,' if Lily's amateur lip-reading was anything to go by. Gladys was nodding her head against his shoulder, but Lily could see her whole body shaking.

Her friend's parents had been killed in the Coventry Blitz. She only had her gran, and Bill, who'd been brought up in an orphanage, had had no one till he'd met Gladys; they were everything to each other. Lily looked away, blinking back a tear of her own. When she looked back, Gladys's face was visible again and Bill was tucking a strand of her light-brown hair behind her ear. As he gently untangled himself, Lily touched Jim's arm and they moved forward again.

The guard was coming down the train closing the doors. Bill grabbed his kitbag, gave Gladys a final kiss and with a thumbs-up to Jim and Lily, squeezed aboard. He'd barely closed the door before the signal changed and the train, with a painful jolt and deafening

4

clanks, chugged slowly out.

Bill leant out of the window.

'Be good!' he called, jovial to the last — or pretending to be.

Others ran down the platform, clutching outstretched hands through lowered windows. That was beyond Gladys, but she waved her hanky, tears rolling down her face. At least she could let herself cry, thought Lily. Bill obviously felt just as torn but couldn't show it.

She stood on one side of her friend, Jim on the other, waving frantically like everyone else left behind. And as the train curved away down the track, every single turn of the wheels chanted their desperate, silent prayer: 'stay safe, stay well . . . stay alive.'

★ ★ ★

Having walked Gladys back home, it was almost dark by the time Lily and Jim felt they could leave her. She lived with her gran, so she wasn't totally on her own, but Florrie Jessop wasn't exactly the twinkly grandma of storybooks. She'd been too long a widow and had had things her own way for too many years before Gladys had come to live with her. As they left, Mrs Jessop was eyeing up the quarter of peppermint creams that Bill had left for Gladys — they helped with her pregnancy indigestion. There was no doubt who'd be scoffing the lion's share of those.

For once, Lily and Jim didn't have much to say to each other as they walked home themselves. Or rather, they did, but neither wanted to broach it. Lily knew Jim would have been affected by the sight of all those servicemen and women; he constantly cursed his poor eyesight for keeping him out of the Army. He made up for it as an air-raid warden and with fire-watching duties, but Lily knew he never felt he was doing enough, and she'd started to feel that way herself. She'd looked sidelong at the Wrens and WAAFs and ATS girls as they boarded the train. Where were they going? What were their jobs? Did she owe the fact that she was here at all to their skill as cypher clerks and plotters and searchlight operators?

At Christmas, Jim had given her a joke engagement ring and promised she'd have the real thing when he'd saved up enough, but he knew she was considering joining up. She'd be old enough this year. He'd promised he'd never hold her back and he meant it, but Lily was torn. She loved him and she loved her job. Joining up would take her away from both, and they might not be the same — her job might not even be there — when she came back. And then there was Gladys. How could she desert her in her hour of need?

Her sigh was audible and Jim squeezed her hand. He knew what she was thinking. He wouldn't try to influence her; this was something only Lily could decide. And that, thought Lily, was the trouble. She didn't have the answer.

★ ★ ★

As she and Jim rounded the corner on their way to work next day, the vicious wind that blew down the High Street at this time of year nearly lifted Lily off her feet. But when she raised her eyes, there was the sight that always lifted her heart: the curved façade of Marlow's on its corner position at the top of the hill. But today there was something different. Jim stopped dead and Lily stopped too. The store's painters were setting ladders against the frontage.

'It's happening!' said Jim exultantly. 'At last!'

At Christmas, the owner, Cedric Marlow, had announced that changes were afoot and the first was to drop the apostrophe from the store's name. 'So it is no longer my family's personal fiefdom' had been his actual words, not that many of the staff understood what 'fiefdom' meant. But Marlow's — with an apostrophe — would in future be Marlows — no apostrophe, like Selfridges and Harrods in London. Hinton might only be a small Midland town, but you had to set your sights high, didn't you?

Lily pressed Jim's arm. Marlows (as it would be from today) had been good to them. It had brought them together, for a start, and seen them both rise through the ranks — Lily to second sales on Childrenswear, and Jim to first sales on Furniture — and, in addition, deputy supervisor on the first floor. That didn't mean they could be late, though, and they set off again, Jim pulling Lily up the hill behind him, puffing and blowing and making out she was a ton weight. Lily went along with it; she loved looking from behind at the shape of his head and the way his dark hair went into a little duck's tail in the nape of his neck.

As they reached the top of the slope, Beryl was unlocking her door. Another friend, she had a bridal hire business in one of the store's former window spaces. After a bomb had landed in the town's main shopping street, damaging several shops and blowing their plate glass to smithereens, Marlows had cleverly turned its damaged windows into four small shop units.

'Morning!' carolled Beryl. With a wink and a toss of her head at the painters, she added, 'While they're

7

here, I might ask them to give me a touch-up.'

Lily smiled. You could count on Beryl for a bit of innuendo — and the brass neck to try and wheedle a free paint job. She'd probably get it, as well — all peroxide and black-market perfume, the Americans would have called her 'sassy'. And the paintwork on 'Beryl's Brides' *was* looking a little tired.

Someone else looking tired lumbered slowly towards them. Gladys was still working, of course — she was a sales assistant on Toys.

'She's a size, isn't she? And the baby's not due till June. How was she when Bill left?'

'Take a guess.' Lily watched Gladys make her weary way. She probably hadn't slept without Bill beside her. 'She's going to need a lot of support.'

'Literally,' added Jim, as he moved away to offer Gladys his arm.

'Such a gent,' nodded Beryl approvingly. 'You've got a gem there, Lily. Even if he hasn't come good with a proper ring yet!'

⋆ ⋆ ⋆

'Mr Goodridge? May I have a word?'

Jim was poring over the weekly sales targets, which might have been achievable if they'd had the goods to sell. Instead, the store mostly relied on unreliable supplies of Utility furniture and people who'd fallen on hard times offering their genuine Sheraton sideboards, which turned out to be repro, and not very good repro at that. He straightened up to see Miss Frobisher, the Childrenswear buyer and first-floor supervisor. Like him, she had a dual role — another wartime economy.

8

'Of course. What can I do for you?'

Tall, blonde, thirtyish, and trim in a bird's-eye checked suit, Eileen Frobisher was Lily's boss and her role model in everything, though Lily had a long way to go to achieve Miss Frobisher's poise — and thank goodness, thought Jim. They'd never have got together if Lily had seemed as remote and unattainable as Miss Frobisher, though he knew very well that her appearance was deceptive and she had her very human side. Spotting potential — or perhaps seeing something of herself in Lily — she'd always taken a special interest in her.

'Miss Collins. Lily.' She never wasted words. 'Once she reaches her birthday, what are her intentions?' Jim frowned, waiting. 'I'm not planning a party,' Miss Frobisher continued with a wry smile. 'I leave that to you. But she'll be eighteen. I mean her intentions about joining up.'

This was awkward. Jim craned his neck to look over her shoulder for Lily. She was absorbed in writing out price tickets for a pile of tiny trousers.

'Wouldn't you be better asking her?'

'If she knew what she was doing,' Miss Frobisher replied crisply, 'she'd have told me by now, I know. So I take it there's an element of doubt.'

Jim sighed. As usual, Field Marshal Frobisher had got the situation taped.

'She's not sure,' he said slowly. 'She wants to do her bit for the war. But you also know how she loves what she's doing here. She's afraid that if she joins up, she won't have a job to come back to.'

Miss Frobisher nodded.

'As I thought,' she said. 'Thank you.'

She swept away, leaving Jim staring after her, as

wise to what she was thinking as he was convinced that his department could meet its sales target. She discussed the other staff quite freely with him, but it was different with Lily because she and Jim were a couple. And Lily *was* different anyway. She always had been. That was the attraction for Jim.

★ ★ ★

On the ground floor, Miss Frobisher sought out Mr Simmonds, the senior supervisor. He was deep in discussion with Gloria, one of the Cosmetics salesgirls, but extricated himself when he saw her and came over.

The staff knew, but no customer who saw them together would have suspected, that they too were a couple. Cedric Marlow didn't encourage liaisons between staff but with the time everyone spent at work, he'd had to accept that they were inevitable. Even so, discretion was his watchword; it might as well have been carved on tablets of stone.

Jim and Lily understood but it didn't stop them snatching a quick kiss if they met on the back stairs. Older and wiser, Peter Simmonds and Eileen Frobisher didn't break the rules quite so blatantly. Instead, he steered her away to a quiet corner where he could smile more openly and where they could speak more freely. They made a striking couple — she tall and fair, he tall, dark, and angular. He'd been a regular Army man who'd had to quit after a trivial, but nagging, shoulder injury.

Eileen smiled at him.

'Don't tell me, Gloria's moaning about stocks of face powder again?'

'Not for much longer,' he replied. 'She's leaving.'

Miss Frobisher, usually imperturbable, gaped.

'She's never been accepted into the WAAF?'

This had been Gloria's long-held ambition, though unlike Lily, duty didn't come into it. Snaring a pilot for a boyfriend — or even better, a husband — was the draw for her.

'She has. She's given me her notice.'

'Well, there'll be someone else doing that if we don't act fast,' said Miss Frobisher briskly. 'Lily Collins. She's thinking of joining up too. So will you please see Mr Marlow and get her promoted to first sales?'

Peter took a step backwards, pretending surprise.

'Speak your mind next time, why don't you!'

'You know I'm right, Peter.' Eileen softened her tone. 'You know how it is in the forces, better pay, better food, better everything, and — Gloria excepted — the feeling that you're doing something for your country. Lily's a girl with a conscience but she'd be completely wasted square-bashing all day and saluting till she fractures her elbow!'

'Thank you. Rubbish my previous career, go ahead!' he teased.

'You know what I mean. She's done nine months, pretty much, as second sales. Please speak up for her. I'm not prepared to lose her — and I don't think Marlows should be either.'

2

Lily had timed her morning break to coincide with Gladys's, thinking her friend would want to talk. Instead, Gladys pushed a coloured postcard across the canteen table. It showed the sun rising over the sea. On the back Bill had written:

Wherever I am, wherever I be,
Nothing can separate you and me.
Our love will go on like the endless seas
And keep us close till we have peace.

Then he'd added:

Love you always and forever, your Bill xxx

'I reckon he made that up all by himself,' said Gladys, awestruck, as if she'd suddenly found herself married to Shakespeare. 'He tucked it under the top sheet. I only found it when I went to bed.'

Lily handed the card back. No wonder Lily's brother Sid, who'd trained with Bill in the Navy, had called him 'a great sloppy date' — and now a poet to boot! Jim was lovely and loving, and clever with words — he loved a crossword and wrote the Marlows staff news-letter every month — but she couldn't imagine him ever saying, or sending her, anything as flowery. And a verse was all very well but not much help when Gladys was having a baby and her husband was half a world away. That was when someone literally close by

12

would be important. Off her mind went again in the same groove: to join up or to stay?

★ ★ ★

'To me . . . about another three inches, I think.'

With Les, Beryl's husband and one of the store's porters, Jim was positioning a newly delivered sideboard. Utility-made, light oak, two cupboards, three drawers, decent workmanship — he didn't see it sticking around for long. Satisfied it was now in prime position, he stood back.

'Thanks, Les.'

Les touched a finger to his forehead in mock-salute.

'Anything to oblige.' He passed Jim a wooden clipboard and Jim squiggled on the form. 'So how's it going? Taken Lily ring shopping yet?'

'Nowhere near! I'm still saving.'

Les did one of his exaggerated eye-rolls; he fancied himself a bit of a comedian.

'Blimey, what for? The Koh-i-Noor?'

'Yes, and a necklace and bracelet to match.' Jim grinned, then frowned. 'What's it to you, anyway? Why are you so keen to hurry it along?'

'Why? I'll tell you for why!' Les rolled his eyes again. 'Me and Beryl married that quick, with our Bobby on the way, we didn't even bother with an engagement ring. Now *she* wants one, doesn't she? So you'd better not set the bar too high!'

★ ★ ★

'No, no, it's out of the question. She's only been at second sales level for what . . . ?' Cedric Marlow, seated

13

at his big mahogany desk, ruffled through Lily's personal file.

'Nine months, sir.'

'Eight, I think you'll find.' Cedric had found the relevant page. It was eight months, two weeks, and two days, in fact. Peter Simmonds had checked, but he didn't correct the older man, who went on: 'You know perfectly well we expect a year at second sales level before promotion to first. Some assistants never move up — and never want to.'

'If I may, sir . . . ' Mr Marlow always needed careful handling. 'That's not the case with Miss Collins. She's already proved she has the potential to go far. And with Miss Frobisher having taken on extra duties . . . '

Cedric raised a warning hand.

'Even so. I like Miss Collins; she's bright and a fast learner. But if we make an exception for her, it sends the wrong message to other staff. It's bad for morale. And we need to keep that up!'

Peter sighed — he hoped not too visibly. He'd already made the argument that Eileen had made to him — and which he believed — that they might lose Lily altogether, but Cedric Marlow was obviously going to dig in his heels. The store's owner might have handed over most of the day-to-day running of things but although he was nearly seventy, he clung on to the power he still had. Perhaps it was precisely because he was approaching seventy, thought Peter with a flash of insight.

Cedric wrote something in his meticulous script on Lily's file, closed it, and re-capped his pen.

'Send Miss Collins to Small Leather Goods for a while. She can change places with the current second sales there. Let her widen her experience on a different

14

floor with different stock, type of customer, and type of purchase. Then come and talk to me again.'

The matter, Peter knew, was closed. For now.

★ ★ ★

'I'm sorry, Lily. This is all my fault.'

Jim and Lily were walking home in the inky dusk. They knew the way almost blindfold by now, and neither wanted to use their torches till they had to, batteries being so hard to come by. Lily couldn't see Jim's profile clearly, but she tilted her head to look up at him anyway.

'Because I've got to wait for my promotion to first sales like everyone else? How do you work that out?'

'Promoting you early'd look like favouritism. Because . . . oh, you know.'

Lily did.

Cedric Marlow was Jim's uncle by marriage but Jim had had nothing to do with his wealthy widowed uncle or his cousin Robert when he'd been young. Jim's family background was much humbler and when he'd needed a job, he'd never expected or asked for preferential treatment — he'd started at the bottom, like Lily, and worked his way up. Maybe his new supervisory role did mean that Mr Marlow had something bigger in mind for him eventually, but as for saying she was being held back because they were a couple . . .

'That's right, make it all about you!' Lily teased, then relented. 'It's fine. I don't mind really. A couple of months on the ground floor on a different department . . . it'll be a chance to get away from you picking me up on things, Mr Deputy Supervisor!'

15

'Honestly? You would tell me if you'd still rather leave and join up?'

'Yes. Of course I would.'

And she would, if only she knew what she really thought. Lily squeezed his hand through two layers of knitted gloves — his and hers, both carefully crafted by her mum. Her mum . . . She always knew what to do. Maybe she'd be able to help her sort it out.

★ ★ ★

As soon as they'd eaten with Dora, Jim, with his armband on, tin hat under his arm, and gas mask over his shoulder, headed out again for ARP duty. With Hitler tied up on the Russian front, air raids had virtually stopped, so Air Raid Precaution these days was more a case of barking 'Put that light out!' at careless householders or businesses working late. But it was still war work, which was more than Lily was doing, just helping her mum wash up.

'I don't know which way to turn, Mum,' she confessed.

Some mothers might have pussyfooted around. Not Dora Collins. Widowed young with the boys, Reg and Sid, under school age and Lily still a baby, Dora had had to stand on her own two feet and speak up for herself — and for others. If you couldn't say what you thought to your own children and give them advice when they needed it, when could you? Dora might mince bread crusts and scrag end, but never words.

'Lily,' she said, scrubbing at a bit of burnt-on sausage on the frying pan, 'you're making a mountain out of mouse droppings here. You love your job. Even if you've got to wait a bit, you're going to get this promotion before too long, that's plain. You're acting as if it's black and white: stay in Hinton with Jim, do your job at Marlows, and do your duty by Gladys, or join the forces or go off to some factory miles away and do your duty by the war. You can easily do both things right here!'

'What? How?' Lily took the clean pan from her mother and balanced it against the crocks already draining. Only the cutlery was dried nowadays, to save wearing out the tea towels. 'Oh, look, if you mean doing ARP or the Auxiliary Fire Service, sitting by the phones all night, when nothing's happening any more, I'm not sure that's for me.'

'Nor am I. Which is why you can start coming with me to the WVS.'

'What?' Lily was glad she'd put the frying pan down or she might have dropped it. 'I can't serve at the tea bar when I'm at work in the day!'

'I know that. Give me some credit!'

'So what can I do? Knit balaclavas? Sew gloves? You know I'm hopeless! And as for the farmworkers' pie scheme, you're the first to say my pastry'd make good shoe leather!'

It was a source of amusement to Jim and of bafflement to Dora, who was an accomplished cook and housekeeper, that Lily was so cack-handed with a pair of knitting needles and heavy-handed with a ball of dough.

'Oh, you don't slide out of it like that!' Lily's mum had a knack of combining what sounded like a scolding with a smile. 'We'll find something for you to do, don't you worry!

Dora let the scummy water out of the sink, shook her fingers dry, and reached for the towel. Like the tea towels, it was worn so thin you could almost see through it.

'We've had twenty sacks of seaboot socks arrive this week. Seems the Navy's got socks coming out their ears, so to speak, when what they really need is polo-neck jumpers. So we've got to unravel the socks, card the wool and rewind it for our knitters. Surely even you can manage a simple thing like that, and if that isn't directly helping the war, I'd like to know what is. And you can do it alongside your job.'

Lily considered.

'Polo-necks . . . for the Navy . . . Some might even end up on Bill's ship.'

'They might well.' Dora dried carefully around her wedding ring, also worn thin. 'Will you do it, then? Will that satisfy your conscience?'

It would be tedious and repetitive, but so was life in the forces a lot of the time, Lily knew, and factory work certainly was. It was still war work — hadn't some minister or other called the WVS the country's 'domestic soldiers'? And if Lily imagined Bill in one of the reknitted jumpers and gave it a human face, well, she could do the work with pride.

'Yes.' She tried out a smile. 'I think it would.'

'Thank goodness for that!' said Dora. She turned away to hang the towel up and to hide a smile. 'We're not all dried-up old biddies in the WVS, you know. There's quite a few younger women, not as young as you perhaps . . .'

That was enough for Lily. She caught her mother round the waist and spun her round.

'You're not a dried-up old biddy, you know you're not! You're still young and you're really pretty, Mum!'

Dora was. She'd never lost her girlish figure, and

her brown hair, cut last year in a more fashionable style, had only a few threads of silver.

'Oh, get away with you!'

Dora sounded pleased, but Lily didn't push it.

Guessing what her daughter was thinking, Dora kissed her forehead, then pulled gently away. Sam, a Canadian corporal, had only been a friend and he was gone now, back home across the sea. But he wasn't forgotten, not by Dora and not by any of them. How could he be, when he'd left them the golden spaniel that he'd adopted and made them promise to take care of?

'Talking of your conscience, it's your turn to take that dog for his night-time lamp post inspection.'

'More like a route march, the way he pulls!' Lily smiled as she took down the dog's lead from the back of the door. Buddy had a lovely temperament but he was only young and, as Dora said, as daft as a bottle of pop. 'But at least it's not square-bashing and it's in my own clothes, not some scratchy uniform!'

3

The following week Lily spent her first evening in the Drill Hall with the WVS, unravelling socks till her eyes went fuzzy. She went to sleep still trying to blink the blurriness away and dreamt she was being chased by a giant ball of wool while a bristling ATS sergeant shouted 'faster, faster!'.

In fact, her evening with the WVS had been far more fun than she'd expected. They'd been a jolly crowd, and though her mum's idea of younger women was not quite Lily's, she'd palled up with a girl not much older than herself. Over copious cups of tea, she'd made Lily laugh about the time she'd tinted her eyebrows with Bisto, only to have it run down her face in the rain. At the end of the evening, Lily had lain down in her own bed, not a dormitory with twenty others with a kit inspection to look forward to in the morning. And she'd still done something worthwhile for the war.

Next day was her first on her new department, so she gave herself a kit inspection anyway and presented herself at Small Leather Goods with well-scrubbed fingernails and a well-pressed blouse. As the Handbags buyer also sourced the department's purses, wallets, and key fobs, Lily would be answerable to the first salesgirl, Rita — Miss Ruddock.

Rita wasn't that much older than Lily — mid-twenties, perhaps, but from asking around, Lily knew that she couldn't be called up because she lived with her father who'd lost a leg in the Great War and had no one else to look after him. Unlike Lily, Rita Rud-dock wasn't very happy with her lot. And despite another Marlows dictum — a cheerful smile at all times — when there were no customers around, it showed.

'I don't know what all this is in aid of,' she sniffed when she'd finished showing Lily where everything was kept. 'Making Betty — Miss Simkins — swap with you, I mean. I hope I'll be getting her back. No offence.'

Why was it that whenever people said that, you automatically did take offence, wondered Lily. And they meant you to.

'They like to move us around sometimes, don't they?' she said innocently. 'To get more experience, to test us out.'

'Betty doesn't need experience, she's got plenty,' said Rita tartly. 'She doesn't need testing, or want to go anywhere else; she's suited here. She's not always got her eye on the next rung of the ladder, like some.'

'Like some'? She meant 'like you', Lily knew. Fortunately, a customer was approaching and Rita moved away; she'd explained that you had to keep an eye on people. Small Leathers was an 'island' depart-ment — four counters in a square — and though most of the goods were under the glass-topped units or in drawers, there was a stand with hanging key fobs and a basket of end-of-line 'oddments' which had to be counted and accounted for at the beginning and end of every day.

Lily smiled at the junior, Annie, who was busy with a duster, polishing an already sparkling countertop. That was a job and a half, as well, with small items constantly being brought out, handled, and put down.

Lily tested herself by opening a few drawers to check that she remembered where things were. At least Rita hadn't skimped on facts, and though Lily suspected it had been more about showing off her superiority than making sure her new assistant was well briefed, she was grateful. She couldn't afford any slip-ups — they'd get back to Mr Simmonds and beyond him to Mr Marlow, Rita Ruddock would make sure of that. Welcome to the ground floor, Lily, she thought.

As the days passed into weeks, however, Lily got to rather like her new role. Rita was no more friendly and Annie was a little mouse of a thing who did as she was told and the rest of the time did her best to make herself invisible. But the ground floor was a livelier place than the first. There were more customers, both male and female — more to see, more going on. The goods Lily was selling were attractive, too. She loved the smell and feel of the leather and enjoyed guiding customers who were undecided, or choosing a gift, asking about colour preferences, or whether the recipient wanted, for example, a little clear window in their wallet where they could put a photograph. As with everything, there wasn't always much choice, of style or of colour, but Rita, Lily had to admit, had an eye for display. She changed the arrangement under the glass-topped counters every fortnight, and sometimes even let Lily help. Lily still watched her step with her, though. She could turn on a sixpence.

Talking about undecided customers, though . . . Lily closed the drawer and placed another purse in front of the woman on the other side of the counter With this last offering, every small coin purse they had was laid out between them, with the customer picking them up, opening and closing them one at a time, laying them back down, then starting the process all over again. There might have been four different colours, but there were only three styles — was it really that difficult?

Still the woman dithered, and Lily's mind wandered — her gaze, too. That was when she saw her — or rather, the back of her. Someone she surely recognised. She was at the neighbouring counter — Scarves, Gloves and Umbrellas.

'Well? Miss Collins?' Startled, Lily snapped back to attention. Rita had loomed up and was standing over her. 'Madam is asking you a question.'

'I-I'm sorry!' Lily exclaimed. 'Erm . . .'

'Perhaps I'd better help the lady myself.' Rita swooped in smoothly. She picked up a calfskin purse, the most expensive style, naturally. 'If I may, madam, this is the one I'd recommend. Beautifully soft, but also hard-wearing.' The woman took it from her. That was all Rita needed. 'And for colour I always think navy's the best. Not as stark as black.'

Mr Marlow didn't really believe in the hard sell, but in this case, Lily could see that it was the only way, and it worked. The customer paid and left, seemingly happy with her decision that hadn't been her decision at all.

Rita nodded to the junior to tidy everything away and pulled Lily to the other end of the counter.

'What the hell were you doing?' she demanded. 'You were miles away! We could have lost the sale altogether!'

'I'm sorry.' Rita was right. 'I saw someone I thought I knew and . . . I got distracted.'

'Someone you thought you . . .' Rita raised her pencilled eyebrows. No gravy browning for her: she

23

had a friend on Cosmetics. 'I don't care if it was the Queen of Sheba! When you're working for me, you keep your mind on the job, OK?'

Lily nodded. She had no doubt that from now on Rita would be on her back with her full weight of authority. That was going to be fun.

Lily had never been so grateful for the working day to end. She'd almost given herself lockjaw, so fixed had been her bright and cheerful smile, and in attempting to please Rita, she'd actually driven one customer away by being too pushy. She opened her locker to get her outdoor things with relief, only to hear the dread words: 'Locker and bag check!'

'Do you know what they're looking for?' she asked the girl next to her.

Spot-checks happened from time to time, usually because there'd been an incident of shoplifting and in case one of the staff was the culprit.

'A scarf, I heard. Jacqmar — one of the pricey ones.'

It would be. But the news came as balm to Lily. She'd been terrified it was something from Small Leathers, one of the key fobs or 'oddments' that could have disappeared while her attention had wandered. In a further panic — not like Lily at all — she'd even wondered if Rita could have taken something herself and would try to blame her for it. She'd better get a grip on herself; she'd be dreaming Rita was chasing her and pelting her with purses next.

The check didn't take long and nothing unusual was found. Lily had never been so glad to get out into the fresh air — nor had Gladys by the look of it.

'You haven't forgotten it's my midwife appointment tomorrow, have you?' Gladys asked anxiously.

She looked exhausted. It was a long day for her

24

now. Lily had asked Jim to keep an eye on her when she'd moved to the ground floor but, like many men, he treated pregnant women like unexploded bombs, so she wasn't very hopeful that he was doing it.

'Half-day closing and a trip to the clinic? I feel quite spoilt!'

Half-day closing meant five hours less of Rita. That was the real treat.

★ ★ ★

Lily's spirits rose even more as she left the store with Gladys again next day. The morning had been misty after rain, but it had turned into a bright and breezy April day by lunchtime. There were bunches of daffs outside the greengrocer's and a sky of china blue. You couldn't help feeling cheerful.

'Remember the old days when we were both young and single and carefree?' she joked. 'Soup and a roll at Peg's Pantry and a matinee at the Gaumont? A pennyworth of toffees each? Now it's meat-paste sandwiches while we wait for the midwife!'

'You don't mind, do you?' Gladys's face had clouded.

'Of course not! The Gaumont's a vile, smoky flea-pit anyway. What were we thinking? This is far nicer!'

The clinic was crowded with women the size of battleships, so Lily stood while Gladys took the only remaining seat, swapping with her when Gladys was called in, and pulling out her murder mystery from the library. The culprit was just about to be unmasked when Gladys reappeared, looking a bit flustered.

'Everything OK?' Lily stuffed her book back in her bag.

'My blood pressure's a bit up since last time. She asked if I was getting enough rest.'

'Does she know what you do for a job? Of course not, you're standing all day!' Lily picked up their gas masks from the floor and stood up herself.

'Not much I can do about that, is there?'

'I'm not so sure. You've got two months to go and you're only going to get bigger. We'll have to think of something.'

Gladys looked horrified. Bill might be a serving sailor, but she'd never been one for making waves.

'Don't be silly, I'm not the first person to have a baby at Marlows.'

Together they moved towards the door.

'And that's exactly what'll happen,' Lily scolded. 'It'll pop out one day on the sales floor if you're not careful.'

She held the door open and they emerged into the street.

'What do you suggest?' Gladys queried. 'I have a lie-down on one of the beds in Jim's department?'

Lily stopped dead, which usually meant she'd had an idea.

'You're on to something there. Not a bed, but why not a chair for you behind the counter?'

Gladys stopped too, in the middle of putting on her gloves.

'Mr Marlow'll never agree to that! Chairs are for customers!'

'A stool then,' Lily improvised. 'Or a ledge for you to perch on.'

'A ledge?' Now they were both laughing. 'You're making me feel like a pouter pigeon!'

Lily took her friend's arm. She decided to drop the

subject — for now. She could always have a word with Jim later.

'Come on, Peg's Pantry for us. You can take the weight off your feet and fluff up your feathers in there!'

Thank goodness she was in the WVS and not the ATS. Here, with her friend, was where Lily's war work lay, no doubt about it.

4

A couple of weeks later, spring had well and truly
sprung and nowhere more so than on the ground floor
of Marlows. With so much leather needed for Army
boots and belts, not much new stock came in to Lily's
department, but those whose goods still managed to
follow the seasons were showing a few different styles
for spring. Plaster hands twirled lacy gloves or gaily
patterned scarves, and tilted umbrellas almost made
you long for April showers. On Costume Jewellery a
stand held a new line in taffeta-covered beads and
bangles which Lily rather coveted. They weren't that
expensive, especially with her discount, and she was
trying to decide whether she could justify a purchase
when she saw her again. This time there was no doubt
in her mind. The woman was definitely someone she
recognised. It was Violet's mother — Mrs Tunnicliffe.

★　★　★

Lily had been thrown together with the pair of them
during an air raid on her first day at work, when
Violet had had hysterics and Lily had calmed her
down. She'd been devastated when the girl had been
killed the following year in an air raid. She hadn't seen
Mrs Tunnicliffe since, but now here she was shopping
at Marlows again.

Lily wondered if she should catch her eye — Mrs
Tunnicliffe was browsing the same bangles Lily had
been looking at. Then, suddenly and very swiftly, she

28

took one and slipped it into her pocket. Lily blinked. That couldn't be right. Mrs Tunnicliffe was very well off. She could have bought the entire display if she'd wanted to. So why was she now leaving the store as if nothing was amiss, smiling graciously as the commissionaire opened the door for her and sweeping out into the sunshine?

'And what planet are you on this time?' Rita, back from her break, caught Lily staring at the store's heavy glass door as it rocked gently shut. 'I hardly dare go on my break; one day I'm going to come back and find you've wandered off!'

Lily would have liked nothing more — not to wander, but to run out after Mrs Tunnicliffe, catch her by the arm and . . . what? Tell her what she'd seen? Ask what was going on? Bring her back to face the music? It was shoplifting, after all.

But Lily couldn't do any of those things, not without thinking through the consequences. And she couldn't leave the department, anyhow, because Rita informed her she was off to 'a meeting' with the Handbags buyer — in other words, a surreptitious cigarette with her on the delivery bay. Still in shock, Lily was left to mull over what she'd seen, though not to understand it. What was going on with Violet's mother? And more to the point, what should she do about it?

★ ★ ★

At dinnertime, she managed to secure a place for herself and Jim at the far end of the staff canteen. When she told him what she'd seen, he stopped shovelling fish pie for a full minute to absorb it.

'What am I going to do?' Lily asked.

29

'You said it yourself,' said Jim reasonably. 'It's shop-lifting. Theft. You have to report it.'

'But Mrs Tunnicliffe . . . How can I?' Lily objected, then sighed. 'You see, I don't think it's the first time she's done it.'

'What?' Jim put down the knife and fork he'd only just picked up again. 'You don't mean you've seen her at it before?'

'No, not exactly. But you remember that scarf that went missing? The Jacqmar one? Mrs Tunnicliffe was in the store and at that very counter the same day. I reckon she took that as well.'

'Come on! You're putting two and two together and getting five thousand!'

'No, she took it, I know. There was something about the way she was acting today — she's done it before, I could tell.'

'But she's got pots of money! Look where she lives, how she lives! She's loaded!'

'I know, I thought that. But money isn't always why people steal, is it?'

Jim took off his glasses, looked at them, and put them on again. It meant he was thinking.

'You mean she's funny in the head? Like Violet was?'

'Violet wasn't funny in the head!' said Lily indig-nantly. 'She had a nervous disposition, that was all.'

'Yes, OK, sorry.' Jim backtracked. 'But she was on tablets for it. Maybe her mother's on tablets too, for some condition or other. Something physical, even. And they make her a bit dopey, so she doesn't know what she's doing. Or maybe it's the . . . well, you know . . . the 'change of life' that women go through.'

'Oh, thanks very much. Us women all go doolally in the end, do we?'

30

'I didn't say that.'

'You didn't have to!' Lily sighed. 'I can't leave it like this, Jim. Whatever I do, I'll have to do something, won't I?'

Miraculously, there was no locker check at the end of the day: either the bangle hadn't been missed, or the staff on Costume Jewellery were covering up its absence in the hope it had been mislaid and would reappear. That happened sometimes with small items — they rolled under a fitment or even under another counter. Ideally, the cleaners would find them overnight. If not, the department would have to report the loss.

All next day Lily turned the problem over and over in her head. She saw the Costume Jewellery buyer talking intently to Mr Simmonds. That evening there was a locker check, as she'd known there would be; obviously nothing was found. Lily knew what she had to do.

'I can't report it,' she told Jim after tea when her mum was upstairs fetching some mending. 'Not just like that. Not till I've given Mrs Tunnicliffe the chance to explain. I'll have to go and see her.'

Jim smoothed the frown from her forehead with his thumbs.

'All right. But I'll come with you,' he said.

★   ★   ★

It was a lovely spring evening for a walk. As they left the narrow streets around Lily's home for the better parts of town, the gardens were exploding vividly into life. Blackbirds and starlings shot in front of them, fearless or desperate, searching for supper for their

31

chicks, while the turtle doves lulled theirs to sleep with their low burbles. Jim had Buddy on the lead. The dog was thrilled by a more exciting walk than his usual trot round the block or along the canal. He slowed their progress, of course, but in the evening sun, neither of them minded.

Mrs Tunnicliffe lived in the smartest part of Hinton, on Juniper Hill, one of the nicest roads. The houses were large with pillars at the ends of their drives and noble-looking trees in the centre of well-groomed lawns which still had flower beds instead of being turned over entirely to veg. The houses had names, not numbers, and on Mrs Tunnicliffe's side of the road, a view over open countryside at the back.

The house looked much as Lily remembered it, with daffodils and narcissi round a monkey puzzle tree on the lawn. But the flowers were wizened and shrivelled and the lawn straggly, the urns by the front door long past their best, and the door-knocker looking tarnished. Jim tied Buddy's lead to the boot scraper while Lily rang the bell and, after a long pause, the door opened.

Last time it had been opened by a maid: now it was Mrs Tunnicliffe herself standing there. Everything fell into place. The maid and the garden boy must have been called up, hence the neglect. Mrs Tunnicliffe was changed, as well, now Lily saw her close to. She'd been well-dressed and elegant before, with hair that was still brown and softly waved. She was still elegant, but her hair had a lot more grey in it, and her tweed skirt looked loose about the waist.

'Yes?'

'You don't remember me,' said Lily. 'It's Lily. Lily Collins? It's been a little while.'

Mrs Tunnicliffe's hand went to the twin rope of pearls at her neck.

'Lily,' she said softly. 'Yes, of course. From Marlows.' There was a note of puzzlement — or was it caution? — in her voice.

'That's right.'

'You've changed. Your hair's different . . . You're taller . . . Your face is thinner.'

Lily blushed.

'Oh, my hair!' Her blonde curls had often been a source of frustration when they wouldn't behave. 'I've got better at managing it, that's all!'

In the last couple of years she'd got much better at taming her hair: it was softly waved now too, and longer so that she could roll it up for work.

Mrs Tunnicliffe nodded vaguely. Lily didn't know how to move things on; they couldn't stand on the step talking about her hair all day. But Jim stepped forward and held out his hand.

'Jim Goodridge. I'm a colleague from the store. And a . . . friend of Lily's.'

'A colleague?' The nervous note was back, then Mrs Tunnicliffe smiled as if she only half-remembered how to do it. 'Oh, Jim! Yes, I remember you. Lily and I talked about you. You're her young man, aren't you?'

'Well, yes, that too,' Jim admitted. 'The thing is — '

'I saw you take the bangle,' Lily blurted out. 'I'm working on the ground floor now. I'm sorry, Mrs Tunnicliffe, but — '

Mrs Tunnicliffe went white. She swayed and clutched at the door jamb. Jim reached out and caught her arm.

'May we come in? I think perhaps you should sit down.'

33

They sat Mrs Tunnicliffe down on a high-backed chair in the hall and let her be. She folded her hands in her lap and kept her eyes low. On her previous visit, Lily had been quickly led through to a sitting room at the back of the house: only now did she notice the lovely Minton tiles on the hall floor. A console table held a vase of peonies reflected in a gilt-framed mirror. But the flowers were faded; a drift of petals had fallen on some unopened letters and into the saucer of a tea cup, which must have been there some time because the dregs were clotted and scummy. Standards had definitely slipped. Something was going on here, more than the loss of a maid and a garden boy.

Lily looked at Jim, who shrugged and mouthed, 'Give her a minute.'

Lily crouched down so she was on a level with Mrs Tunnicliffe.

'Can I get you anything?' she asked. 'A drink of water? A cup of tea?'

She didn't know where the kitchen was but guessed she could find it.

Mrs Tunnicliffe shook her head.

'No, no, I'll be fine. Thank you.' Her shoulders rose and fell as she gave a deep sigh. She looked up at them. 'I just needed to gather my thoughts.' Pressing heavily on the arms of the chair, she stood up. 'You'd better come with me.'

Lily looked at Jim, who nodded agreement. Mrs Tunnicliffe didn't take them to the sitting room, as Lily had expected. She began to lead the way upstairs. Jim and Lily followed in silence.

At the top, there was a large square landing. Mrs Tunnicliffe turned to the left and stopped in front of a closed door. She took a key from the pocket of her skirt, put it in the lock and turned it. Then she stood back and indicated that they should go in.

Jim stood back to let Lily go first. As she stepped through the door she knew at once it had been Violet's room. The wallpaper was just what she would have chosen herself: a trellis pattern entwined with honeysuckle. Sun streamed through the window between the lemon-coloured curtains that matched the skirt on the kidney-shaped dressing table and bounced off its triple mirror.

Lily turned to say something to Mrs Tunnicliffe about how pretty the room was and then she saw it. The bed with its silky coverlet was behind the door and it was covered with things — a powder compact, a lipstick, a comb, a purse, a velvet hairband, tins of talc, and a bar of soap — and two more which Lily recognised at once. A taffeta-covered bangle and a Jacqmar scarf.

Mrs Tunnicliffe was speaking before Lily had a chance to say anything and once she started, it seemed as if she couldn't stop.

'I can't help myself,' she said. 'It's for Violet. They're all for Violet. She loved pretty things, Lily, you know that. And before . . . before it happened, and before the war, if I saw something I knew she'd like, I'd buy it and stow it away. And by the time her birthday or Christmas came around, I'd have a proper little hoard to give her. I'd wrap up them up and her face when she opened them . . . I can see it now . . . She could never believe I'd been saving all these things up for her, buying them bit by bit. And she'd fling her arms round me and — '

She was looking unsteady again and Jim guided her to the bed, where she sat down among the sad offerings.

Lily was feeling a bit wobbly herself. The poor woman. She was trying to keep Violet alive — no, to bring her back from the dead.

There was still one nagging question, and Jim asked it.

'Mrs Tunnicliffe,' he said gently. 'You have the money. Why not buy these things?'

'Oh but don't you see?' Mrs Tunnicliffe shocked them with intensity of her reaction. 'It was different when she was here! I wouldn't have dreamt of taking anything! Never! But now . . . to make it a financial transaction, that would ruin it! This way it's as if the things are still a secret, but a secret between me and Violet together. Just the two of us.' She looked at them, pleading, hopeful. 'Does that make sense?'

Not much, thought Lily, and then . . . well, yes, maybe. Who was she to say what losing a child did to you? She crouched down by Mrs Tunnicliffe and, boldly, took her hand.

'I can understand that, I think,' she said. 'But it can't go on, can it? Not now we know.'

Jim had been standing by the window, but he came over to add weight to what Lily was saying.

'You're not a professional shoplifter,' he said. 'Sooner or later you'll be caught, and publicly, and that would be dreadful for you.'

'And for Violet,' added Lily, because as far as Mrs Tunnicliffe was concerned, Violet was ever-present.

'I know. I know. But what's going to happen?' asked Mrs Tunnicliffe pathetically. 'Do you have to report me? And what about all these things?'

'These aren't all from Marlows, are they?' said Jim. 'I can see that by looking, but they're not the most important thing right now. As Lily says, we know, and

36

we have to do something about it.'

'You mean go to Cedric Marlow.' Mrs Tunnicliffe was holding back tears. 'What if he goes to the police?'

Lily and Jim knew the answer to that. Most stores had stern notices pinned up — 'Shoplifters: We Always Prosecute!' — but Mr Marlow wasn't of this persuasion. He thought any involvement with a criminal investigation would damage the store's cherished reputation; apart from advertisements and good news stories, he'd do anything to keep the store's name out of the papers. And certainly out of court.

'He won't,' said Jim. 'I can guarantee it.'

'So you needn't worry about that.' Lily gently squeezed her hand, feeling awkward about what she had to say next. It felt so wrong to be talking to the older woman like this. 'But please, Mrs Tunnicliffe, for your sake, and for Violet's, you can't go on doing this. At Marlows or anywhere else.'

Mrs Tunnicliffe closed her eyes briefly, then opened them and scanned her haul of treasures. She reached out and touched the powder compact and the scarf, then the hairband and the bangle.

'She'd have loved them, I know she would,' she said.

5

Lily and Jim were quiet when they left Mrs Tunnicliffe's. Even Buddy seemed to sense their mood and trotted meekly along, looking wistfully at the privet hedges and not lingering for long at the lamp posts he simply couldn't resist. Finally Lily spoke.

'I hope it's OK to leave her on her own,' she fretted. 'You don't think . . . you don't think she might do something stupid?'

The thought had crossed Jim's mind, but he'd dismissed it. And his job now was to bolster Lily up.

'Lily!' he soothed. 'Come on. We gave her all the reassurance we could.'

Lily had made them all some tea, and, daringly, a sandwich for Mrs Tunnicliffe, because she couldn't see any evidence of an evening meal. She still hadn't touched it by the time they'd left.

'She's not looking after herself properly. Why aren't her sons visiting, or at least checking up on her?'

Like Lily, Violet had two brothers.

'They're both doing some top-brass jobs in the war, aren't they?' said Jim reasonably. 'They might be abroad by now and even if not, they're most likely working all hours with all these rumours that we're about to invade Europe.'

'Could be.'

Lily stopped to let Buddy inspect a dandelion sprouting from a crack in the pavement.

'I can see what's going to happen,' Jim sighed. 'You're going to take her on as a cause. I know what

38

you're like.

'I feel sort of responsible for her,' said Lily, 'if she's got no one else. I always thought people like her were copers, you know — their big houses, breeding, stiff upper lip and all that. But think about it, Jim. You can't keep anything private, can you, where we live, good or bad. The walls are thin, everyone's in and out of each other's houses all the time — '

Jim made a noise that was a cross between a laugh and a snort.

'Like Jean Crosbie?' Dora's next door neighbour was a known busybody. 'Popping in on the pretext of borrowing a pastry brush, when she really wants to pass on the latest scandal?'

Lily shook her head impatiently.

'OK, maybe not her, but others — they'd be the first to help out. Mrs Tunnicliffe'd never be left on her own to manage like she is. Give me our set-up any day of the week, not some big house behind a long drive where nobody calls or knows how lonely or miserable you are, or because of their 'breeding' doesn't like to ask and you don't like to tell them.'

'But the colonel's lady and Judy O'Grady are sisters under their skin,' said Jim thoughtfully. 'Kipling,' he added when Lily looked baffled. 'A poem. Well, more of a ditty — it's a bit coarse, really, but you get my drift.'

Lily shrugged.

'If you mean they feel things just the same, then yes, I do. It's like the WVS. At first some of the posher ones, like the organiser, Mrs Russell, the doctor's wife, they seemed a bit standoffish, bossy — but actually they're perfectly nice. Ordinary. And when you get them talking, they're scared for their husbands and sons too, fed up with queuing and the blackout and Make Do and Mend, just like everyone else. And then they remember who they're talking to, and it's like they've let the side down and it's all gung-ho again.'

Jim suddenly dipped his head down and kissed her.

'What was that for?'

'Do I need a reason?'

'Yes!'

'All right. For being you,' he said. 'I love it when you suddenly spout off, thinking it out as you go.'

Lily smiled up at him. She felt the relief and happiness she always felt, that she could always tell Jim her thoughts, however halting and half-formed, and he'd somehow understand.

Buddy indicated he was finally ready to move on and bit by bit they left the leafy avenues and crescents behind and returned to their own sort, to the roads and streets. But Lily had learnt something that evening — or rather, she'd had something reinforced. She'd always try her hardest, go as far as she could in her job, and hope that she and Jim, when they set up home, might be a bit more comfortably off than her mother had been, having to scrimp and save. But she had no envy for really monied people and their way of life. She was very happy where she was.

* * *

By next morning, she and Jim had come to another important conclusion. It was Lily who should go to Cedric Marlow and tell him about Mrs Tunnicliffe.

'You saw her do it,' Jim concluded. 'And you know her better than I do. You knew Violet. If Uncle Cedric does cut up rough, though I don't think he will, I think

40

you'll put up a better defence.'

Lily had to agree. Admitting she'd witnessed an incident of shoplifting and not reported it at the time might not do much for her promotion prospects, but Marlows wasn't the only one with a reputation to protect — Mrs Tunnicliffe had one too. What was Lily's promised first sales status when set against that poor woman's loss?

It was unusual for one of the sales staff to see the store's owner directly and Mr Marlow's secretary tried to deflect her. But Lily stuck to her guns and was grudgingly granted ten minutes at noon. All she had to do was make sure she got the first dinner break which started at 11.30 — easily done as Rita always bagged the more reasonable time of 12.30 for herself. The poor junior would have to wait for her dinner today.

At twelve sharp Lily presented herself at Mr Marlow's door, knocked and waited for his 'enter!' command. She'd rehearsed what she was going to say and managed to get out the facts without too much hesitation. Cedric, small and bald behind his big desk, listened with what looked like increasing amazement, and Lily began to falter. He clearly couldn't believe that Lily had let such blatant pilfering go on under her nose. But when he spoke, that wasn't the reason at all.

'Daphne Tunnicliffe?' he exclaimed. 'But her late husband was in the Chamber of Commerce with me! We served on the Golf Club committee together! Years ago, of course, he's been dead a long while, but even so . . . he can't have left her badly off. I can't believe it! Some of the pilferers we get here one can understand, but why would a woman in her position do such a thing?'

41

Lily was tempted to quote Jim, and Kipling, but instead she said mildly, 'She lost her daughter, sir, in the Baedeker raids on Bath. There was a small paragraph in the local paper at the time, but perhaps you didn't see it?'

Cedric's face creased.

'No, I didn't,' he said. 'How dreadful. I'm so sorry. But how does that justify . . . ?'

'It's not just the things we've lost from Marlows,' Lily explained. 'She's been taking things from other shops over the whole two years since Violet was killed. They're all gifts for her, you see, and somehow it makes sense to Mrs Tunnicliffe not to pay for them. It's a sort of secret pact between them.'

As the words came out, she thought what little sense they made, but, sobered, Cedric Marlow nodded.

'I see now,' he said. 'Grief is never rational. That's the one sure thing about it.'

Lily looked down. Mr Marlow's wife had died soon after giving birth to their son.

They sat in silence for a moment, then Mr Marlow stood up, a sure sign that Lily's time with him was over. She stood up too.

'Leave this with me,' he said. 'I'll deal with it from here.' And when Lily looked alarmed, he added, 'Don't worry, Miss Collins, I shall be as tactful as you've been.' Seeing Lily's relief, he went on. 'I remember now your connection with Mrs Tunnicliffe and her daughter and I quite understand why you acted as you did. Thank you. You may go.'

Lily scuttled out on jelly legs. She'd done all she could — though she was intrigued by two things. Some of the chat in the staff canteen reckoned Mr Marlow was past it and out of touch, but he clearly remembered from almost three years ago — her very first day — why and how Lily had come into contact with Mrs Tunnicliffe and Violet in the first place; she also wondered what his 'tactful' dealing with Mrs Tunnicliffe might entail.

★ ★ ★

'Are you all right up there, Dora?'

Gladys, holding the stepladder, watched as Dora strained to reach a cobweb in the corner.

'I'm fine! And if I fell, you'd give me a soft landing!'

'Don't even talk about it! I'd never forgive myself! It's so kind of you to help.'

'We can't have you shinning up steps and bending down to wash skirtings in your condition, can we?' The cobweb caught in a duster, Dora climbed carefully down. 'And if Jim's going to distemper this weekend . . . '

'The paint smell will go, won't it, by the time the baby comes?'

'Yes, love, of course it will. You've got weeks yet!'

'Five,' sighed Gladys. 'I feel like I've been pregnant for ever!'

'Baby'll be here soon enough. And what a lucky little mite to have his or her own nursery!'

'Yeah.' Gladys smiled. 'It's so good of Gran to let me have the box room.'

Dora pursed her lips. Didn't help you move any of the stuff that was in here, did she, she thought, but didn't say it. Gladys wouldn't hear a word against her gran.

'The thought of you, the size you are, lugging stuff up to the attic!' she said instead. 'Why didn't you ask me or Lily or Jim to help, you silly girl!'

43

'Oh, well . . . ' Gladys shrugged. 'I couldn't expect Gran to do much. Her lumbago was playing her up.'

Was it indeed, thought Dora. Funny how Gladys's gran's many ailments were always things you couldn't see or hear. Never a proper wheezy chest, just 'this terrible tight feeling, like a vice', never actual sickness, just a 'sick headache' or 'shocking indigestion'. Which came from stuffing her face, in Dora's view. In fact, the thing wrong with Florrie Jessop was bone idleness — and greed.

All right, she was in her sixties, but the way she acted you'd have thought she was a hundred. It was a terrible thing to say but the death of her daughter and son-in-law in the Blitz had been a positive blessing for her. Her sweet, obliging granddaughter had come to live with her and Florrie had made her into her personal slave.

'Time you had a sit-down and something to eat,' Dora told Gladys now. 'We'll leave washing down the walls till after.'

She'd brought round a plate pie for herself and Gladys but if Florrie got to it first there wouldn't be enough left to fill a hollow tooth. Sure enough, when they went down, Florrie was sitting at the kitchen table with the pie in front of her, pouring the top of the milk on what was obviously her second slice.

'Nice bit of pastry, this,' she commented, shamelessly taking up her spoon. 'Did you grow the rhubarb yourself, Dora?'

'Yes, we did,' Dora replied curtly. 'But I'm surprised at you touching it. I wouldn't have thought one helping of rhubarb would agree with you, Florrie, with your delicate digestion, let alone two.'

'I thought I'd risk it, just the once. Vitamins, isn't it?'

44

'Have you had yours today, Gladys?' asked Dora sharply.

The Government gave expectant mothers vitamins, cod liver oil, orange juice, and extra rations. Dora could well imagine who benefited from that lot while Gladys was out at work. Thanks to Lily's suggestion, she now had a low stool behind the counter for when there were no customers around, but Dora would much rather Gladys had given up work already.

She made them each a sandwich and freshened the pot — Florrie had managed to make some tea, at least. Gladys didn't eat much — 'No room,' she explained — and when she went to shake the dusters in the yard, Dora rounded on Florrie.

'I hope that wasn't Gladys's top of the milk you were having. And you must see how tired she's getting.'

'What of it?'

'I know how much she does for you, the shopping, the cooking, your bits of washing — it's too much for her. Couldn't you do a bit more?'

'That's nice, being attacked in my own home!' Florrie reddened and defended herself. 'It's that shop that's wearing her out, not me, and it's her own doing!'

'Nonsense. She's only staying on for the money, to give the little one the best start in life!'

Gladys came back in and Dora noticed her puffy ankles.

'We're only getting in each other's way in that little room,' she said. 'I'll finish up. You have a rest. Put your feet up and listen to the wireless.' And she couldn't resist adding, 'Take a leaf out of your gran's book.'

The look Florrie Jessop gave her would have curdled not just Gladys's extra pint but every bottle on the milkman's cart. Dora didn't care. If Gladys wouldn't stand up for herself, and Bill wasn't here to do it for her, well, at least Dora Collins was up to the job.

6

Cedric had telephoned in advance, so when his taxi drew up on the gravel sweep in front of Daphne Tunnicliffe's house, he knew he was expected. Telling the driver to wait and climbing the steps to the front door, he too noticed the neglected plants in the doorstep pots. Like the beloved Humber that he'd given up in 1939 — now probably serving as a staff car, if not an ambulance — they were all part of the collateral damage of the war.

He rang the bell, and Daphne answered almost at once; she must have been watching from a window. He handed her his hat and coat and followed her down the hall to the sitting room. Beyond 'good evening' and 'thank you for coming' she hadn't said a word.

Cedric sat on one of the chintz-covered sofas; she sat stiffly in an armchair like a prisoner about to be interrogated. Cedric had kept his telephone call brief, and now he kicked himself for it. She was clearly expecting a lecture, if not actual punishment. He should have been more reassuring.

'Mrs Tunnicliffe,' he began. 'Daphne — if I may?' She nodded. 'I don't want this to be any more awkward than it has to be. I knew your husband slightly, as you may know.'

Her face showed that she hadn't. Well, fair enough; they'd met and moved in exclusively male preserves. Cedric didn't smile easily — he took life too seriously for that — but he tried one now, a kind one, he hoped.

'I know what you did,' he said, 'and I know why you

did it.'

She went to say something but he held up his hand to stop her.

'I lost my wife at a young age,' he said. 'I know what grief can do to you. It's a madness of sorts, a temporary madness, one hopes, but no one can tell you that — or predict how long it will last. And it affects everyone in different ways.'

Mrs Tunnicliffe spoke for the first time.

'You're very kind, making excuses for me. But it was stealing — from you and from other shops. Stealing!'

'I'm not making excuses,' Cedric insisted. 'It's a fact. Grief sends you to extremes. I threw myself into my work. I see now I was lucky to have it, but it was selfish. I neglected my son, packed him off to boarding school, and didn't have much to do with him in the holidays either. It was excessive and he suffered — our relationship suffered. I'm not sure it's ever recovered. Your relationship with your daughter was obviously the opposite — very, very close. And you were trying to preserve it.'

Daphne Tunnicliffe sighed. She pulled at a loose thread on the arm of her chair.

'Well, thank you for that. But if you're trying to make me feel better — '

'I'm simply trying to say that as far as Marlows is concerned, as far as you and I are concerned, the incident is explained and forgotten. The only question now is . . . ' He paused. This was delicate. 'The question now is what you're going to do instead.'

'Do?'

'To keep yourself occupied. To fill that void. Maybe to do something else that your daughter would approve of.' He gave a self-conscious laugh. 'I'm not expressing myself very well. Violet' — he saw her flinch at the name — 'she wouldn't want you to be in trouble for . . . for collecting a few trinkets for her, would she? I'm sure she'd far rather have you do something — again, if I may — more worthwhile with your time.'

She lifted her eyes to his — very blue eyes, he noticed. She sounded puzzled, but also hopeful.

'Such as?'

'There are so many things a woman like you could be doing!'

Her shoulders sagged.

'Oh, you mean voluntary work.' It was as if she'd thought he had some miracle to offer, and her disappointment had a touch of exasperation too. 'I do that already, all of it! I've made pounds of jam; the scarves I've knitted laid end to end would reach the Middle East and back!' She shook her head impatiently. 'If you knew how sick I am of khaki and navy blue! How I'd love to knit something sky blue or magenta!'

'I'm sorry.' Cedric retreated rapidly. 'I should have realised — '

'No, no, I'm sorry.' She retreated even further. 'I shouldn't take it out on you, of all people! But you men have no idea. They say it's important work, and I know it is, it is — ' She sighed, frustrated. 'Maybe if Violet were here, we'd do it together, and it would mean more, be fun even. But to me, alone, it simply seems pointless.'

This was a blow; Cedric had been sure he'd had the answer.

'I'm sorry,' he said again. 'But I'm sure all you do is valued. And essential.'

49

'Yes,' she said resignedly. 'Yes, I know you're right. I shall carry on with it and . . . well, now I don't have my other little time-filling exercise, I shall be able to do even more, shan't I? But enough of that. To business.' She reached down for her handbag. She took out a cheque book and a pen. 'I'm grateful, of course, that you've taken a personal interest in this. And that you don't want to pursue the matter.' He could see her steeling herself to say it. 'To prosecute. But I must compensate you for what I owe. Which, I believe, is two pounds twelve shillings and sixpence. And of course, I'll give you the items back.'

'Don't be ridiculous!' Cedric was unusually impassioned. 'I don't want the money and I don't want the things back! They've been written off already. And I can assure you the same will apply to anything you'd, er, acquired from other stores.'

'So what shall I do?' she asked, nonplussed. 'I was going to send the other things back anonymously. I can't keep them! I don't even want to look at them.'

This time, Cedric was prepared.

'I suggest,' he said, 'that you parcel them up and send them to a charity of your choice — not round here, for obvious reasons. They can hand them out or sell them as they see fit.' He tested out another smile. 'Think of it as another sort of contribution to the war effort.'

Worry disappeared from her face like lines erased from a page. She still sat upright, but the tension in her shoulders had gone. The china-blue eyes found his again, relief and thanks in them this time.

'I'll do that. Thank you.'

They chatted a little more about the usual things — the weather, the progress of the war, a couple of mutual acquaintances. But it was time to go. She saw him to the door, gave him back his hat and coat, and they shook hands.

'Thank you so much,' she said. 'But you're a busy man — please don't let this take up any more of your time. I shall be quite all right now.'

'I hope so. Goodbye.'

'Goodbye.'

The taxi driver put away his paper and started the engine. Cedric touched his hat to her and got in. As they drove off, he raised his hand in a wave. Framed in the doorway, watching him go, she waved back.

He hadn't solved things quite as neatly as he'd hoped — she was already doing the voluntary work he'd thought would be the perfect substitute to fill her time. He frowned. All over the world, people were suffering losses like Daphne Tunnicliffe but something about her loneliness in that large house had moved him, reminding him of his own grief.

*   *   *

Day by day, week by week, Jim had watched the columns in his Post Office book fill up. At Christmas, when they'd first talked about getting engaged, he'd given Lily a pretend ring out of a cracker. He'd said at the time that he'd never dare choose her a ring as she had such decided ideas of her own, but as time had passed, he'd changed his mind. He wanted to surprise her. For once in his life, he was not going to be sensible, sober, doing-as-he'd-said Jim. He was going to be bold, daring, dashing even. He was going to take a risk.

And it was about time he got on with it, he thought,

reverting to his sensible self. Les's teasing was becoming even more pointed.

'Had a reply from the Palace yet?' he asked when they met on the loading bay. 'If the Queen can't spare you the Koh-i-Noor, how about some sparkler from a tiara she doesn't wear much?'

'I was going to tell you,' said Jim with dignity. 'I've started looking.'

Les punched him lightly on the arm.

'About blooming time! I never thought your Lily had that much patience. What have you got in mind?'

'I don't know,' said Jim. 'I'll know it when I see it.'

The problem, as he'd found out from a quick tour of Hinton's jewellers, was that jewellers didn't display their prices. Peering through the criss-cross grilles that covered their windows was tricky enough, but the minute price tags were always cunningly tucked away in slits in the velvet display pads. Jim thought he had enough money, but he dreaded pointing out a ring he liked the look of only to find it was five times as much as he had to spend.

'You're lucky you and Beryl married so quickly,' he told Les. 'There's so many to choose from, I can't remember what I've seen where — and there's no prices on any of them.'

'They're not daft, are they, jewellers?' Les retorted. 'That's to lure you in. Want me to do it? I don't mind asking the price. I'm not proud!'

'No, thanks,' said Jim. 'It's my engagement, I'll do it.'

'Let me know the worst!' Les grimaced. 'Lord knows how I'll afford the kind of ring Beryl's on about unless I win on the horses and the chance of that's less and less with Aintree a blooming prisoner-of-war

52

camp and an anti-aircraft battery at Epsom!'

'Les! Not by betting! You know it's a mug's game!'

'I like that!' snorted Les. 'It's all your fault, anyway, you and Lily! Beryl's leaving film magazines all round the house now, with Ava Gardner sporting some great rock! If the nag I've got my eye on doesn't come good at Newmarket, nag'll be the word! I'll be in trouble, I can tell you!'

★ ★ ★

Jim kept a lookout for any *Picturegoer* magazines left open at theirs, and for Lily slowing down when they passed a jeweller's, but there was nothing. It was puzzling; months had passed and it was true, she wasn't known for her patience. But Lily had other things on her mind.

'Do you think we should call round to Mrs Tunnicliffe?' she fretted to Jim one Sunday as they took a stroll along the cut. There were catkins on the willows and six fluffy, yellow-brown goslings were still finding their sea — or rather their canal — legs, listing uncertainly in their parents' wake. 'I can't stop thinking about her, and how sad it all is . . . that sort of shrine to Violet.'

'I know it's tough,' Jim agreed. 'But Uncle Cedric said he'd deal with it. And he will have done; he's a man of his word.'

'I wish I knew how, and what he's done exactly!' Lily burst out. She hated unfinished business. 'She's so alone in that great house. I mean, what's she doing this afternoon? Wandering about the place? Staring out of the window?'

'Maybe she'll start directing her energies into the

garden. It could do with it.'

Jim instantly he wished he hadn't spoken — Lily'd be suggesting they went round and gave her a hand. But she was hardly listening.

'And what's happened to all those things she took?' she sighed.

'We may never know,' said Jim. 'Sometimes, Lily, you have to accept you've done all you can.'

Lily screwed up her mouth in a way he recognised. It meant that she wasn't going to argue any more. It didn't mean she'd let the matter drop.

Next day she was determined to buttonhole Mr Marlow when he made his tour of the store. He did it every morning, greeting customers with his old-fashioned half-bow, conferring with buyers, pulling straight a display stand, picking someone up on a sloppily-tied shoelace. Though 'buttonhole' was hardly the word. Miss Frobisher had warned Lily from the first that when Mr Marlow stopped at your department, it was like meeting royalty. You didn't speak till you were spoken to.

He was agonisingly slow, of course. He lingered on Jewellery, where flimsy clasps were a concern. Then he got stuck on Handbags while Rita's friend expounded at length about clutch bags. Finally, he made his way to Small Leathers. Rita smiled her most ingratiating smile. Lily smiled too, hopefully.

'Good morning, Miss Ruddock,' he said, as courteous as ever. 'Miss Collins.'

Lily looked at him beseechingly as she replied. He didn't appear to notice.

'Any problems?' he asked, running his eye over the brass-handled drawers, the glass tops of the counters, and the goods within. Lily could sense the junior holding her breath.

'Nothing to report, sir,' Rita replied. 'All running smoothly.'

Thanks to me, was the implication.

'Good, good,' murmured Mr Marlow. Lily's eyes scanned his face like searchlights; it was a wonder he wasn't shielding himself from the glare. She willed him to look up and he did.

'Miss Collins,' he said evenly. 'A word, please.'

Lily felt Rita stiffen beside her but Mr Marlow drew her away to the furthest end of the counter, where even Rita, however much she strained, wouldn't be able to hear.

'You have the reputation,' Mr Marlow began in his usual dry manner, 'of being something of a terrier, Miss Collins. So I daresay you're curious about the conclusion to the incident you witnessed.' Had he been to one of those 'Psychic Fairs' you saw advertised, Lily wondered; he'd read her mind accurately enough. 'I visited the lady and the matter has been fully resolved. I assured her that none of the stores would want the items back so they'll be donated to charity. There's no more to be said.'

There was a lot more as far as Lily was concerned, but Mr Marlow had neatly wrapped up the business side of things, anyway. She nodded and smiled as unresignedly as she could.

'Thank you, sir.'

He looked at her with something which, if it hadn't been Cedric Marlow, Lily would have said was almost a twinkle.

'No more to be said . . . except perhaps about the lady's state of mind, which I'm guessing is of equal concern to you. She promised me that she is, and will be, using her time more productively in future. And rest assured, I've made sure someone is keeping an eye on her.'

Lily's smile this time was genuine. Jim had been right, as usual, blast him!

'Oh, I am glad!'

Mr Marlow had known her husband; maybe he'd contacted one or both of her sons and told them how lonely and bereft their mother was. They must be doing a better job of keeping in touch.

'Good. Now back to work please.'

Dismissed, Lily scuttled back along the counter. Rita was ostentatiously rearranging the oddments. She turned on Lily at once.

'What was all that about?'

'Nothing,' Lily flannelled.

'Nothing? You looked very chummy!'

'Not at all!' Lily wondered how she could phrase it without telling an outright lie. 'He just wanted to let me know that things would be, um, getting back to normal.'

'Meaning . . . ? Oh, I see! You'll be going back to Kidswear, and Betty'll be coming back here?'

'Hmn,' said Lily, trying to make it sound as much like an agreement as she could.

'Did he say when?'

'I didn't ask him that,' said Lily truthfully.

'Fair enough. Still, good to know, eh?'

Rita's mood had changed rapidly. For the rest of the morning, she was almost pleasant, and after lunch and the canteen's brave but ill-advised attempt at curried mutton, she even offered Lily a surreptitious peppermint.

In his office, meanwhile, Cedric Marlow was

inscribing something in his pocket diary. He'd just made a phone call, part of his 'keeping an eye' on Daphne Tunnicliffe and, as he'd hoped, had managed to get himself invited to tea on Sunday.

★　★　★

The month of May went on its merry way — and there was merriment, or at least relief, when the long battle for Monte Cassino in Italy, which had cost so many Allied lives, was finally won and their flags fluttered above the ruins of the hilltop abbey.

A week on, and while the inside pages were still giving details of the victory, the headlines had moved on.

PHEW! WHAT A SCORCHER!

they blared, and:

BRITAIN BAKES IN 90° HEAT!

In the last few days of the month, the heat built up alarmingly. Gladys was feeling it intensely.

'I don't know what to do with myself!' she moaned, shifting uncomfortably in the back room at the Collinses'. 'I'm sticking to this chair! There's not a breath of air!'

This was unfair but true. The back door stood open and the sash window was thrown right up. Lily was seated on the rush-topped stool fanning Gladys with a copy of *The People's Friend*, but she was only really moving the warmth about.

Dora laid aside her knitting.

'I'll fetch you some more cool water,' she said,

stooping to retrieve the enamel bowl. 'Pop your feet on the towel a minute, there's a love.'

Gladys put her dripping feet on the towel Dora had laid down.

'Thank you,' she said pitifully. 'You are good to me, all of you.'

Dora smiled thinly. Poor girl, she deserved it; she was still getting no consideration from her gran. Dora had called on Florrie the other week to make another appeal of Gladys's behalf but still found the old besom unmoved and unmoveable.

'I was stood standing in the laundry where I worked till the day before I had Gladys's mum,' Florrie had declared. 'Had her the next night, nobody to help but old Mother Cooper that lived over the back of us, no training or nothing bar the six kids she'd had herself. Gave me a rag to bite on and told me to hang onto the bed frame, that was all the assistance I got!' Dora opened her mouth to reply but Florrie wasn't to be interrupted. 'Back at work two days later, couldn't afford to lose the pay, and look at it now! All this free stuff and running back and forth to this clinic for 'check-ups'! Girls today,' she added without any sense of irony, 'they don't know they're born!'

'Have you seen her ankles?' asked Dora sharply. 'Like footballs, they are!'

'Tch! Hypochondriac. Her mother was the same.'

Somehow Dora managed to not say anything about pots and kettles. The only way to take care of Gladys was to have her round at theirs as much as possible, which was why she was in the stuffy back room that hot night.

Even when the burning ball of sun had dipped below the roofs of the houses, the heat remained. In fact it seemed even more oppressive, and the thought of having to put up the blackout once they needed the lights on was unbearable. Buddy was lying at full stretch on the tiled scullery floor and Jim had gone out to water the veg. Lily's arm was aching from flapping the magazine; it was making her even hotter, but she didn't like to complain. Gladys had her eyes closed. She really was a size, Lily thought, as she watched her friend's face. She dropped her eyes and suddenly noticed a dark patch on the front of Gladys's chair. She looked again. The light was going . . . was it a shadow? She put out her hand and touched it. When she took her hand away, her fingers were damp.

'Mum!' she hissed. 'Mum!'

Dora looked up and Lily signalled her over.

'I think Gladys has wet herself.'

Dora shook Gladys's shoulder gently.

'Gladys! Gladys, dear. Wake up. That's it, you had a little doze . . . Can you stand up for me?'

'Eh?'

Dazed and still dopey, Gladys stood up. It was a good job the bowl was there, because as she did, liquid poured out of her, splashing into the bowl and over its sides. Lily gasped.

Gladys swayed, though Dora was holding her arm.

'I feel a bit funny,' she said.

'Your waters have broken, love,' said Dora. 'The baby's coming!'

7

It was chaos after that. Jim was sent off for the midwife, while Lily and Dora somehow managed to get a still-bemused Gladys upstairs. Dora led the way into her own bedroom and told Lily to fetch all the towels in the house.

'And get some water on to boil, lots of it, and bring me up the dustsheets off the front room furniture,' she added in a low voice as Gladys, seated numbly on the edge of the bed, began to unbutton her dress. 'You never know what we might need.'

Lily dashed off, while Dora helped Gladys to undress and rummaged in the chest of drawers for her oldest nightdress to preserve what was left of Gladys's modesty.

'I'm so sorry,' she was murmuring. 'Your chair! I'm so embarrassed!'

'Don't be daft,' said Dora smoothly. 'It's only water, more or less! There's a lot more to come than that to embarrass you!'

'Why can't I feel any pain?' Gladys looked up at her. 'I thought it was supposed to — Ooh. Ooh. That felt funny.'

'What's that?' Dora helped Gladys to unhook her bra.

'Not a pain exactly, but a bit like . . . a sort of swirling, back and front, like the washing when you're pushing it round and down with the dolly.'

'There you are then,' Dora smiled. 'That's the start. The midwife'll be here soon and before you know it, you'll be holding your little one in your arms.'

Gladys clutched her hand.

'It will be all right, won't it, Dora? I thought I had a few weeks yet!'

'Of course it'll be all right!' Dora spoke with all the certainty Gladys needed to hear, even though she knew full well that any birth was a trip into the unknown. 'Babies decide when they're going to make their appearance and this little one couldn't wait to meet you, that's all!'

With Dora's nightdress straining over her belly, Gladys lay back against the pillows. Dora busied herself laying Gladys's clothes over a chair and tidying away everything on the chest of drawers; the midwife would need somewhere to put her things. For all her reassurance, for all Gladys's large size and discomfort, she'd expected the baby to go over its due date, not come early. *Hurry up, Jim,* she thought. *I want that midwife here.*

Lily reappeared, half hidden behind a pile of towels. Dora took them from her, hoping they wouldn't all get ruined; the midwife would at least bring a rubber sheet for the mattress.

'How are you feeling?' Lily asked Gladys.

'Funny,' was all Gladys replied. 'It just feels . . . funny.'

Helpless and out of her depth, Lily wasn't sure what to say but didn't have to reply as she heard feet on the stairs. A second later a small, slender figure, not much older than Lily herself, appeared in the doorway.

'Well, thanks very much!' she said. 'I'd just run myself a cool bath and was about to get into it! And now I'm hotter than ever!'

She certainly looked it — she must have biked over

at top speed to get here so fast. Although she'd gone with Gladys to the clinic, Lily had never seen the midwife and she was astonished. She'd expected a stout, motherly figure with arms like hams and hands like a bunch of bananas. Was this tiny creature really going to deliver Gladys's baby? It seemed she was.

'I'm Marie,' she said, already opening her bag and getting out her things. 'And you're Lily and Dora, Jim explained. That's marvellous you've got things all ready. Let's have a look at you then, Gladys.'

'Lily, pop down and put on some hot water?' asked Dora meaningfully and Lily could have hugged her. She wasn't sure she was up to seeing Gladys poked and prodded about, let alone the rest of it and, glad to have something to do, she skittered down the stairs where Jim, thankfully, had reappeared.

'That midwife's a case!' he exclaimed. 'Left me standing, shot off on her bike!'

They boiled the kettle and Lily went carefully back up with the steaming bowl in time to hear Marie declare that Gladys was obviously going to be one of the lucky ones who could shell them like peas. Hope so, thought Lily, making her escape again.

★ ★ ★

It was the longest evening she'd ever spent — and Jim agreed. As dusk began to fall they stood outside where a sulky sort of breeze had got up, stirring the tops of the trees on the railway embankment and raising a gritty dust which made the moist air even thicker, heavier, and hotter. In the west the sky was the colour of an angry bruise.

'The weather's going to break,' said Jim. They

were standing side by side against the wall of the privy — hardly romantic, but it never got the sun and felt cool against their backs. It was too hot to touch each other. There was a low growl of thunder in the distance. 'Hear that? It's going to chuck it down.'

Buddy came out of the house and sniffed the air. He gave a little whimper.

'It's coming,' said Jim. 'He can tell.'

The thunder growled more purposefully. Buddy whimpered again and went back inside. When they'd taken him on, Dora had sworn the dog would never be allowed inside the house, but that hadn't lasted long. He slept outside, but he was too endearing and they were all too fond of him to stick him in the yard and have him scratching at the door in the daytime.

Lily closed her eyes and leant her head back against the bricks. She was dead tired and there was work tomorrow. Perhaps it was time to try sleeping standing up, which her brother Reg, who'd done hours of sentry duty in the Army, had told her was perfectly possible. It wasn't to be. Jim was watching the horizon.

'Lightning,' he reported.

It was followed by more thunder: the growl had turned to a snarl. Lily wondered what was going on in the bedroom at the front of the house. Beryl's labour with her son Bobby, she knew, had gone on all night — was it going to be the same with Gladys? She ought to go and see how things were going, and if they needed anything.

The window to her own room was open and suddenly her mother was calling.

'Lily! You might want to come up!'

From inside, far off, there was a high-pitched wail.

'Oh Lord, she's had it!' Lily seized Jim's hands. 'Already! The baby's here!'

She raced inside and up the stairs. The door to her mother's room was standing open and Dora was holding a tiny bundle, wiping its face with the corner of a towel. Lily looked to Gladys in delight, only to see another baby on her chest. Marie was cleaning a fearsome looking implement that looked like giant spoons.

Lily looked from one to the other and back again.

'What . . . two?' she stuttered. 'Twins?'

'A boy and a girl,' said Marie triumphantly. 'A pretty good evening's work.'

'Gladys has been marvellous.' Dora came over and held the baby out for Lily's inspection. It had dark hair and pink cheeks. Its eyes were tight closed and the little mouth worked as if chewing a toffee. 'This is the little girl, popped out first with a bit of help, and the little lad straight after.'

'Oh, Gladys!' Lily moved towards the bed. 'That's incredible! Two babies! Oh, you are clever! Wait till we tell Bill!'

Gladys was cradling the baby. Her eyes, far away, looked up at Lily as if she'd never seen her before. The baby's dark head, still smeared with a bit of blood and some waxy white stuff, was so tiny it pretty much fitted in her hand. Lily bent down to look at the minute features, the perfect nose, and the miraculously complicated little ears. Then, as she marvelled, Gladys closed her eyes, threw her head and shoulders back, and seemed to go as stiff as a board. Marie dropped what she was doing and snatched the baby away, thrusting him into Lily's arms. Gladys had started to jolt and twitch like some ghastly puppet.

'Ambulance,' shouted Marie. 'Now!'

Dora quickly took the baby from Lily and she ran down the stairs, racing through the kitchen, where Jim had his back to her, boiling another kettle.

'I thought a teacup in a storm would be a good idea — ' he said, then, as Lily flung open the back door, 'Lily?'

'It's all gone wrong!' she called back over her shoulder.

'What, the baby?' Jim followed her at speed down the yard.

'Babies!' cried Lily, yanking at the gate. 'She had twins! And now — oh Jim, I'm so scared! She's having some kind of fit! I've got to phone for an ambulance right now!'

As she ran full pelt along the cinder path, grit in her eyes, stones in her shoes, the storm broke. There was a whiplash of lightning, a ferocious rumble of thunder and then it was as if someone had taken a knife to the sky, slashed open the clouds, and all the moisture the sun had sucked up in the last few days was released. Lily had run out in her thin cotton dress and canvas shoes; she was instantly drenched and the ashes under her feet churned to black slush, splashing up the backs of her legs.

Panting, her heart hammering, she turned into the street. The rain was bouncing off the pavements and coursing along the gutters. Her hair was in her eyes, her dress slapping wetly against her legs, her shoes slopping up and down on her feet. What did *she* matter? Something dreadful was happening to Gladys, and if — God forbid — it was as serious as it had looked, what about the babies . . . not one, but two? Her breath was coming hot and fast in her chest, her heart banging against her ribs. The thunder rolled and the lightning flashed. In every way, for Lily, for Gladys, what should have been a moment of bliss had turned into something hellish.

* * *

They all went with Gladys in the ambulance, piling in before anyone could object, taking corners on two wheels, bell ringing, rain still pelting down. Lily was still wearing the soggy shoes and soaking dress in which she'd run to the phone box, so the ambulance driver wrapped her in a blanket.

At the hospital, they whisked Gladys away, and the babies, and took Dora with them too, so she could give them Gladys's details and fill them in on what had happened at the birth. Seeing Lily shivering, a kind nurse gave her some overalls belonging to one of the auxiliaries; they were too big and a bilious green. Her shoes were like leaky canoes, so the same nurse found her a pair of rubber clogs. They wore them in the operating theatre, apparently; Lily didn't want to think about why.

Even when she was dry, somehow she couldn't quite get warm.

'You look terrible,' said Jim in concern. 'And I don't mean the outfit, though I don't think it'll catch on, somehow. I hope you don't catch your death.'

'I'm fine,' jittered Lily. 'And don't even say that word! I'm not really that cold any more. I think it might be the shock.'

'I'm not surprised.'

Jim led her to a couple of hard chairs and they sat down. He put his arm round her and pulled her against him. He kissed the top of her damp head and there they sat as the hospital clock clicked the minutes and hours away.

★ ★ ★

It was after midnight when Dora reappeared. While Jim nipped to see if there was any chance of a cup of tea, she filled Lily in before going back to sit with Gladys.

By the time Jim was back — minus tea, unfortunately — Lily was ready to explain it to him.

'It was all because of her blood pressure,' she began. 'Gladys's was high, and then . . . I'm not quite clear but with having the babies quickly one after the other, it must have yo-yoed up and down too fast, that's what caused the fit. They've given her a shot of something to level it out and put her to sleep for a bit. Mum's gone back to sit with her.'

'What a drama!' Jim grimaced. 'And Gladys, of all people, who never likes to make a fuss! She'll be mortified!'

'Yes.' Lily smiled ruefully. Then: 'Jim, Mum and I . . . we're going to stay. But if you want to go home, get some sleep . . . '

'You must be joking!' Jim replied at once. 'I'm not leaving you here! And you're not to come into work tomorrow,' he added. 'Well, today. I'll explain to Mr Simmonds. And the dreaded Rita.'

Lily looked dubious.

'She'll think it's favouritism. She picked me up quickly enough when Mr Marlow spoke to me.'

'It's called friendship,' said Jim stoutly. 'Consideration. Loyalty. Kindness. Though that's an unknown

67

concept to Rita Ruddock.'

'She did once give me a peppermint.'

Now she had an explanation for what had happened to Gladys, Lily was beginning to feel a bit more normal.

'Oh, bosom buddies!' he grinned. 'She shouldn't mind you having the time off then, should she?'

At that moment, Dora came back, looking more hopeful.

'I think she's coming round,' she said. 'Do you want to come and see her, Lily? High jinks and holidays, eh?' she added drily to Jim.

She was sounding relieved, though, thought Lily; the worst was surely over. The babies were safe in the hospital nursery and Gladys was in good hands. The doctor had told Dora they'd keep her in for a few days 'for observation'.

Jim said he'd wait outside. Lily went with her mum and took a chair at one side of the bed while Dora stood on the other. Gladys still looked dead pale. She was moving her head on the pillow and frowning as if she was trying to remember something.

'Gladys,' said Lily softly. 'Gladys, you're all right. We're all here, me and Mum and Jim. You've had the babies — two of them — and they're beautiful! A lovely little boy and a perfect girl. You've done so well.'

Gladys let out a great shuddering breath and slowly opened her eyes. She turned her head towards Lily. She seemed to be trying to focus.

'Lily,' she said. 'Is that you?'

'Yes!' cried Lily. 'I'm here, right here!'

Gladys blinked. She wriggled and pushed herself up a bit in the bed, wincing.

Dora bent towards her.

68

'Don't strain yourself,' she said gently. 'Shall I shift your pillows a bit?'

Gladys turned towards the sound of her voice.

'Dora,' she said. 'Oh, Dora! Where am I? What happened?'

'Bless you, love, you're in the hospital.' She mouthed to Lily, 'Let's keep this simple.' Then she explained to Gladys: 'They brought you in to make sure everything was all right.'

'All right? But I'm not all right!' Gladys groped for Dora's hand. 'It's all dark. I can't . . . I can't see! I can't see a thing!'

8

Gladys began to cry.

'What is it? What's going on? What's the matter with me? I can't see, I can't see! My babies . . . where are my babies? I want to see them! I have to see them!'

Helpless, transfixed, Lily stroked Gladys's hair off her face while Dora pressed the call bell and kept her finger on the button. They could hear it shrilling down the hall. A nurse came hurrying, then a doctor. He shooed them out of the room and took charge. In the corridor, Jim was on his feet.

'What is it now?'

Lily felt as if a ton weight was pressing on her chest. She wasn't sure how she got the words out.

'There's something else. She's awake but she can't see!'

'What?'

None of them knew what to do with themselves. Dora, totally drained, sat down; Jim paced the corridor; Lily stationed herself like a guard dog at Gladys's door. All her tiredness had passed: terror had replaced it.

The nurse came out but waved their searching looks away. She bustled down the corridor and hurried back with a trolley of implements and covered dishes. The door closed behind her and gradually they heard Gladys's sobs subside into silence.

Books always said 'after what seemed like hours' — well, it was an hour, just about, before the nurse and the doctor emerged. Dora, Lily, and Jim

70

fell on him like lions.

'I think I know what it is,' he said slowly. 'I've never seen it before. It's a chance in a million — two million, maybe. It's the blood pressure again.'

'How can that affect her eyesight?' demanded Lily. 'I don't get it.'

'It's called cortical blindness,' the doctor explained. He was only in his thirties but looked older, exhausted, with shadows under his eyes and a day's worth of beard growth beginning to show. Hospitals were having to manage with fewer staff — the forces needed all the medics they could get. 'Her body's been through so much in such a short time that it's in shock. A bit of it has shut down. The part of her brain that should process messages from her eyes to enable her to see just isn't working.'

'Can you do anything for it?' Always practical, that was Jim.

'I'm afraid not.'

'What? It's not . . . permanent is it?' Dora voiced all their fears.

'No, no, it's not. There's nothing actually wrong with her eyes. They're working — it's only the messaging that's gone wrong.'

'Like a telephone line being cut?'

Jim always liked to relate something abstract to something he could understand.

'Exactly.'

'But how long will it go on?' It still sounded serious to Lily.

The doctor shook his head.

'I'm sorry, I can't say.'

Jim wasn't going to let him get away with that.

'You must be able to give us a clue!'

'I don't want to commit myself. Her blood pressure will stabilise, we can help with that, but . . . full recovery can take days, weeks, or months. The chances are that her sight will return, bit by bit.'

The chances? That didn't sound great.

'And what about the twins?' asked Dora.

'We'll keep them here in the nursery. A midwife can help to get feeding established; there's no reason why she can't feed them herself when her milk comes in. Apart from the problem with her sight, she's really come through the birth very well.' He looked at them as if he'd just given them some wonderful present. Their faces told him he hadn't. He opened his hands wide, palms upwards. 'I'm sorry I can't tell you more. Now, if you'll excuse me, I've got to write this up for the day shift.'

Jim thanked him; Lily and Dora were too numb. But they were all thinking the same thing. How long was this going to go on? How would Gladys cope? How would any of them? And how on earth — *what* on earth — were they going to tell Bill?

★ ★ ★

Lily did go to work next day. It wasn't because she was scared of Rita, but if Jim was going in — which he was determined to do — then she felt she should as well. She'd had literally no sleep and felt strangely light-headed, but a stocktake was due and if she could lurk in the stockroom and not have to be on show she felt she could cope. Her mum promised she'd visit Gladys in the afternoon; Lily would go in the evening. Dora was also going to send the crucial telegram to Bill on his ship. Sid would know how.

72

In the end it hadn't taken long to compose: they'd decided they'd only tell him the good news. He wouldn't get shore leave for months; surely all this would be a ghastly memory by then?

Jim wrote it out on a bit of paper for Dora to take to the Post Office:

TWINS BOY AND GIRL DELIVERED SAFELY CONGRATULATIONS!

The usual rider of 'mother and babies doing well' was missing, but in his excitement and delight, they hoped Bill wouldn't notice that.

Lily's wan appearance didn't go unnoticed, but there were plenty of pallid faces and obvious yawns among the staff — the thunderstorm and the rain that had followed had kept a lot of people awake.

'Thought the heavens were falling in!' Rita remarked.

She'd overdone the rouge in an attempt to disguise how much sleep she'd lost and it gave her long face with its downturned mouth a slightly clownish appearance. Lily would normally have wanted to smile; today she just nodded agreement.

Apart from spreading the good news that Gladys had safely delivered not one but two babies, Lily and Jim had decided to keep the rest under wraps. Jim was going to tell Mr Simmonds; Lily told the full story to just one other friend in the store, known always as Brenda from Books. And at dinnertime, she got a pass out and went to find Beryl in her shop.

'Dear God!' Beryl cried, when the customer she'd been advising had settled on oyster crepe, paid her deposit, and departed. 'Isn't there anything the doctors can do?'

'Nothing. Just watch and wait.'

Lily was so tired and dispirited she could hardly get the words out and Beryl moved from shocked to subdued as the full implications of the news sank in.

'Puts everything else into perspective, doesn't it?' she sighed. 'Even this wretched war.'

'What war?' said Lily.

★ ★ ★

She went straight to the hospital from work. Thoughtfully, they'd kept Gladys in the side room. It would have been too cruel to put her in the maternity ward with the other new mothers who could do everything for their babies and marvel at their tiny and perfect faces, fingers, and toes.

Gladys was sitting up in bed. Her eyes weren't bandaged and they were open; they looked perfectly normal. They had last night — that was what was so unsettling. She turned her head towards the door when Lily opened it, but Lily might as well have been a nurse. Gladys looked blankly at her till she spoke.

'Hello! It's me.'

Gladys recognised her voice.

'Lily,' she said. 'Thanks for coming.'

'How could I not?' Lily pulled up a chair and sat down. The miracle she'd been praying for all day — that Gladys's sight might miraculously have come back — obviously hadn't materialised.

'You must be tired out after last night and a day at work, that's all.'

Trust Gladys to be thinking about everyone else.

'Don't be daft! What about you?'

'I'm OK.'

Until Gladys mentioned her sight or lack of it, Lily didn't like to bring it up. The next obvious thing to ask was about the babies: where were they, had Gladys seen them? But then she couldn't actually *see* them, could she?

'Are the babies in the nursery?' she hazarded. That seemed a safe bet.

'Yes,' said Gladys flatly. 'They won't let me have them with me. Too risky, they say.'

'Well, I suppose they have to play safe.' Lily chewed her lip. They had to get onto something a bit more cheerful. Ah! Inspiration. 'But what about names? I'm dying to know what you came up with!'

Gladys had agonised. She favoured something modern, she'd said: Roy or Graham for a boy; Angela or Pauline for a girl. Bill, on the other hand, liked the more traditional names: William or George, Katherine or Anne. They were never going to fall out over it — it wasn't in their natures — but there'd been some animated discussions while Bill had been at home, and Lily knew they'd continued back and forth in letters. But she suspected that Bill would give way to Gladys in the end — she'd done the hard work, after all.

'They're M. I. Webb and F. I. Webb.'

M. I.? F. I.? Lily couldn't remember any of the names under consideration that began with those letters. Maybe Gladys had decided, in the end, to keep the final choice a secret between herself and Bill. Michael? Malcolm? Or was the little boy the 'F'? Frederick maybe, or Frank? And Ian, perhaps. And what about Gladys's daughter? Marianne? Mary? Frances? Isabel? Iris?

'Right!' she said brightly. 'And what do they stand for?'

'Male Infant Webb and Female Infant Webb.' Gladys's voice had started to wobble. 'How can I give them their names, Lily, names they'll have all their lives, till I can see them and see what they look like?'

'Oh, Gladys!' Lily seized her friend's hand. 'I'm so sorry about all this! You don't deserve it! It's so unfair! It's always the wrong people! And you're being so brave!'

'I'm not.' Gladys loosed her hand from Lily's and groped for her hanky. Lily could see it on the coverlet, and gently pushed it towards her. Gladys put it to her eyes. 'I thought I'd cried all my tears. All morning I was at it and had another good go when your mum was here. This stupid eye thing doesn't seem to affect that!'

Lily was welling up herself, but she had to be strong — or at least sound it.

'I know it's hard, so hard. It's the cruellest blow. But it's not for ever. Your sight will come back, the doctor told us.'

'So they say.'

'You have to believe it, Gladys! It's going to be all right!'

Gladys turned her head away.

'You try lying here all day, hurting, empty, no baby in your arms, and tell yourself that.'

Lily didn't stay long. Gladys said she was tired and in the stuffy atmosphere of the hospital, Lily was almost falling asleep herself. When she got home, completely wrung out, she had a good cry too, and all over Jim's good work shirt. And she started again when she saw the telegram that the ecstatic Bill, in his ignorance, had wired straight back.

76

OVER THE MOON TELL GLAD I LOVE HER CAN'T WAIT TO SEE THEM ALL xxx

Three days passed with no change in Gladys's condition. At work, Lily moved through the hours robotically but on Gladys's fourth day in hospital, Mr Marlow, on his rounds, motioned Lily aside again. Rita threw her a meaningful look which she ignored. For once, Cedric ignored the formalities.

'Mr Simmonds has apprised me of Miss Huskins — Mrs Webb's — situation. I've sent flowers and a basket of fruit.'

'I've seen them, sir,' said Lily. 'Thank you. Gladys was very touched. She'd write if she could — '

'Goodness, I don't need thanks!' Cedric waved the idea away. 'It's the least I can do. But as her employer I want you to know that if this situation continues, I'm prepared to do more. If the doctors here in Hinton can't do anything for her, I'd be very happy to pay for a second opinion — or in the future, any treatment that might help. You must tell her that.'

Lily was dumbfounded.

'Oh, I will! That's very good of you!'

'Not at all. I'd do the same for any of the staff who found themselves in a medical emergency,' Mr Marlow replied. 'But this is especially sad. It's a terrible thing when congratulations have to be mixed with condolences.'

Lily could only nod. He'd put it very well and she knew why: the death of his wife so soon after giving birth. He knew what he was talking about. Mr Marlow smiled his reedy smile.

'Now, back to work. Business as usual. The show must go on, eh?'

And he moved away.

'Well?' Rita loomed up. 'What's he got to say this time? Any date for Betty coming back?'

Lily was too bamboozled, weary, and preoccupied to score points.

'No,' she said. 'Nothing about that. But,' she added feelingly, 'I really hope it won't be long.'

That evening, as usual, she went to see Gladys. Her milk had come in and they were bringing the babies to her one at a time so she could feed them. She was trying to feed the little boy when Lily got there. The nurse motioned her to come in, but also to sit quietly while Gladys concentrated.

Male Infant Webb was having trouble latching on and with him flailing around and unable to see his little mouth, Lily could see what a struggle it was for Gladys. His face scarlet, he was yelling with hunger and frustration, trapping his hands in his nightgown and getting all hot and bothered. Gladys tried and tried without success and it wasn't long before she began to cry too. The nurse frowned and nodded her head at Lily to go and she crept silently away.

Jim was out on ARP duty, but thankfully, her mum was home when, in black despair, Lily got in. Dora was at the stove, reheating the end of yesterday's stew stretched out with pearl barley and cabbage.

'What are we going to do,' Lily worried, 'if this goes on? Mr Marlow can pay for all the specialists he likes, but right now . . . Gladys can't stay in hospital for ever. Who's going to look after her, let alone the babies? Not her gran; she's only been to see her once as it is!'

Lily took the dreary National Loaf out of the bread crock and put it on the board.

Dora sighed. She'd been having the same worries herself, and another one she didn't dare voice: even when Gladys got her sight back, as the doctors kept assuring them she would, what if, God forbid, Bill never made it through the war?

'I went round for another word with Florrie today,' she said. 'All she could do was moan about how one baby would have been enough trouble, but Gladys had to go one better by having two. And as for this eyesight thing . . . the way she was talking, you'd think Gladys had asked to go blind.'

Lily sawed savagely at the loaf, wishing the crust was Florrie's neck and the crumb her puddingy face.

'And to cap it all,' Dora went on, 'we've had another telegram from Bill. Rambling on, no thought to the cost, sent when he'd been wetting the babies' heads if you ask me. He wants every last detail and photographs of Gladys and the little ones! How long can we keep it from him, that's what I'd like to know!'

9

After a beautiful spring and the heat of May, the next few days were anything but 'flaming June'. Lily shivered as she and Jim walked to work on the first Monday of the month.

'A week,' she marvelled. 'A week, that's all, since Gladys had the twins. It seems like years ago.'

Jim said nothing. He felt for Gladys, of course, but he had other things on his mind. There were staffing problems at work. Toys were a man (or woman) down as, to save on costs, Gladys wouldn't be replaced. On Childrenswear, Betty Simkins was no substitute for Lily, with no interest in the stock and even less in her young customers. There was another edition of the *Marlows Messenger* to fill. Should he print the simple fact — that Gladys had had twins — or hold back till her sight returned and he could add a quote from the happy mother? And then there was the question of Lily's ring. All that had been put on hold.

Neither of them was unduly cheerful when they presented themselves on their departments, but as ever it was not just best foot but best face forward for the customers. Lily had quite a successful morning, notching up three sales, including a wallet and purse set in navy calf — one of the best they had. That would be something to tell Gladys when she saw her. Beryl was going tonight which was just as well — Lily was running out of chirpy chat and poor Gladys had nothing to contribute.

She was all set to put a good face on things, then,

when she ran into Miss Frobisher in the Ladies' at dinnertime. Her back was turned and she was half leaning out of the window but Lily would have known Miss Frobisher anywhere: the bird's-eye check suit, the sleek roll of honey-blonde hair. She was having a crafty smoke. She jumped and spun round when she heard the door, but relaxed when she saw it was Lily.

'I know, I'm supposed to have given up!' she sighed.

Mr Simmonds didn't like her smoking, Lily knew. He wasn't a smoker, unusual for ex-Army, but then he'd been a PT instructor and made a big fuss about lung capacity.

'I won't tell,' she smiled.

Miss Frobisher took another long, delicious drag and stubbed her cigarette out on the sill. The end was stained with her crimson lipstick.

'I have cut down,' she said. 'But really, after Miss Simkins was almost rude to Mrs MacRorie . . . '

'She wasn't!'

Mrs MacRorie was a long-standing and loyal customer, and with three boys to clothe, a valuable one.

'Don't worry, I've made representations.'

'Have you? Good!' Despite her resolve, the words were out before Lily could help herself. Miss Frobisher pounced on them.

'Are you not enjoying life on the ground floor?'

Lily quickly backtracked.

'No, no, really, it's fine,' she said. 'I had three sales this morning.'

'That wasn't quite what I asked. And I daresay you'd rather be . . . well, in more familiar surroundings when you're so worried about Gladys.' Miss Frobisher was one of the few people who'd been told the full story.

She took a miniature tin of Parma violet sweets from her suit pocket and offered one to Lily. She took one out of politeness; they were too highly perfumed for her, but they disguised the smell of a cigarette pretty well. Miss Frobisher popped one in her mouth, snapped the tin shut, and stowed it away.

'It must be devastating for her — even if they do say it's temporary. How long is temporary, after all?'

'That's what we'd all like to know.'

'I'm sure.' Miss Frobisher pulled down her suit jacket and checked her lipstick in the mirror. 'Still . . . by the end of the day, I hope you'll be getting some good news. Even if there's none from the hospital.'

Then, with her most enigmatic smile — she was good at those — Miss Frobisher was gone.

Good news? Had she served her time? Could she dare to hope . . . ? Lily practised an enigmatic smile in the mirror, but it just made her look like a constipated cat. Giving up, she went back to her department, hoping that soon her smile would be a genuine one.

Sure enough, when she emerged after a long, dull afternoon — not a single sale — Jim was waiting for her at the staff entrance. If he'd been a cat, he'd have been the Cheshire cat in *Alice in Wonderland*.

'Back to Childrenswear!' he said. 'Next Monday! And as first sales!'

'What?'

'Simmonds told me I could tell you. Happy?'

'Oh yes, yes, yes!' Lily dropped her bag and gas mask and flung her arms round his neck. He gave her a smacking kiss. 'Now all we need is good news for Gladys too!'

The breakthrough, when it came, though, was one that no one had expected. The next day, as Miss

Frobisher was off seeing a supplier, Lily took her dinner break early, and Jim managed to get on early dinner too. So they were both in the canteen when the wireless, which the canteen ladies always had on in the background, was suddenly turned up loud. The clatter of knives and forks and the sound of voices was stilled amongst warnings of 'Shh!' and 'Quiet!'

'What's going on?' Lily whispered across the table to Jim.

He shrugged and put his finger to his lips as they heard:

'Here is a special bulletin read by John Snagge.'

He paused. Then there was just the crackle of the wireless over the ether before the announcer continued:

'D-Day has come. Early this morning, the Allies began the assault on the north-western face of Hitler's European Fortress. The first official news came just after half-past nine when Supreme Headquarters of the Allied Expeditionary Force — usually called SHAEF from its initials — issued Communique No. 1. This said:

Under the command of General Eisenhower, Allied Naval Forces, supported by strong Air Forces, began landing Allied Armies this morning on the Northern coast of France.

It was announced a little later that General Montgomery is in Command of the Army Group carrying out the assault. This Army Group includes British, Canadian, and United States Forces.'

That was it. There was a stunned silence, then whoops and cheers from their fellow workmates. Lily felt tears leaking from her eyes and she wasn't the only one.

'Thank goodness!' she said, grabbing for Jim's

hand. 'Thank goodness it's come at last, but thank God that Sid and Reg aren't anything to do with it!'

Sid was in a desk job at the Admiralty; Reg, who'd fought in the Western Desert with the Eighth Army, was still in North Africa, working on the reconstruction of Libya. He'd met his fiancée, Gwenda, out there — she was a driver with the MTC. Her sister was out there too, in the WAAF.

Jim nodded.

'Yes. It won't be a doddle, though. I don't suppose Hitler's going to sit by doing a jigsaw while we march on Berlin.'

Jim was right, but even so, thought Lily, even so. Mr Churchill had said that the victory at El Alamein was the end of the beginning. Could this, at last, be the beginning of the end?

There'd been rumours of a big push to recapture Europe for a while, and puzzlement when it hadn't happened in May when the settled weather offered clear skies and a calm sea. The main thing was that it was happening now.

There was lots to talk about, then, when Lily visited Gladys the next day. The news about her return to Childrenswear and her promotion had been received with exclamations and hugs from Dora, naturally, but Lily felt almost guilty about telling Gladys her good news. At the same time she knew that Gladys was a good enough friend — and person — to be pleased for her even though her own situation still seemed so hopeless.

Sure enough, when Lily told her, Gladys reached up at once to give her a hug. She was now considered well enough to be up and dressed and was led up and down the corridor every day by a nurse 'to get those muscles working again!'. As Lily had learnt more about this strange cortical blindness thing, it had emerged that Gladys could tell the difference between light and dark, roughly. She could tell when they shone a light in her eyes; she could tell that the window side of her room was lighter than the side with the door. Beyond that, she couldn't make anything out. But it didn't stop her being Gladys, and she was thrilled for Lily.

'What did I tell you!' she exclaimed. 'I said at Christmas you'd be first sales before long!'

'It's felt long enough, putting up with Rita's sneering,' Lily grimaced. 'But I am pleased, of course I am. And thank you for being pleased for me.'

'Oh, don't be daft,' said Gladys. 'Sit down and tell me what else has been going on.'

Lily pulled up a chair and sat down with her back to the window. It was another typical Midland evening, fine after a dull day.

'Well, you know we've landed in France, don't you?' she began. The papers had naturally been full of it — not that Gladys could read them. 'They say — '

'Hang on,' Gladys interrupted her. She put out a hand. 'Lily, you're sitting over here, aren't you?' She extended a hand towards Lily's chair.

'Ye-es.'

'I can see you! Well, I can't — but I can see your shape against the light! I can't see your face, but I can see . . . it's blurry, but I can see the outline of your head and your shoulders, definitely I can!'

'Oh Gladys! That's wonderful! You're starting to see again? Shall I get the doctor?'

The doctor came. Gladys found that she could see him, too, at least when he stood with his back to the

85

light. He was cautious. He couldn't promise anything, and he still couldn't give any kind of timescale, but he confirmed it was definitely a step in the right direction.

Lily floated back home. Ages ago, in one of the darkest periods of the war, she'd taken the advice in one of her mum's magazines to write down Three Good Things that had happened every day.

On Monday she'd written:

Sold three items AND
Going back to Childrenswear next week.
As first sales!

Yesterday she'd written just one thing, but in huge letters:

D-Day!

When she got home from the hospital that evening, though, she couldn't stop writing.

Gladys started to see again!
Gladys started to see again!!
Gladys started to see again!!!

And then, as three times simply wasn't enough:

Gladys started to see again!!!!

Next evening, they both went to visit Gladys, Lily and Jim together. This time, Gladys wasn't just sitting out, she was standing, feeling her way round the bed, straightening the cover. She turned when they opened the door and moved cautiously towards them. This was an improvement already: they hadn't got the full light of the window behind them. She peered at them for a moment.

'Lily!' she said. 'And you've got a light dress on, with a lighter collar, your blue, is it? And a scarf or a hairband in your hair?'

'Yes!' cried Lily. 'You can see all that?'

Gladys nodded. She peered upwards. Jim was six feet tall. 'I'm having to crane my neck, so it must be Jim!'

'Spot on!'

Gladys beamed and Lily turned to Jim, biting her lip. It was so moving to see her coming back to life.

They sat down and talked. Gladys welled up when she told them about seeing the shape of the twins' heads for the first time and their little hands and feet, even if she couldn't see all their features properly yet. Then they talked plainly and honestly about what Gladys had been through. Only now did she confess how desperately low she'd felt, and what she'd tried so hard not to show her visitors: the terror that she'd never see again, that she'd never be able to be a proper mother to the twins or wife to Bill. In other words, exactly what Lily, Dora, and everyone who cared about her had been feeling and hadn't wanted to say either.

'And not just that, but the little things that got me down as well!' she said. 'I say little, but they're not really, when you do them every day. You try cleaning your teeth and spitting out into a cup that someone else is holding when you can't see. Try it when you get home! Close your eyes and try eating anything that you can't pick up with your fingers, and even then, finding your mouth every time! Try drinking a cup of tea and getting it back on the saucer . . . let alone daring to take a single step on your own or think about finding a job you might be able to do.' She shook her head. 'It taught me a lesson or two. I swear I'll never again go past a blind war veteran begging on the street without giving them something.'

Gladys spoke from the heart and Lily felt her own heart wrench. What had she ever had to complain about, she thought guiltily, remembering how she'd chafed about Rita or fretted over a snagged stocking or a miserly helping of custard in the canteen. The picture Gladys had painted was shocking and they all sat in silence for a moment. It was a 'there but for the grace of God' moment — not the first in five years of war, and probably not the last, either.

Then Jim cleared his throat and said something about the news from France. Gladys and Lily leapt on the subject gratefully; Gladys was taking more of an interest in things now. On convoy duty in the Northern Exchanges, Bill's ship was always at risk of U-boat or air attacks, but Gladys was relieved that he hadn't been in the thick of the landings in Europe.

Now, at last, they could tell her how they'd managed to fill their letters to him with a lot of guff about how the boy looked like him and the girl like Gladys, which at this stage was nonsense — as Jim had remarked, they both looked like the Prime Minister, though without the Homburg hat and cigar. They'd managed to say nothing about Gladys except that she was doing a wonderful job of feeding the babies and that they'd both regained their birth weight. They apologised for the lack of photographs, saying there was no camera film to be had — this at least was true, as was the fact that Gladys hadn't finally fixed on the babies' names.

'I'll be able to write to him myself soon I hope,' Gladys smiled. 'Or dictate a letter you can write for me, Lily. We can say I've got my hands full, which'll be the reality!' It was so good to see her smile again, a proper smile, not the pinned-on one for visitors. 'Oh, and by the way,' she added casually, 'I've decided what to call them.'

'What? Well, go on then!' cried Lily. 'What?'

10

'It came to me this morning,' Gladys explained. 'I'd fed them, and we were all having a cuddle and a little chat, with them in my arms' — and as Lily looked surprised — 'well, don't look at me like that, I was doing all the chatting, obviously!' She sighed happily. 'It's just so . . . and now I can start to see them a bit . . . they're so perfect and so beautiful and such a miracle. You just feel so filled with love . . . I can't explain. Anyway, we were sitting here and the sun was coming through the window. And the nurse came in to take away my breakfast and said it had been on the wireless about how we were doing in France, how we'd got five miles inland and taken some town where there's a famous tapestry, Bayoo or somewhere.'

'Yes?' urged Lily. This was typical Gladys, taking ages to get to the point. 'Go on!'

'I looked down at them, and I thought about how I was feeling, just so full of happiness, now I could start to see their little faces, and how thrilled Bill is going to be when he sees them for the first time . . . And I was so full of it I could have burst and I thought to myself, joy, that's what this is, pure joy. So that's what I'm going to call her.'

'Oh Gladys! Joy! What a lovely name!' Lily glanced at Jim. He was no tough guy, but he didn't often show his emotions. Even he was swallowing hard.

'And what about the boy?' he asked.

'That just came to me as well,' said Gladys simply. 'It's obvious, with us going into France and everything.

90

He's going to be called Victor.'

Right on cue, the nurse brought the two little scraps in to be fed. Jim immediately excused himself so Gladys could have some privacy, but Lily leapt up to help with the pillows as Gladys settled herself on the bed. Both swaddled in white, Lily couldn't tell which twin was which, but by craning at the wristband, which still said F. I. Webb, she realised that the nurse was handing over little Joy. Then she promptly handed the other screaming shawlful to Lily and disappeared through the door, explaining over her shoulder that she had six other babies to deal with.

'He doesn't seem very impressed,' Lily said nervously as M. I. Webb —Victor, as she must learn to call him — showed his displeasure by turning up the volume and trying to bury his hot, red face into Lily's chest.

'He's rooting,' said Gladys, crooning to Joy as she calmed her down before trying to latch her on. 'Thinks you're his milk tank.'

'He's in for a big disappointment then!'

'Give him your finger to suck,' advised Gladys, 'but suck it yourself first to give it a clean.'

Lily did as she was told and the punishment of her eardrums subsided.

Gladys turned back to her daughter.

'There's nothing to cry for, precious,' she murmured. 'It's all right, Mum's got lots of milk for you. Yes, you're hungry aren't you? Let's get you settled.'

Then, as Lily watched, she tucked Joy neatly under one arm and, with the baby's head supported on a pillow, latched her on. The baby clamped her mouth, Gladys winced, then stroked the soft skull as she started to suck.

'Now for you, trouble,' she said, holding out her free arm towards Lily.

'You're doing them both at once?'

Lily didn't know whether to be amazed or aghast.

'I've got to, if I don't want to be sat in a chair all day with my bosoms hanging out,' said Gladys practically.

Lily blinked. What a lot Gladys had learnt in a short time! And without being able to see, as well! Her admiration for her, which was already sky-high, rocketed. Grateful, she handed the baby over and while Gladys held her daughter's head in place, helped to secure the little boy under her other arm and angle him so he could feed.

Mission accomplished, she sank into Gladys's vacated chair. Apart from the surprisingly loud sound of suckling, peace reigned.

'And you have to do this how many times a day?'

Gladys laughed.

'Oh, Lily, I feel for your Jim, I really do! It's every few hours, day *and* night! You may be forging ahead at Marlows but outside of work, you've still got a lot to learn, haven't you?'

★ ★ ★

It was another week before they let Gladys out of hospital, with strict instructions that there must be no unnecessary stress and she mustn't get overtired.

'Have they listened to themselves!' snorted Dora. 'She's got two-week-old twins, for goodness' sake — and they've never met Florrie!' The old woman's selfishness was staggering. She'd visited Gladys just once in the hospital, and that only to raid the fruit basket and the bedside locker. 'There's nothing for it,'

92

Dora added. 'I shall have to go round every day.'

So she did, fitting in a visit between the daily round of housework, queuing for food, washing and cooking, plus the afternoon duties she'd resumed at the Red Cross and WVS tea bar. Poor Buddy was sorely neglected, or felt he was, fretting and whining in the backyard, to the displeasure of Jean Crosbie next door, who never failed to report it to Dora. Lily suspected Buddy was trying it on, hoping that Jean would throw him a bit of bacon rind or a bread crust over the fence, because in the evenings he'd got used to being thoroughly spoilt by them all. Feeling guilty about leaving him, Dora sweet-talked the butcher into extra bones and scraps, and for walks Jim had started taking him along on his night-time ARP patrols. And Buddy needed the exercise, what with the biscuits he was fed by the kindly wardens when they got back to the ARP post.

Dora might be back on the tea bar rota, but the WVS was on Lily's conscience. With all the visits to Gladys, she also hadn't been able to do so much, not at the Drill Hall anyway. Now though, she and her mum could both rejoin the merry throng refashioning the unwanted seaboot socks into the famous polo-neck jumpers and sewing the thick shoulder and elbow patches that they'd cut at home onto hefty crew-necks for the rifle brigades. After her initial enthusiasm, Lily found it pretty dull, but at least she was doing something — and she could still help Gladys too, which consoled her when she saw other girls in uniform.

One evening towards the end of June, Lily was late getting to the hall. She'd called on Gladys after work, as she often did, but had been held up. After Victor had been fed and changed, he'd promptly soiled his clean nappy. Lily had had the job of stopping him throwing himself off the chest of drawers that was used as a changing table while Gladys went to fetch another off the clothes horse.

Lily arrived at the hall, though, to find it in even more of a flurry than she was. The usual circle of chairs for companionable chat wasn't in place; instead, Mrs Russell, the organiser, was bustling about with a clipboard, while helpers sorted piles of blankets and what looked like children's jumpers, shorts, and dresses.

As Lily hung up her jacket, Dora came over.

'You won't believe it!' she said. 'Evacuees on the way!'

'Evacuees?'

Lily was baffled. Then she realised what it must be. The wretched doodlebug bombs — officially V1 rockets - that had started to rain on London.

'Evacuees . . . ' she repeated. 'How many?'

'We don't know yet. But a good few. All the really safe billets in the countryside have been taken up long ago so they've got to resort to towns like us.'

'Are we going to take one in at our house?'

Dora shook her head.

'I'd like to help, but where'd they sleep, in Buddy's kennel?'

'The front room?' said Lily.

'I can't put them in there, with that damp that's come through. It might not hurt Sid on the occasional night he's home, but no one's going to thank me for giving their child TB, are they?'

Lily had to agree. The damp patch was growing, even in summer.

'No, there's nothing we can do,' her mother resumed. 'Except . . . it's your half-day tomorrow, Lily. Will you come to the station with me and the others and meet them off the train?'

'Of course!'

'We've got to do squash and biscuits for them when they arrive, then keep them occupied while we try and sort them out,' Dora explained. 'Mrs Russell only got warning of it last night; she's been ringing round ever since trying to rally a few people to take them in. But we'll end up walking them round the streets, I reckon, knocking on doors. Not much of a welcome for the poor little mites, is it?' Poor little mites was about right. As the children straggled off the train the following afternoon, Lily thought what a sorry-looking bunch they were. There were about thirty of them, the oldest perhaps ten or eleven, the youngest only about three. They'd come from Bermondsey, Bow, and Mile End itself, where the very first buzz bomb had dropped. They were among London's poorest districts and just as much a target for the new breed of bombs as they had been in the Blitz. All because they cradled London's docklands.

A few of the children looked around curiously, almost excited. The rest were mute, disorientated, and fearful. Tearful, too — some of the smaller ones were crying, whether from anxiety or exhaustion it was hard to say. There were two adults with them as chaperones, a hawk-faced woman and a hollow-eyed man. Mrs Russell, in her full WVS rig of green suit and felt hat, bustled towards them, clipboard at the ready. The beaky woman produced a list of names from her bag and the complex negotiations over who might go where began.

'Come on.'

Taking Lily's arm, Dora made for the massed crowd

of children. She clapped her hands and the little faces turned towards her. Close to, Lily could see just how scruffy they were. It came as no great surprise.

Last year, a quest with Gladys to track down Bill's mother had taken them to Stepney where he'd grown up in the orphanage. Lily had been shocked. Hinton was her home town and for that reason she loved it, but without it being exactly ugly, she knew it was nothing special. Beyond a few old Georgian buildings and the central shopping streets, it was a web of small factories, warehouses, pubs, corner shops, and terraces, like her own, crowded around the railway line and canal.

Her own home was nothing grand but in Stepney she'd seen proper slums, cramped and insanitary even before the Blitz. Add a layer of dust and grime, broken bricks, broken houses, broken windows, and half-cleared bomb sites and the sum total was a vision of hell. However, it had been home to these children and was all they knew. It must have been a wrench to leave. She hoped they'd settle in Hinton somehow.

The numbers were about even, boys and girls. Some were obviously siblings, the older ones either protective or dismissive of the little ones' tugging hands. Some of the older boys were boisterous, pushing and shoving, some of it genuine, some bravado, Lily suspected. The older girls looked resigned or bored. In the early days of the war, there'd been mass evacuation of children from the big cities, but in the months of the phony war, many had gone back, only to be caught up in the Blitz. Off the children had been sent again, only to be reclaimed or to drift back home when the bombings had eased off. For some of these children, this might be their third journey into the unknown.

'Now listen,' Dora was saying to them. 'Over there at the tea bar there's refreshments for you while we try to sort a few things out. But — No, wait —'

It was too late. The children had already started streaming noisily towards the offer of food and drink.

'Get after them, Lily!' cried her mother. 'We don't want to lose any! Here was I thinking I could get them into a nice orderly crocodile!'

They chased after the children and tried to corral them.

'I should have brought Jim's fire-watching whistle,' Lily grinned when finally the children were slurping noisily at squash and stuffing arrowroots and malted milks into their mouths and pockets.

'No choclit?' complained one lad. 'When I was evac to 'Ereford we got biscuits *and* choclit when we got there!'

It was a taste of things to come.

★ ★ ★

When Lily had told him she'd be busy that afternoon, Jim was delighted — not that he showed it. They normally spent every hour of their free time together, but after the hiatus caused by Gladys and the babies, Lily's offer to help with the evacuees meant he could resume his secret ring shopping.

He'd settled on his chosen jeweller's — Samson Newman and Son, jeweller, watch mender, and silversmith — whose window, he felt, held the best selection. Still in his work suit to give the impression of being a serious purchaser, his Post Office book in his pocket, Jim headed for the shop. He paused before the window to straighten his tie, and as he did so, a hand poked through the velvet drapes at the back and removed one of the pads of rings.

'Knew I was coming!' thought Jim and pushed open the door. A bell jangled prettily and he blinked, adjusting his eyes to the dark interior after the sunshine outside. Once he had, he could see there was another customer in the gloom at the back, bending over the pad of rings. The jeweller, an old chap alone behind the counter, stepped to one side.

'Would you mind waiting, sir,' he said with an old-fashioned deference. 'I'll attend to you as soon as I've finished with this gentleman.'

It was a nuisance, but Jim was there now. It had taken him long enough, so what was another few minutes?

'No problem,' he replied.

The other man wheeled round.

'Jim!'

It was Peter Simmonds.

11

When the children had drunk and eaten their fill, Dora, Lily, and the other WVS volunteers marched them to the Drill Hall. There, the council's billeting officer, Mr Parfitt, would be waiting alongside the women Mrs Russell had rounded up the day before who'd expressed a willingness to take a child.

On the way, Lily and Dora had counted and recounted every few minutes, terrified one of the children might make a run for it. Amazingly, numbers were intact on arrival, but once in the hall, the children rapidly scattered. Energised by their refreshments, they re-formed the gangs and groupings they knew from home with high-pitched squeals and shouts.

Mr Parfitt wasn't immediately impressive — receding hair, receding chin, receding manner. It was left to poor Mrs Russell to try to restore order, but it was a hopeless task and the would-be foster mothers didn't help. There was a positive scrum as they scrambled towards the children. Girls were everyone's first choice — they were more biddable and ate less — and the smallest and best-dressed, cleanest and prettiest, were the first to be claimed. Off they were hauled to be ticked off on Mr Parfitt's list.

Appalled by the chaos, Lily was comforting a little scrap with a grubby teddy bear who hadn't yet been chosen when there was a ruckus nearby. A woman had swooped on a boy of about ten and a girl of about five and was trying to prise them apart. The boy yanked the little girl towards him.

'No! Get your hands off! Our mum said we was to stay together!' he shouted. 'She made me swear to look after Barb! Me and my sister's going together or we're not going at all!'

'I don't think you have much say in the matter, young man!' the woman shot back.

Mrs Russell scurried over to see what was going on, and the boy — Joe, according to the label round his neck — repeated what he'd said, several times over and at increasing volume. It turned out the woman in the dispute was a friend of Mrs Russell's.

'I can promise you,' Mrs Russell said kindly, 'that your sister will be going to a very good home. I know this lady and she's had evacuees before, earlier in the war. Barbara would be very lucky to be there.'

'Only if I go as well!' insisted Joe.

Mrs Russell turned in mute appeal to her friend, who shook her head.

'You know how it is, Irene,' she said firmly. 'I have my husband to consider. He works hard all day. A little girl who I can keep tidy and who'll be in bed by seven is one thing. A great big growing lad thumping about the place is a very different matter. I'm sorry, but no.'

Joe held a wide-eyed Barbara's hand even tighter. In desperation, hoping he'd exert a bit of authority, Mrs Russell appealed to Mr Parfitt, but he, as Les would have said, was as much use as an inflatable dartboard. Eventually, force had to be used. Little Barbara, by now almost hysterical, was prised off her brother and led away, being told 'not to be so silly now' and to 'wait till she saw the pretty room that was waiting for her.'

All the remaining children were staring. Barbara's

wails had set off some of the other younger ones and Lily saw Joe turn away, biting the inside of his cheek and dragging the ragged sleeve of his jumper across his eyes.

She went over and put a hand on his shoulder.

'She'll be all right,' she said. 'I know that woman didn't go about it very well, but she didn't look a bad sort.'

'Yeah?' he muttered.

'You did your best,' she said. 'It's not your fault.'

'I hate this bloody war!' he said. 'I hate it, I hate it here and I hate all of you! Got it?'

★   ★   ★

'Cheers!' Peter Simmonds raised his glass and chinked it against Jim's. They'd just caught dinnertime last orders, a happy state of affairs as Peter was in a celebratory mood, and no wonder. In his pocket, in a small leather box, was the engagement ring he'd bought for Eileen Frobisher.

'You realise you're in on a secret,' he said when they'd both wiped the froth from their lips.

'Wild horses,' Jim reassured him.

He was still coming to terms with what the ring — an oval sapphire in a frill of diamonds — had cost. Not that Miss Frobisher wasn't worth it, but it put a screaming brake on his ambitions. Jim had been eyeing a sapphire for Lily; she wore a lot of blue. Perhaps not as big a ring as the one Peter had chosen, admittedly, but now he knew that anything of that order was far beyond his pocket.

It was a bitter blow, but in a way he was grateful. Peter had looked at six or seven rings of all shapes and sizes before he'd settled on his chosen one, and Jim had noted the prices as the jeweller reeled them off. It had saved him the humiliation of asking to see any rings himself, then having to creep away saying he'd 'think about it'. He'd spent long enough serving customers at Marlows to know that that was code for 'way out of my league' or even 'you won't catch me setting foot in here again!'.

'So what were you there for, really?' Peter asked, looking at him sidelong. Jim had blathered some story about needing a watch mended, saying he'd bring it in another day, and Peter had obviously seen right through it. 'If I had to take a guess, I'd say you were ring shopping too.'

Jim pulled a splinter off the leg of his chair. He did it automatically now; he'd heard enough complaints from Lily about ripping her precious stockings on them.

'OK, you got me,' he admitted. 'But I'm not as far along in the process as you.'

'But you and Lily are unofficially engaged already, aren't you? You're much further along than me!' Peter exclaimed. 'I haven't even broached the subject yet. And' — he fiddled with his glass — 'it's difficult.'

'How?'

Peter Simmonds opened his hands in a gesture of helplessness.

'There's the question of young John. I'd like to surprise Eileen with the ring, but I can't. I can't drop it on the poor kid out of nowhere.'

Miss Frobisher's background was complicated. She had a five-year-old son whose father had long since disappeared, never to return.

'You get on with John well enough,' objected Jim.

'I've seen you with him at the cricket. He surely won't mind; he seems to idolise you.'

Jim and Lily sometimes went to see the store's football and cricket teams in action; Peter Simmonds managed the football team and captained the cricket side. He also wrote up the matches for the *Messenger*, but Jim liked to do the odd spot-check. Peter had been known to get carried away in his reports, accusing the cricketers from Timothy White's of exaggerating a broken finger and gloating that the ARP footballers had 'played like girls'. Jim didn't like to think of the treatment he'd have received on his next ARP shift if that claim hadn't been edited out.

'It's kind of you to say so,' Peter acknowledged. 'But a few hours a week isn't quite the same as asking him to share his mother with me full time. She's been on her own with him since he was a baby. They have a very special bond.'

Jim nodded.

'Yes, I suppose you're right.'

'I need to think about how to approach it. So don't say anything to anyone about today, please. Not even to Lily.'

Jim picked up his glass and tipped it towards Peter.

'Why?' he said. 'What happened today? I really can't remember — this beer must be stronger than it tastes.'

★ ★ ★

In the end, with the evacuees, it was just as Dora had predicted. When the initial fuss had died down, the remaining children were allocated to their new homes. Off the luckier ones went, child-sized gas masks bumping against their little bodies, their pathetic bundles of possessions in their arms. Left behind were the poorest, the shabbiest, and the least attractive — a rabble of boys and a few of the older, more lumpen girls, the ones who looked as if they wouldn't be cheap to feed.

'Look at them!' Jean Crosbie, another WVS volunteer, crimped her lips in her usual way. 'We'll be traipsing round town with this lot till midnight!'

There were thirteen of the thirty left, but Mrs Russell, to her credit, had come prepared. Every volunteer was allocated a few of the remaining children. Lily and Dora had three — a boss-eyed twelve-year-old girl, a pasty boy of about seven, and a sullen Joe. Mrs Russell then gave them a street plan of the part of town where they were to try to house them. Lily wasn't over-hopeful. It was one of the poorer districts of Hinton, most of the houses already crowded, but as Dora pointed out, rather cynically for her, that might work to their advantage.

'There's ten and six a week in it for anyone who takes an evacuee,' she said in a low voice as they set off, trying to keep the children together. 'Plus the rations they're given to start them off, plus their ration book . . . It might be a temptation for some.'

'That's hardly the motivation we want, is it?' queried Lily. 'Filling the larder for free!'

'The milk of human kindness doesn't put milk in the jug,' was Dora's pithy reply.

They had no luck at all in the first street they tried, but that came as no surprise to Lily. Jim was always swotting up on anything to do with sales and he'd told her that whether you were selling lucky heather or ladies' underwear, the success rate in cold-calling was a maximum of three out of every hundred doors you knocked. Lily counted eighty-eight houses in that first street, but when in the second street another twenty doors were virtually slammed in their faces, her hopes really began to fade. Then came a breakthrough, and in the space of ten houses they managed to allocate two children almost one after the other. The girl was taken in by a voluble widow who said she'd like the company, someone to talk to — or perhaps at, thought Lily. The seven-year-old was taken in by a harassed-looking woman with two children roughly the same age, who said one more couldn't make much difference, though by the shabbiness of what Lily could see of the house, ten and six a week perhaps would.

That left them with Joe. Lily wished she could tell him to cheer up — it might make him more appealing — but she knew it would do no good.

'We're going to end up taking him home with us, damp or no damp,' she whispered to Dora.

But her mother was firm.

'Lily, I'm sorry, I can't take on any more waifs and strays! First Jim, then the dog . . . I'm over with Gladys and the twins every day, then my WVS and Red Cross in the afternoons. Are you trying to send me to an early grave? We've got to find him a home somehow.'

It was mid-afternoon now, and as they passed the Fox and Goose, the landlord's wife was ejecting the last drinkers. Dora knew her slightly — as girls, they'd worked together at Hinton's corset factory.

'Afternoon, Ethel,' she said.

'Dora. What are you doing round this part of town?' Then, noting Dora's WVS uniform, she added, 'Oh, evacuees, is it? I heard they'd sent a load.'

'This is Joe,' said Lily, pushing the boy forward. 'He's looking for somewhere to stay.'

Ethel Pearson eyed him.

'Big lad, isn't he? Eats his own weight in bread and scrape every day, I'll bet.'

To Lily's surprise, Joe thrust the brown paper bag he was carrying towards her.

'There's corned beef in here,' he said. 'Two tins. And condensed milk the same. And before you ask, I've ate the chocolate.'

'He speaks, then!' But Ethel's mind was obviously working. 'Well, I suppose I might be able to help you out. No harm in doing my bit.'

'Would you?' asked Dora. 'If you're sure . . .'

'Go on then.' Ethel addressed Joe. 'Get inside. Go through the back. My daughter's in there. Tell her who you are, get her to give you a cup of tea and a slice.'

To Lily's further amazement, Joe went — without a backward glance or a goodbye to Lily or Dora, and without a thank you to Ethel, but he went. As Dora went through the paperwork with his new foster mother, Lily peered into the pub. The bar was basic but looked clean. Maybe Joe would be no worse off here than anywhere else.

As they walked away, though, it seemed Dora had doubts.

'I'll make sure Mr Parfitt keeps an eye on him,' she said in a low voice. 'Ethel might seem hard, but she has to be, running that place, and she's not bad really. Her husband's another matter. I didn't come in on the last coal barge. Joe'll be put to heaving crates and washing glasses if I'm not mistaken.'

Lily knew that working them was definitely not

part of the arrangement for evacuees, and Joe's sudden acceptance of his fate was bothering her too. She couldn't help feeling that the problem of Joe and his sister was not entirely resolved.

12

Across town, another Lily-related problem wasn't entirely resolved either, but Jim, emboldened by Peter Simmonds — or more likely the whisky chaser Peter had insisted on — was determined not to let it linger. When he and Peter had parted, he hot-footed it straight back to the jewellers.

The old fellow was on his own in the shop, polishing up a tray of lockets.

'Good afternoon again,' he said. 'You've brought the watch?'

'No,' Jim confessed. 'I'm sorry, there is no watch. I'm after a ring myself, but I didn't want to say so in front of my colleague.'

The old chap nodded.

'I understand. I think. So what can I show you?'

Jim laid his Post Office book on the counter.

'I may as well be honest,' he said. 'My girl means just as much to me, but I'm not in the market for something as pricey as he could afford.'

The old man picked up Jim's book and looked at it. He laid it down again.

'I'm sure we can find something to suit,' he said kindly. 'Have you anything in mind? A particular stone? A specific design?'

Jim sighed.

'I was thinking of a sapphire,' he admitted. 'Lily wears a lot of blue — it brings out the colour of her eyes. But I know even a small one's out of my league.'

The old man pursed his lips.

'And what sort of person is your Lily?' he asked. 'Is she the traditional type? Or — '

Jim almost snorted with laughter.

'Anything but! She's . . . she's special. Not just to me.' The jeweller waited, his head on one side. He seemed to want more, so Jim went on. 'She stands up for what she believes in — she'll fight for it. She's not hard or ruthless, but she hates injustice, or unfairness, or seeing people suffer. Sometimes she jumps in with both feet — though she's got a bit better at that lately — but it's only because she cares. She'd go to the ends of the earth to help someone out; she's got the biggest heart of anyone I know. Oh, she can be annoying at times with what she takes on herself but it's impossible not to like her! And I love her for it.' It was only when he took a breath that Jim realised he'd almost been giving a speech, and a passionate one at that. 'Funny,' he said, slightly embarrassed. 'I don't often put it into words. But there it is.'

The old fellow smiled.

'Maybe you should put it into words more often. Blue eyes, you say. One moment.'

He disappeared into the back of the shop and came back holding a ring between his fingers. He held it out to Jim.

'This is an aquamarine,' he said. 'For my money, even prettier than a sapphire, and perhaps more suitable for a young girl, as I take it your Lily is. As you see, the stone's not large, but it's clear, which is important, and it's a pretty shape, I think, with the two small diamonds each side?'

Jim took the ring. Even in the austerity lighting, the diamonds winked back at him.

'It's beautiful,' he murmured. 'I can just see it on

109

Lily. And I can afford it?'

The old man waggled his head from side to side like a tortoise.

'I made a good sale to your colleague. It's more a case of I can afford for you to afford it.'

'Oh, thank you! Thank you.'

'My wife will kill me,' said the old fellow. 'Says I'm too soft-hearted. But young love . . . who can resist?'

The deal was sealed.

★ ★ ★

Jim was thrilled with how the afternoon had worked out, but it was a good job he had no thoughts of presenting the ring to Lily immediately — when and how was another thing he had to consider — because when he got in, she was full of her afternoon with the evacuees.

'Oh Jim,' she said when they went for their customary walk after tea. 'The things those children have seen! There was one lad boasting about the bottles of gin he'd pinched when the front of a pub was blown off. Another who told me in rather too much detail about a man with a huge shard of glass sticking out of his shoulder. The bloke reached round and pulled it out himself and the blood ran all down his arm.'

Jim winced. Then she told him about Joe and Barbara.

'They've been sent here for safety but what's the point of that if it makes them so unhappy?'

'After what you've just told me about things in London? Come on, Lily, they'll settle down. They'll have to.'

'I'm not so sure. And Mum's not very sure about

where we had to leave Joe anyway.'

'Oh Lord,' groaned Jim. 'Here we go. Good Cause number ninety-three — or should that be ninety-four? — since I've known you.'

Lily punched him on the arm and he gave her a kiss in return. What had he said in the jeweller's? Lily and her causes were one of the many reasons he loved her.

Dora had had a word with Mrs Russell, who'd made a note on Joe's form for Mr Parfitt, but Lily couldn't imagine that nondescript individual fighting the boy's corner very vigorously even if he suspected any wrongdoing. She thought about it all next day at work, and by the evening, she'd decided to do her own spot-check. Jim was on fire-watching duty on the roof of Marlows — not that he'd have been able to stop her; he might as well have tried to stop a tank in its tracks.

After tea, and Dora's departure for her WI Knitting Circle — it was hats on circular needles tonight — Lily set off for the Fox and Goose. When she got there, the noise from the open doorway suggested some kind of tournament was going on — darts, by the sound of it. Good. The bar would be busy with players and drinkers; Ethel and her husband would be occupied. Lily made her way round the back.

There was an untidy yard piled with casks and crates of empties. The back door to the pub was open and she ventured in. On the right-hand side, another door stood open and she peeped cautiously round. It was obviously the family's living room, and their office, too — on the table the remains of a meal jostled with a litter of papers. There was no sign of Joe. Had he, as Dora had suspected, been put to work out front, collecting glasses and mopping tables?

111

Just then, she heard footsteps behind her and froze. Being caught snooping wasn't going to endear her to Ethel Pearson or her husband. But when she slowly turned, it was Joe.

'What are you doing here?' he demanded.

'Looking for you, actually!'

'Fine private eye you are! I saw you come in the back.'

'Must do better,' smiled Lily. Then, relieved, she asked:

'They haven't got you working, then?'

Joe sniffed.

'The old feller said something about washing up but I'd like to see 'em try.'

'Good. So . . . were you up in your room? You do have a room of your own?'

Joe tossed his head.

'I've got a camp bed. In a box room with some broken bar stools and old lamps.'

And Dora had been concerned about a bit of damp!

'That doesn't sound very suitable.'

Joe shrugged.

'I've never had a bed of my own before, so that's something I s'pose. But it don't matter anyway 'cos I'm not staying.'

'No, I thought perhaps not. Look, it's all right,' soothed Lily. 'We'll find you somewhere else.'

'Are you deaf or daft?' scorned Joe. 'I'm not staying here and I'm not staying in this stinking town. I'm going to find my sister and we're going home!'

'Joe! You can't! How are you going to get there? What are you going to do for money? And how are you going to find Barbara in the first place?'

'You're going to help me.'

'How do you get yourself in these situations?' demanded Jim when Lily told him what had happened.

He knew the answer perfectly well; he'd explained it in the jeweller's. The ring was burning a hole in his pocket, but how could he stage the proposal when Lily had other things on her mind?

They were on their usual Sunday afternoon stroll, walking aimlessly, Lily taking no notice of where they were going. Buying time, pretending she'd do some investigation for him, she'd persuaded Joe to stick it out, but she knew he wouldn't wait long.

'I can't do anything till the WVS on Tuesday,' she sighed. 'We're bound to talk about the evacuees. Maybe I can talk to Mrs Russell about it and sort of subtly find out the address of the woman who took in Joe's sister.'

'Yes, and say you do, then what? You're going to yank her away just because you've taken this lad to heart? You might find the little girl's perfectly happy there.'

'She won't be happy. She knows as well as Joe that their mother insisted they stay together. She's got a weak chest. He says she'll pine and not eat and get sick.'

'He would say that, wouldn't he?' protested Jim. 'So what's your plan? Smuggle her away in the dead of night? Buy the two of them tickets to London? Come on, Lily, you can't!'

'I know I can't! They need a place together, here in Hinton. I thought I could work on the woman who's got Barbara to take them both.'

'But Mrs Russell tried that on the day they arrived! It was a no-go.'

'But if I explain that I've seen Joe, and . . . Jim! We've come miles!'

Lily had suddenly realised where they were.

'Doesn't time fly when you're ranting on,' said Jim mildly.

They were almost at Juniper Hill, where Mrs Tunnicliffe lived. Lily stopped, hesitated, then turned to Jim.

'Do you think we could call on her?'

'What for?'

'Just to see how she is. As we're here.'

'Hang on . . .' began Jim, pretending to think. 'Remind me . . . she was your Good Cause number seventy-one, wasn't she?' Lily threw him one of her looks. If only she knew how like Dora she looked when she did that, Jim thought, but also thought it better not to say. 'Anyway, Uncle Cedric told you someone was keeping an eye on her. You can't have everyone in Hinton on your conscience, Lily.'

'I know that,' agreed Lily. 'If there's a car there, or if when we ring the bell she's obviously got company, we'll come away. But Sunday can be a long day when you're on your own.'

It had been Florrie Jessop's constant complaint if Gladys went out on a Sunday. Now, of course, Florrie's gripe was the opposite — not a minute's peace.

Jim pulled Lily towards him and gave her a kiss.

'I don't know how you found room for me in your heart,' he said. 'But I'm glad you did.'

There was no car on Mrs Tunnicliffe's drive, so that was the same as before, but there were some notable differences. The pots on the step were planted with begonias and the knocker had had a fairly recent polish. And when they rang the bell, Mrs Tunnicliffe came to the door almost immediately.

'Lily!' she exclaimed.

'I hope you don't mind,' Lily began. 'We were passing and — '

Mrs Tunnicliffe smiled. She was looking better as well, in a pale linen dress.

'Of course not,' she said. 'You're just in time for tea.'

She took them into the sitting room, which was as Lily remembered from her visit after Violet's death, with its chintz-covered chairs and silver photo frames. She insisted on making the tea herself without Lily's help.

When they were all nursing their cups ('Very little sugar, I'm afraid, and no cake — you must think me a very bad hostess!') the conversation ran surprisingly smoothly. Out of sensitivity, Lily avoided mentioning Marlows, but Mrs Tunnicliffe brought the subject up herself. Jim told her about Lily's promotion and Mrs Tunnicliffe asked about a typical day.

'There's no such thing!' Lily laughed, but ran through the basic duties which had to be performed every day — the tidying, the displays, the filling in of counterfoils, and the counting of coupons.

Mrs Tunnicliffe seemed intrigued.

'It's fascinating to hear about the shop from your point of view,' she mused.

'And have you been busy?' Lily finally dared to ask.

'Oh, I keep myself occupied,' said Mrs Tunnicliffe. 'The WVS and the Red Cross, you know, and my sons have got me involved with fundraising for various military charities, the Spitfire appeal and so on.'

115

The usual round, thought Lily. It was useful work, of course, and it filled time. But did it really fill the void left by Violet?

'I go to the WVS now, with my mum,' she volunteered. 'At the Drill Hall on the Tipton Road.'

'Ah, the East Hinton branch.' Mrs Tunnicliffe nodded. 'You had to deal with the evacuees.'

'That's right!'

'You had quite a job placing them, I heard.'

'Yes,' Lily sighed. Out of the corner of her eye, she noticed Jim shift in his seat. She turned back towards Mrs Tunnicliffe. 'They're not all in the best homes. Some in the same family had to be split up, I'm afraid, a girl here, a boy there. There was one boy we had to place in a pub.'

'That's most unfortunate,' said Mrs Tunnicliffe.

'I know, but we had no choice. There weren't enough people willing to take more than one. Some had had evacuees before, not always a great success, and most people don't have the room or the time to give two children the attention they deserve, poor things.'

Jim gave a little cough and covered it with a 'sorry'.

'No, I can see that,' mused Mrs Tunnicliffe. 'Poor things indeed. Oh well . . . ' She lifted the silver pot. 'More tea?'

★ ★ ★

'You planned that,' said Jim, when they were back down the drive. Lily was stroking the grey cat which had taken up its position on top of one of the stone pillars at the gate.

Lily turned innocent blue eyes to his.

'Planned what?'

116

'You're hoping she'll take Joe and Barbara. That's why you wanted to call on her.'

'I don't know where you got that idea,' objected Lily. 'She brought up the WVS and the evacuees, not me!'

Jim shook his head, half admiringly. 'Yes, and if she hadn't, you'd have found a way to drop it in. You certainly laid it on thick enough. You don't seriously think she could be persuaded to take them, do you?'

'I don't know what you're talking about,' said Lily blithely. 'It never crossed my mind.'

The cat — the disc on his collar gave his name as Theo — lifted his chin and Lily tickled the thick fur underneath. He began a rasping purr.

'Don't ever play poker, Lily. You're a terrible liar.' But Jim was smiling. 'Though I suppose that's a good thing about you. Well, there's certainly no more you could have done. Or can do for now.'

'There is one thing,' said Lily. She reached up and kissed him, holding the back of his head in a way he loved. 'You've given up all your Sunday afternoon for me, one way and another. I'm sorry, Jim. How do you put up with me, and why?'

'I won't answer that,' smiled Jim. But he knew perfectly well.

13

Lily wasn't even sure herself if she'd consciously thought of Juniper Hill as a possible home for Joe and Barbara. Well, all right, the thought had crossed her mind, then had crossed back again, if only because she thought she should approach the matter the official way, through Mrs Russell. But when the subject of the evacuees had come up quite spontaneously, it had simply been too tempting. And so obvious! There was Mrs Tunnicliffe, all alone in that family house, which was crying out to be a family house again . . .

On Tuesday, it was the WVS meeting. The minute they arrived, Dora made straight for the latest mountain of Army socks that had arrived for darning, but Mrs Russell beckoned Lily over.

'The evacuees that you and your mother were worried about,' she began. 'Joe and Barbara Wilson.'

Lily's heart started banging away like a trip-hammer. It was impossible to read Mrs Russell's tone.

'Oh yes?' she stuttered.

Had something happened? Had Joe run away? Was she in for a ticking off?

'I had a telephone call on Sunday evening,' Mrs Russell went on. 'From Daphne Tunnicliffe.' She paused. She obviously couldn't work out quite how Lily knew someone like Mrs Tunnicliffe outside of Marlows. 'I gather she's an acquaintance of yours?'

Lily swallowed hard. Mrs Tunnicliffe had seemed sympathetic, but had she felt that Lily was interfering, taking the plight of the evacuee children too much to

118

heart? Or had she — could Lily dare hope — had she taken the hint?

'It came half an hour,' Mrs Russell went on, 'after my friend — the one who'd taken in Barbara — had left my house in tears. The placement wasn't working out. The child was unhappy, not eating, not sleeping, crying, wetting the bed . . . ' Lily's trip-hammer heart pounded even faster. 'In short, Daphne's call was manna from heaven. Your mother had already told me her concerns about leaving Joe at the Fox and Goose. I understand why you had to do it — if someone offers, you can hardly turn them down, and goodness knows, we were desperate. But placing a child in a public house, whether he's put to work or not, is hardly ideal.'

The situation at the Fox and Goose didn't matter now.

'But what did Mrs Tunnicliffe say?' Lily could hardly get the words out.

'She suggested she meet the children to see whether she could offer them a home together.'

'Oh, that's wonderful! I'm so pleased!'

'There's more,' Mrs Russell looked almost smug. 'I took them round myself yesterday afternoon and they moved last night.'

'No!'

'Yes! It's a relief to me as well,' Mrs Russell confided with a smile. 'Though Mr Parfitt isn't too happy. He droned on about people taking matters into their own hands, but his main gripe was having to have his master list retyped, and carbon paper being like gold dust. Well, if that's all he's got to worry about, he's a lucky man! Now, have you seen the socks that are waiting for us? You'd better get started!'

Lily took her place at a long table next to her mum, already busy with her needle.

'What was all that about?' queried Dora.

'Joe and Barbara!' Lily beamed. 'And it's all good news!'

She told Jim about it too when she and Dora got home. He rolled his eyes and shook his head with his usual patient affection — he'd warned her so many times about trying to fix everyone's problems. It made Lily almost embarrassed that things had worked out as she'd hoped, but she was relieved that they had without her having to get any more embroiled. As time went on, however, that didn't stop her being intrigued by the new set-up at Juniper Hill.

★ ★ ★

'Wouldn't you like a little walk to see how she's getting on?' she asked Jim a couple of weeks later. It was a fine summer's day, and Jim had planned to use their afternoon off to sow spring cabbage in the veg beds in the yard.

Fatal. Buddy, sniffing around, heard the word 'walk' and started his crazed Jack-in-a-box routine.

'Go on,' urged Lily, trying to calm a yapping Buddy down. 'Before Jean Crosbie sticks her head over the fence and moans about the noise.'

'Oh, all right.' Jim gave up. 'But don't blame me if you haven't got any fresh greens on your plate come March.' Then, almost as an afterthought, he added, 'Let me get my jacket.'

Off they went, Buddy nosing his way along the pavements like the hunting dog he was supposed to be, though the scents he'd pick up in Hinton were more

120

likely to be old fish-and-chip papers than pheasant.

Lily was free to enjoy the scenery, and as they walked that included Jim. She stole a sideways look at him. He'd never have called himself good-looking, but he was — tall, with a finely drawn face, chestnut hair and deep brown eyes. He had so many good qualities, too; he was thoughtful, intelligent, funny. And he was so kind and patient, shortening his long stride to her leg length, listening to her rabbit on, trying to support her even when he didn't always agree with her, but not afraid to stand his ground when he thought she was off on completely the wrong tack. She sighed happily.

'What?' he asked.

'Do I need a reason?' Lily smiled. Then she answered her own question. 'Just happy.'

★ ★ ★

There was no answer when they rang the bell at Mrs Tunnicliffe's.

'Maybe she's taken them out,' suggested Jim. 'On a walk or something.'

'Yes. Oh well. We tried.'

They turned and were about to walk away when they heard laughter — children's laughter. It was coming from the garden at the back.

'Come on, she won't mind.'

Lily took Jim's hand and led him round the side of the house. Buddy, thrilled to have somewhere new to explore, pulled at his lead on Jim's other arm. The gravel path crunched lightly under their feet, but when they came to the corner, Jim hauled Buddy back and held Lily back too.

'Let's not barge in.'

They peeped round. Joe and Barbara were on the lawn playing Blind Man's Buff, Barbara squealing excitedly as she evaded her brother's outstretched hands. There were toys scattered on a rug — a doll, a bat and ball, a toy fort and a Noah's Ark. Under the cedar tree, four chairs were grouped around a wrought-iron table. Tea was standing ready — the silver tea set and the china cups, plus a plate of sandwiches and a cake. A muslin cloth weighted with glass beads protected a jug of lemonade from flies. In a basket chair to one side sat Mrs Tunnicliffe, watching the children indulgently. And in another, close beside it, sat Cedric Marlow.

'Wha-at?' Jim exploded. 'What's he doing here?'

'Shh!' Lily dragged him — and Buddy — a few paces backwards, the gravel skittering under their feet.

'But . . . but . . . Uncle Cedric! And Mrs Tunnicliffe!'

'Isn't it sweet?'

'Sweet? How long d'you think it's been going on?'

Safely out of earshot, Lily stopped.

'What's been 'going on'?'

'You know, seeing each other!' Jim looked dazed. 'Aren't they a bit long in the tooth for all that?'

'All what? Honestly, Jim, I never knew you were such a prude! You sound like some old fishwife!'

'Well . . . and here were you thinking she was lonely!' marvelled Jim. 'It's a wonder she's got time to take on two children! As for him, I don't know whether to call him a dark horse or a dirty dog!'

'Don't be so awful! I think it's lovely. We wanted someone to keep an eye on her and he must have kept in touch. Now come on!' Lily piloted Jim and Buddy back down the drive. 'The children are obviously fine

122

and we don't want them to catch us spying, do we?'

Shaking his head in disbelief, Jim obeyed mutely, Buddy rather more reluctantly, and they made it safely back to the road. Jim was still dumbfounded at his uncle's secret life.

'Older people do form friendships, you know,' Lily told him. 'Attachments, even. Fond attachments. Look at Mum and Sam.'

'That's different. Your mum's years younger.'

'Well, whatever, it's none of our business.'

'Huh! That's rich, coming from you! You're usually the first to go jumping into everyone else's affairs!'

'Not this one. Now come on, as we're here, let's go and look at our favourite view. I'll race you to the top of the hill!'

When they'd first come over to Juniper Hill, Jim had discovered that at the top on Mrs Tunnicliffe's side of the road there was a magnificent view. Beyond the edge of Hinton lay the wider countryside, the houses dwindling away into a few cottages in a valley between green hills and a road winding into the distance. After the terraced streets they usually tramped through, the uninspiring park and the canal, it was a literal breath of fresh air. It was a view to make you throw your hat in the air and dance a jig. It made you feel you'd taken your brain out and given it a wash.

Emerging from the overgrown footpath that led to it, the sun beaming down, the view was more splendid than ever. Jim let Buddy off the leash and he shot off like a greyhound in search of his own imaginary rabbit, though he'd find none this close to town. Jim and Lily flopped down on the grass.

Jim lay back and Lily snuggled into the crook of his arm.

'Remember when we first found this place?' he asked. 'Two whole years ago now.'

'Funny, isn't it? It seems like longer. And it seems like yesterday.' She flipped onto her side to look at him. 'That was the day we first properly admitted we liked each other. It took us long enough, didn't it!'

'Yes.' Jim's face was just inches from hers. 'I was a bit slow off the mark.'

'Well, we got there in the end. Oh Buddy!'

The dog had come back, all slobbering enthusiasm. Lily pushed him gently away and sat up. Jim sat up too.

'Lie down, Buddy, lie down.'

Buddy took a moment to think about it, then, surprisingly, did as he was told, settling with his chin on his outstretched paws. Jim cleared his throat.

'I, er, I've got something to say to you. I've been waiting for the right moment but I can't wait any longer and . . . Stand up.'

'What?'

'Stand up.'

Lily scrambled to her feet, Jim too. He stood to face her and took her hands in his.

'I want to say this looking into your eyes. I love you, Lily, and I want us to be together forever. So will you — '

'What?' Lily interrupted. 'No, no, no, no, no, hang on! If this is what I think it is, if this is my big moment, can we please do it properly?'

'Properly? Oh, you don't mean . . . ?'

'I do,' grinned Lily. 'Go on! It won't kill you!'

Sighing, shaking his head, muttering something about her being impossible, Jim went down on one knee.

'I love you, Lily,' he repeated. 'Always have, always

124

will.' Reaching into his pocket, he produced the ring box, opened it and held the ring up to her. 'Will you marry me?'

'Oh Jim! Yes, yes, of course yes, you know I will! Oh, you can stand up now! But let me see . . . ' She drew back as Jim stood and held the ring out to her again. 'And a ring! You got that too! Oh, it's lovely! Will you put it on for me?'

Jim slid the ring onto her finger. Lily looked at it in wonderment.

'It's perfect! Beautiful! Oh Jim! You did all this by yourself, the ring and everything! I wondered why you had to fetch your jacket when it's so warm! Oh, I love it and I love you! I love you so!'

She threw her arms around his neck and even Buddy, who'd leapt up and was running round them in frantic circles, barking his congratulations, couldn't interrupt their kiss. Finally breaking away, Lily turned the ring on her finger, letting it catch the sun and examining it properly.

'It's an aquamarine,' Jim explained.

'Beautiful,' murmured Lily again.

'And different,' said Jim. 'Just like you.'

Time passed, as it does when the man you love has just asked you to spend the rest of your life with him, and especially when you can't believe it has actually happened. They stood, they sat, they lay, they kissed, they looked out at the view, and Lily looked at her ring. They were alone on the hillside, in their own world, on top of the world. In all the time they were there, only a couple of people came past — two men with rucksacks and stout boots, hikers on their way to some unknown destination. They had to pass right in front of Lily and Jim, who were sitting entwined, so

125

they could hardly not speak to them.

'Afternoon,' they said in a stilted way, seeing they were interrupting, and scuttled off so quickly that one almost lost his footing on the sloping downward path and stumbled into the bracken. Lily and Jim had to stifle their laughter.

'If they were French or Italian they'd have smiled and kissed their fingertips to the sky and gone on about *l'amour* and whatever the Italian word is,' Jim smiled. 'You could tell they were English. Thoroughly embarrassed.'

'More fool them,' said Lily, turning her ring on her finger again and then turning her face to be kissed once more. 'Whatever you call it in whatever language, I can't get enough of it. Oh, Jim. I'm so happy I could burst.'

'Don't do that,' said Jim. 'If you haven't gathered, I rather like you the way you are.'

14

'The first person we've got to tell is Mum,' said Lily as they walked home grinning like idiots at each other and at everyone and everything they passed. Dogs, trees, shop fronts — even sandbags basked in the glow of their happiness.

'Of course,' replied Jim easily. He'd expected to feel happy, but he hadn't known how much the feeling of sheer relief — that he'd done it and that she'd said yes — would add to it. He'd been planning to wait till Lily's eighteenth in a couple of weeks — now he didn't have to. He squeezed Lily's hand. 'Now, as we're nearly there, how about one more kiss — just a little one?'

It wasn't a little one, of course, and when they finally got home, Dora was in the middle of a mammoth letter-writing session. The table was littered with paper, envelopes, and stamps for Sid, and air letters for Reg in North Africa, and Sam in Canada.

She looked up as they came in, and Lily ran towards her, hand extended. Dora knew at once what it must mean. Jim hadn't asked her permission, but she'd given him that at Christmas, over the proxy ring.

'Oh that's wonderful!' she cried, jumping up and hugging them both. 'Some proper good news! Oh, where's my hanky?'

'Oh, Mum, don't cry!'

'They're happy tears!' Dora tucked her hanky back in her sleeve. 'And let's see. Oh Lily! What a beautiful ring!'

'It's an aquamarine.' Lily rolled the word around her mouth, drinking in the bounty of all the world's oceans. 'I can't stop looking at it, can I, Jim?'

'I had to stop her walking straight out in front of two vans and a Jeep!'

Dora clucked, then added, 'Look, I haven't sealed these letters yet. Do you want to put a PS?'

'Mum! I can't fit how I feel into a PS!' Lily gave a huge, happy sigh. 'You do it; it's your good news as well. I'll write properly to Sid and Reg later. Anyway, we've got stuff to do before tea — I must tell Gladys and Beryl!'

'Now?' queried Jim.

'Oh, looking for a get-out already?' teased Lily. 'This isn't the kind of news that'll keep! Or are you going to change your mind?'

Jim took her in his arms. They were always discreet in front of Dora — affectionate, but never wanting to embarrass her. Today, however, was different.

'Step outside and say that!' he challenged. 'But look, you go, if you don't mind. I've got stuff to do myself.'

'Lie down in darkened room, I expect,' observed Dora wryly from the table. Having used up every inch of available space on the air letters already, she was squeezing a PS up the side in tiny writing. 'I know what your brothers'll say — they never expected any-one'd be mad enough to take you off our hands! And Sam'll be thrilled. He's very fond of you both.'

A celebratory cup of tea, a quick brush-down of the back of Lily's cardigan — strangely covered in tufts of grass — and Lily and Jim were off out again.

'What's this 'stuff' you've got to do?' Lily asked as they parted on the street corner.

128

'That'd be telling.'

Jim wasn't about to tell her that he wanted to go back to the jeweller's to thank the old man and share with him what a success the ring had been. And to put down a deposit on the wedding ring to go with it.

★ ★ ★

'Oh my Lord!' Beryl shrieked. 'He's finally done it! D'you hear that, Les? Jim, who's too slow to catch cold! And look at this ring! Isn't it gorgeous? I hope you're taking note!'

Les, who'd been building a tower of bricks with Bobby, got up from the rug and dutifully came to inspect.

'Very nice,' he judged.

'It's more than nice, it's a one-off,' said Beryl sternly. 'So the dress'll have to be as well. Not something I've already got in stock that's been worn a dozen times. You shall have new, Lily — well, you know what I mean, new if I can find any liquidated stock, or worn once, and new for around here if not. You must tell me what you fancy.'

'Yes, and then you'll go and find me something completely different!'

'There is a war on, you know!' chanted Beryl, the standard excuse. 'Anyway, you'll love it, whatever I find!'

After Beryl's years of experience in the business, Lily had to admit that this was probably true. She had a knack of knowing what would suit.

'So when's the big day?' Beryl persisted. 'How long have I got?'

'Give us a chance!' laughed Lily. 'I've only been

engaged a couple of hours!' She repeated it in wonder, 'Engaged. I'm engaged . . .'

Beryl snapped her fingers in front of her face.

'Oy, you on cloud nine! Give me a clue! What's your thinking? This year, next year, sometime, never?'

'I don't know,' insisted Lily, smiling. 'We haven't talked about it!'

'Oh, come on! This side of Christmas?'

'I shall have to consult my fiancé,' said Lily primly, to more shrieks from Beryl.

Gladys was less forthright, but more specific.

'When you do set a date, Lily,' she said, after the congratulations, the happy tears and several milky hugs were over, 'if Bill can't be there — and he probably won't be, let's face it — can you try and pick a time to coincide with the twins' sleep? I don't want to miss a second, and if they need a feed and start yelling, I'll have to take them out, so as not to spoil things for you and Jim, and then . . . '

Lily held up her hands in mute appeal.

'Gladys,' she said firmly. 'Jim and I haven't given it a thought. I'd like to enjoy being engaged for a bit before we think about all that, please!'

'And you shall! Do you hear that, Joy? Victor? Your Auntie Lily's engaged!'

So she could hug Lily, Gladys had propped the twins up with cushions in an armchair. On hearing the news, Victor yawned ('typical man' said Lily) but Joy gave an obliging gurgle.

As Lily left, her heart was light. Gladys's worries, Beryl's quest for a dress for her and heavy hints about a ring for herself . . . they were all for another day. Right now, she wanted how she felt at this moment to last forever.

Across town, in contrast, Peter Simmonds had his eye on the time: he was trying to hurry young John along. On his afternoon off, he'd agreed to help Eileen by collecting John after school and taking him to the park. She had some housework to do — to wash the windows and tackle some mould in the bathroom.

Peter had armed himself with a bat and ball but John hadn't wanted to play cricket; he said he'd rather look for 'treasures' to swop at school. They'd found a stripy stone, a few tiny conkers fallen early, and a miraculously intact snail shell. Honour had been satisfied. Now, Peter felt, John was trying it on.

'Come along now,' he urged as the boy lingered by the duckpond.

'I'm watching the dragonfly.'

'And I'm watching the time. Mummy said to be back by six o'clock, didn't she? For your tea.'

John stuck out his bottom lip.

'You can't tell me what to do. You're not my daddy.'

Peter blinked. John had never said anything like it before.

'No,' he said slowly. He knew Eileen had always been straight with the boy when he'd asked about his father. 'I'm not. You know your daddy went away before you were born. That happens sometimes.'

John scuffed his sandal on the tarmac.

'If you lived with us would that make you my daddy?'

That brought Peter up short. He crouched down so he was at John's level.

'Would you like that? If I lived with you? All the time?'

John's grey-green eyes met his. His face was serious.

'If it stopped Jessie Walters teasing me at school.'

131

Playground insults, so that was it. At the same time . . .

'Is that the only reason?'

John gave it some thought.

'I suppose you could read me more stories. And we could play football or cricket every night, not just when you came round.' He thought some more, then added, 'And we could finish my Hurricane quicker. You're better at making models than Mummy. She hasn't got the patience.'

Peter bit back a smile. That was true enough; Eileen was the first to admit she hated the fiddly things. But had Jessie Walters, whoever she was, with her jibes, cleared the way to asking the question Peter had been putting off? Was John giving him permission?

'If I was to live with you,' he said carefully, 'I'd have to ask your mummy to marry me.'

'I know that!' said John impatiently. 'Why don't you then?'

Peter could have hugged him. The ring was in his pocket; he carried it everywhere, every day, in case the moment arose.

'Do you want to know a secret?' he asked.

John nodded vigorously.

'Then let me show you something,' Peter said.

★ ★ ★

'Hello? We're back!' called Peter as he let himself and John into the flat, John dancing about like an excitable puppy.

'Already?' From the echo, they could tell that Eileen was in the bathroom. 'You're early, aren't you?'

'No, bang on time.'

132

'Well, I'm afraid I haven't done anything towards tea yet!' She sounded cross. 'And don't come in here, I'm still scrubbing! I stink of bleach and — '

John couldn't contain himself any longer. He tugged on Peter's hand, dragging him along the hall. Peter pulled him back.

'Shall we wait till Mummy's finished?' he said quietly. 'Till after tea?'

'No!' hissed John. 'You said you were going to do it right away! You're not scared, are you?'

'Me?' As a regular soldier, Peter Simmonds had served in the Far East and in Palestine. He'd had some scary moments in his time, but this one knocked them all into a general's cap. At the thought of what he had to do, his throat was closing like a clam shell. 'Of course I'm not scared.'

'Well, come on then!'

John dragged him into the bathroom. With her back to them, Eileen, in a pair of old slacks and a shapeless shirt was on her knees in the bathtub, scrubbing at the grouting on the tiles. Hearing them come in, she turned her head. Her hair was swathed in a turban from which a couple of strands had escaped. She blew them out of her eyes. Her cheeks were pink from her efforts.

'I said not to come in!'

Peter knew she'd be embarrassed to be seen like this — she was always immaculate, even off-duty. To him, she'd never looked lovelier; in her view, she might as well have had blackened teeth and be dressed in stinking rags.

John jabbed Peter from behind.

'He's got something to ask you.'

'What? Can't it wait?'

Peter gulped. John gave him a glare.

'No,' said Peter abruptly. He dropped to his knees beside the bath and produced the ring box from his pocket. He opened it and held it out.

'Eileen,' he said. 'Will you do me the honour of being my wife?'

* * *

'Honestly,' Miss Frobisher smiled next day as she and Lily ticked off a delivery, 'as romantic proposals go, it was hardly on a level with Mr Darcy! But to be fair, I wasn't very gracious myself to begin with. And John's thrilled, bless him.'

Miss Frobisher angled her hand so that her ring caught the lights — she was doing a lot more with her left hand than usual, but then Lily was doing the same herself. She stole a glance at her own perfect ring. The weight of it there still felt strange, but in a way that gave her a shiver of excitement.

'I'm so happy for you.' Lily turned to stow some baby leggings in a drawer. 'It's strange that they both got galvanised into action on the same day!'

'From what I can gather, my son practically bullied Peter into it! But I'm very happy, as you can tell. And I'm very happy for you too, Lily.'

Certainly Miss Frobisher had never looked so visibly happy, and she'd certainly never spoken to Lily so openly before at work, using Mr Simmonds's first name and everything. She probably never would again, but today she was like a young girl asked out for the very first time. But getting engaged did strange things to people, as Lily could testify.

'Have you thought any further?' Miss Frobisher

asked. 'Set a date?'

'Not you as well!' Lily wanted to say, but she simply shook her head.

'We haven't really thought about it. It's taken Jim years to get round to proposing — hardly a whirlwind romance — so I doubt he's going to rush me down the aisle!'

'I'd pretty much given up hope of Peter getting round to it at all.' Miss Frobisher examined the stitching on an envelope-neck vest and snipped off a tiny thread with the scissors attached to her belt. 'But having got this far, we . . . well, we don't want to hang around. I'm telling you because as first sales' — she smiled — 'you won't be able to take any leave at the same time. We'd like to get married in October and have a few days away. It'll be John's half-term, you see.'

'Oh! Right!' Lily was rather thrown by this decisiveness, but Miss Frobisher was over thirty and Mr Simmonds must be nearly forty. No wonder they wanted to get on with it. 'Of course I'll be here. I don't know that we'd be getting married that quickly anyway.'

'Well, we won't now,' said Jim when she told him at dinnertime. They'd finally fended off the colleagues who'd besieged their table to offer congratulations and coo over the ring, to Jim's embarrassment and Lily's delight. 'We can't very well pre-empt them, what with seniority and everything. And then it's the run-up to Christmas and then it's the January sale . . . no chance of time off then.'

Lily leant across the table and jabbed him lightly with her fork.

'Thanks! The romance didn't last long! Work comes

135

first!' But she'd thought the same herself. 'So we'll get married in the spring. That'll be lovely.'

Jim wrinkled his nose. His foot felt for hers under the table.

'I'm not sure I can control myself till then.'

Lily hooked both her feet round the backs of his calves.

'It'll be worth the wait, I promise,' she told him.

15

In truth it did feel a little disappointing not to be getting married in the next few months but there it was. Into every engagement a little rain must fall, and there was still plenty of excitement. Lily had her birthday, which was a double celebration now. A parcel had arrived from Sam in Canada, something soft and pliable. Lily tore it open — proper American stockings? Several pairs? A soft and luxurious scarf or jumper? No — a set of sheets for her bottom drawer!

Lily had to laugh.

'I'd better get used to it, I suppose,' she smiled. 'It's all practical presents from now on, not pretty ones.'

But Beryl, when she brought round a wedding dress for Dora to repair, was green with envy.

'A ring and a set of sheets!' She shook her head. 'No sniff of any blinking ring for me yet, and I'm darning darns on ours!'

The question of Beryl's ring was becoming pressing. Jim had had an alarming conversation with Les in which he'd floated the idea of paying for it by snapping up some knock-off tins of peaches and selling them on the black market. Jim had sternly counselled against it, but he wasn't sure Les had taken any notice.

'What's the use of a flashy diamond if it's Exhibit One in court?' he worried to Lily. 'Les is a great bloke, but he's not the sharpest knife in the drawer. He's bound to get ripped off, beaten up, or be the fall guy for some proper crooks!'

'You've been reading those thrillers again,' smiled

Lily, but there was another ring — of truth — in what Jim said.

The war news was worrying too. Paris and then Brussels hung out the flags when they were liberated one after the other, but as a result Hitler was directing all his venom at the British. At the beginning of September, another kind of bomb landed in London, even more terrifying and deadly than the doodlebug. The new ones arrived with no warning at all. When the first one hit, the Government, taken by surprise, had tried to pretend it was a gas explosion, but that didn't wash. And as the doodlebugs were still falling as well, Londoners lived in double dread.

'Can't you get posted somewhere safer?' Lily begged Sid in one of their pre-arranged phone calls. She called Sid at his digs from the phone box by the chip shop, but on the last two occasions, he hadn't been there; he'd had to work through the night, he'd told her afterwards. But tonight her pennies hadn't been wasted.

'Yeah, sure,' mocked her brother. 'How's it going to look if the Admiralty and the War Office go all yellow-bellied?' Then he softened. 'Look, Sis, there's no need to worry. We've got a reinforced bunker at work, and when we're off duty, then like everyone else, it's get to the shelter or under the stairs, or roll the dice and stay in bed.'

'You can't keep throwing double sixes, Sid,' warned Lily. 'Get yourself posted somewhere up north. Please? Back up to Scotland, maybe?'

But she knew he wouldn't. Sid had moved to London for a very specific reason. He was the looker of the family, for sure — he could have had his pick of any girl in the country — and when he'd lived in Hinton, he had. But Sid had confessed to Lily something she'd never suspected. He wasn't attracted to girls. It was men he liked.

Lily had been shattered, and it had taken her a while to reconcile the brother she'd grown up with in an ordinary family in an ordinary street in an ordinary town with what he'd confided. She'd spent a long time going over things, looking for signs she could have spotted, but Sid had concealed it so well — he'd had to — that she'd never suspected a thing.

Now she knew he'd lost one love already — Anthony, a pilot in the Fleet Air Arm who he'd met while training — but in London where, he said, men like him had more freedom to meet and mix in the anonymity of a big city, he'd met someone else: an American, Jerome.

'Let's change the subject, shall we?' Sid said now. While she'd been thinking, she'd heard him light up a cigarette. 'How's the blushing bride-to-be?'

'Nothing to blush about yet,' Lily told him. 'All we know is it'll be sometime in the New Year. Spring, maybe. Beryl's looking for a dress for me.'

'Hinton in the spring, mm, mm, mm . . .' trilled Sid, cannibalising the popular song about Paris in springtime. 'Love is in the air, mm, mm, mm. Life's a love affair — '

'The pips are about to go and I've no more money!' Lily cut him off mid-note. 'You will give me away, won't you, Sid? I know Reg is the elder, and it's his right and all that, but he's not here and you are!'

'Thanks very much — how to make a fellow feel second-best!' chaffed Sid. 'Course I will. But you've got to fix a date first!'

But Lily and Jim had other things to think about.

At Marlows, Miss Frobisher and Mr Simmonds might have been there in body, but their minds were totally focussed on their wedding and after that, their romantic getaway to a cottage in the Lake District. This meant that all the planning for the store's Christmas season had fallen on Jim's shoulders — and then Beryl lobbed something else into the mix.

'How about that, then?' she trilled when she next called round, extending her left hand. Nestled next to her simple gold band was a huge five-stone diamond. Lily darted a look at Jim.

'That's, er, stunning, Beryl!' she stuttered.

'Mind it doesn't catch in the lace!' warned Dora, handing over the mended dress. 'I don't want to be mending another rip! And you'll have to watch it in the shop!'

'I put it on my bill spike when I'm doing a fitting,' explained Beryl. 'But I don't let it out of my sight, I can tell you!'

'What on earth can Les have got himself mixed up in to afford a ring like that?' Lily despaired to Jim when Beryl had left. 'Robbed a bank? Coshed an old lady?'

Jim shook his head.

But when he bumped into Les next day at work and asked him — tactfully — Les just tapped his nose and said, 'Ask me no questions and I'll tell you no lies,' which was about as annoying as being told as a five-year-old that it was 'wait-and-see' pudding. But then Les volunteered something else.

'Here, when Beryl was leaving yours last night, she saw something funny next door. At the Crosbies' place. Funny peculiar, that is.'

'Oh yes?' Jim's interest in Jean Crosbie and her

140

family — husband Walter and twelve-year-old son Trevor, was minimal at the best of times and certainly not when he was trying to decide if last year's Christmas grotto would do as it was, or if it needed a repaint.

'Yes,' continued Les determinedly. 'There was a young bloke, no more than twenty, twenty-two, letting himself in the front door with a key!'

'So?' Regretfully, Jim decided a touch-up would be needed. The grotto's plywood walls had previously been part of an Easter display, and the Easter bunnies, quickly whitewashed over last year, had made a ghostly reappearance. Hardly seasonal.

'It's obvious!' said Les. 'Jean's got herself a young feller on the side!'

Obvious to Beryl, maybe, thought Jim.

'Jean Crosbie? And right under Walter's nose?'

'He wasn't there,' declared Les in triumph. 'He was on ARP; Beryl saw him on Union Street. And before you say it, it was after half nine — Trevor would have been in bed.'

Jim turned from his examination of the grotto.

'I'm sorry, I don't buy it.'

'No, neither do I, to be fair,' Les acknowledged. 'Not that boot-faced old crow. But how about this, one better. It's her illegitimate son from years ago! She could have been a right looker for all we know, and a bit of a goer, too!'

'And she could have been a pioneering scientist who discovered uranium,' said Jim mildly. 'But she wasn't. The nearest she ever got to it was selling liver pills at Boots before she got married. She's lived in Hinton all her life. Dora's lived next to her for the last twenty-odd years. I think she'd have known if Jean had a past.'

'It's always the quiet ones,' said Les. If he taps his nose again, thought Jim . . . But Les didn't. He clearly considered his points scored and the subject closed. 'Want these carting away to the paint shop then?' he asked.

Jim nodded.

'I'll fetch my trolley,' Les replied. But the subject wasn't quite closed, because he added cheekily, 'But talking of quiet ones, with all this love in the air, romance, rings, and what-not, has Dora heard from that Sam lately?'

★ ★ ★

As it happened, as she walked back from Gladys's next day with Buddy beside her on the lead, Dora was thinking about Sam, all those miles away in Canada. She never took the dog inside, but whenever Gladys put the pram out to give Joy and Victor some fresh air, he'd lie quietly beside it as if he knew exactly what a precious cargo it carried. He might be a bit of a scamp, but Sam's parting gift had his sensitive side, just like his master.

Dora missed Sam, and no mistake. He'd brought more than just variety and interest into her life — and she didn't mean the ready supplies of tinned jam, ham, and Spam from the Canadian NAAFI. They were both too old for moons and Junes and hearts and flowers. Theirs had been a bond built on friendship, companionship, and mutual respect for the people they both were, or had become, through some hard knocks in life — the loss of her husband, the loss of his son, and his wife's subsequent mental breakdown. But Sam was still married; he'd had to go home on a

142

compassionate discharge, and he wasn't coming back.

She shook herself back to the present. Gladys needed some gripe water for the twins, if there was any to be had, though Dora's main gripe was still with Florrie and her ways. Florrie had grumpily agreed to do a bit of cooking, as Gladys didn't have the time, but she rarely washed up, and since she also squirreled away food in her own room she'd accumulated a stack of dirty crocks up there. Dora had only discovered them when they ran out of plates.

But Gladys had had some good news which had blotted out every little niggle.

'It's Bill's mate that he bunks in with!' she'd begun in her usual rambling, convoluted way, which was even more rambling and convoluted these days because she was sleep-deprived with the babies. 'The ship got caught in a storm and he got thrown against a bulkhead — or was it *the* bulkhead, I forget . . . anyway it doesn't matter — this is about two weeks ago now. Anyhow, this feller broke his leg!'

'Oh dear,' Dora managed to insert.

'Yes but anyway, it was a good thing because they airlifted him off on a stretcher to . . . I dunno, some place I'd never heard of, some island that's neutral or something — and he's coming home!'

'Who? The fellow with the broken leg? I should hope so!'

'No, Bill!' cried Gladys, as if it was obvious. 'He sneaked a letter under his mate's blanket to post on to me — '

'Wait a minute. Bill's coming home? He's not hurt as well, is he?'

'No, he's fine! It's the ship! It's coming to Portsmouth for a refit! Next month! And it could be in dry

143

dock till next year!'

'Oh Gladys! That's wonderful! And they won't post him away again while it is?'

'No, he doesn't think so. They'll keep him down on the coast, he reckons, not near here, but he'll be shore-based. So much safer! And he'll get leave and at least he can be in touch!'

A weight had dropped from Dora's shoulders. Gladys was doing her best, but she depended on Dora's daily visits.

Almost home, Dora unclipped Buddy's lead as they reached the entry and he trotted ahead to wait at the back gate. Over the fence, she could see Jean Crosbie with her hair in a turban and a pinny wrapped round her skinny frame beating the life out of a carpet in her back yard. Dora hoped she could get indoors without Jean seeing — she didn't want to be on the end of one of her diatribes. But Buddy let her down. As she reached for the latch he let out a happy yelp. Jean raised her head.

'Dora!' she called out, her voice sharp.

Inwardly groaning, Dora looked over.

'Hello, Jean!' she said brightly and was surprised by her neighbour's anguished face. 'Is everything all right?'

To her astonishment, Jean burst into tears.

'Oh Dora,' she sniffed. 'It's dreadful . . . have you got a minute? Can I come over?'

Surely Beryl hadn't been right after all about the mystery man she'd seen letting himself in? Dora had been looking forward to a quiet sit-down, but she said at once, 'Of course you can, Jean. I'll put the kettle on.'

16

The whole story came out over a pot of tea, as stories usually did amongst neighbours in Brook Street.

'His name's Kenny,' Jean explained, her handkerchief a damp ball in her hand. 'He's Walter's nephew, his sister's son.'

That put the tin lid on Beryl's wild speculations, thought Dora. She nodded encouragingly.

'We hardly knew him growing up,' Jean went on. 'Or the family — there's another two boys and a girl. Walter thought his sister had married beneath her, you see, a navvy her husband was, from Liverpool. Anyhow, all the boys went into the Army, from what Kenny's told us, one's out East and the other was in Crete, the last that was heard of either of them.'

'I see. And Kenny?'

Jean gave a heavy sigh.

'Kenny was took prisoner at Dunkirk. He's spent four years being shunted around different camps in Germany. But he's managed to get himself back to England on the Prisoner Exchange.'

Dora had heard of this. It had taken a while to set up, but certain categories of prisoner could qualify — often those with TB, which the Germans didn't want to spread among their own population. Maybe Kenny was one of those.

'But why's he here?' asked Dora. 'If his home's in Liverpool?'

'He went there,' Jean began, 'but there's nothing left. The whole street where they'd lived had gone.

145

Turns out the three of them — mum, dad, and sister — got killed in the Blitz in '41. We didn't hear of course, 'cos Walter hadn't spoken to his sister in years. I mean, we didn't know them really, but to think of all of them killed, just like that . . .'

Jean trailed off, pushing a strand of hair that had escaped her turban off her face.

'And Kenny? He never knew?'

'He thought he hadn't heard from them because he kept being moved and the letters never caught up with him.'

'Poor lad!' Dora's heart went out to him. 'Three years and no letters at all?' Reg — and Sid, when he'd been posted further away — had always said how much letters from home meant to them. 'So you've taken him in, have you?'

'What choice have we got?' said Jean. 'He's got no one else. It's took him weeks to find us from some dim memory of what his mum told him about growing up here and knowing her maiden name.'

Dora nodded. It was a very sad, but not uncommon, story of the war.

'So what's the problem?' she persisted. 'Has he got TB or something?'

'If only!' Jean burst out, then shook her head. 'You know the Germans, whatever you say about them, they don't put the prisoners to work — it's some treaty or convention or something that they do at least stick to. But our boys can volunteer for work, and after four years of hanging about, Kenny did. Volunteer, that is. And he was put to farm work.'

'Right . . .'

'Well, he got hurt, didn't he, gashed his arm real bad, and it got infected.'

146

That explained how he'd qualified for Prisoner Exchange, though to Dora, the tale was getting more confusing, not less, the way Jean was telling it.

'Well, that's all right. He'll build himself up again in time, and find something to do, either here or in Liverpool. He must still have some friends there at least. What job did he do before?'

'That's just it!' wailed Jean, the handkerchief back in use again. 'He was a joiner, but they've amputated his arm so he can't go back to that, and he's not right! He just sits about the house, smoking his head off, which sets off our Trevor's adenoids, and then goes out drinking, or brings bottles in from the offie. Walter's not happy and neither am I and . . . and . . . '

'What?'

Jean sniffed again. Her eyes were swollen and her nose red raw.

'I know it's awful of me, Dora, but the sight of his . . . his stump . . . it just turns me up! I never have been good with that sort of thing. When you see them amputees from the First War — I know it's not their fault and God knows it's terrible for them — but I can't help it, it makes me feel sick. And Kenny will sit about and walk about the house in his vest. It's like he's doing it deliberately!'

Jean descended into another torrent of sobs. Self-pitying maybe, when it was Kenny who deserved them, but also those of a woman at the end of her rope, Dora could tell.

'Look, Jean,' she said, 'it's like all these things. They look like Mount Everest at first, like you'll never overcome them, but bit by bit they look more and more like a pile of matchwood. And really, however bad it is for you, it's a heck of a lot worse for Kenny. Think of what he's been though, kept behind wire for four years, losing an arm, family dead and gone without a goodbye, and who knows if those that are left — his brothers — are dead or alive? No wonder he's a bit sunk in himself. As time goes on, he'll get used to things, you'll get used to things. Like you say, there's no choice.'

Jean gave a shuddering sigh and sniffed again. She pressed the backs of her hands to her eyes.

'I wish I could believe you, I really do. I don't feel good about it, but at the same time . . . I dunno. I haven't got your saintly patience, that's the trouble!'

She attempted a smile and Dora patted her hand.

'Look, I'll tell Jim and Lily if that's all right with you. Maybe Jim and Les can take Kenny out for drink one night. Perhaps with a bit of company his own age, he might start to come round a bit.'

'Oh, would you?' Jean lunged at the idea like a pick-pocket in the blackout. 'I'm sure that'd help. It'd help me, anyway,' she admitted with a tinge of guilt.

At teatime, Dora did as she'd promised and though Jim wasn't a great drinker, he went straight round and asked Kenny, who was smoking in the yard, if he'd like to join him at the pub on Saturday.

Kenny was tall and thin. His hair had grown out since his POW days and fell lank and greasy over his forehead. His face was sallow, his eyes red-veined. At Jim's offer, he shrugged.

'What for?'

'No reason,' Jim said. 'Just being neighbourly.'

Kenny shrugged again.

'Up to you,' he said, stubbing out his cigarette on the wall.

'Well?' asked Lily when Jim came back.

'Yes, we're on,' said Jim, covering up Kenny's lack of grace. 'It's the least we can do.'

★ ★ ★

On Saturday night, as Jim got ready to go out, Lily pretended pique.

'That's right, leave me to a bit more WVS wool-winding. I notice you never take me out for a drink!'

'No, I don't,' said Jim, pulling her close, 'because there's no nice private back row at the pub like there is at the Gaumont. Ever thought of that?'

After the reception he'd had last time, as Jim knocked on the Crosbies' back door, he was wondering if Kenny would actually come, but Kenny answered the door himself. The reddened stump which Jean found so hard to look at was protruding from the short sleeve of his shirt. Jim pinned on a smile.

'Great. Let's get going,' he said.

To say conversation was sticky on the way to the pub was like saying the Western Desert was a bit bigger than Bournemouth beach. Kenny didn't make things easy, answering only 'yes' or 'no' to most of Jim's questions and they'd both dried up long before they arrived at Les's local, the Bunch of Grapes.

Les broke away from a couple of off-duty soldiers he'd been talking to and came over.

'How do, Jim,' he said chirpily, 'and Kenny, isn't it?'

Then, unfortunately, he went to shake Kenny's hand before realising it simply wasn't there. Awkwardly, Les retracted his own in a sort of jerky salute, which made him look like a half-hearted member of the Hitler Youth.

149

'Drink?' said Jim quickly. 'What'll you have, Kenny?'

He bought them all a pint. Jim willed Les not to say, 'Good health' or even worse, as he often did after the first swig 'Ah, this is what your right arm's for!' Thankfully he stuck to 'Cheers.'

They found a table, and, still covering his embarrassment, Les launched into a story from the local paper, the *Chronicle*, about a pet parrot with a nice line in swear words. Jim topped it with his favourite from the paper, which had held the front page on the day after D-Day with the headline 'Calamity on the Canal', not a story about a brave attack that had seen the Nazis on the run in France, but a narrowboat slipping its moorings near the local locks. Kenny listened stony-faced.

'Did you have a newspaper in the camp?' Jim asked, trying to bring him into the conversation. 'One you all wrote, I mean?'

Kenny stared at him. 'When you're doing sweet FA all day there's not much to shout about, is there? Bunked up thirty to a hut, you know when someone's broken wind. You don't need a newspaper to tell you.'

Now it was Jim's turn to be embarrassed, but Les leapt in.

'Talking of FA,' he said, 'what about football? Who's your team, Kenny? Are you a Liverpool man or Everton?'

This was a subject on which Kenny could, and did, become animated and Jim leant back and left them to it. Les was a keen Aston Villa supporter and was quick to point out Villa's triumph over Everton in the 1887 FA Cup. Kenny rejoindered with Everton's punishment of Les's team the following year by beating them in the Premier League. They traded statistics

150

and insults happily for twenty minutes, then, carried away with camaraderie, Les overstepped the mark.

'How about a game of billiards?' he suggested. 'Settle some old scores that way!'

Kenny put his drink down so hard the beer slopped over the top of the glass.

'Billiards?' he said. 'You taking the mickey? How about darts? Want to see someone blinded with me chucking left-handed?'

Les coloured scarlet.

'I'm sorry, mate,' he said. 'I didn't . . . um . . . '

'You didn't think!' said Kenny. 'Nobody does. Nobody knows what it's like! You can stuff your drink!'

And he left.

'Sorry, Jim,' said Les. 'I — We were getting on so well, it just seemed natural . . . My mouth ran away with me.'

'It's all right,' said Jim. 'It's not easy. But it's far harder for him.'

The war had come home to Hinton, and to Jim, in a way he hadn't felt since he and Lily had been caught in the bomb blast that had ripped into Marlows. He knew from that experience that their physical injuries had been the least of it: the mental and emotional scars were far worse. They'd had to steel themselves to go into the town centre to see the devastation and to appreciate what a narrow escape they'd had; two people had been killed nearby. Jim and Lily had got over it; they had each other, and loving friends and family around them. Kenny had had no one for four years, no one when the accident happened, and no one who meant anything to him, or to whom he meant anything, now. Poor beggar, thought Jim. And when the war was over, and thousands, millions of

151

servicemen — and prisoners — God willing, came back, Kenny wouldn't be the only one. It was a sobering thought. For the first and only time since he'd been rejected by the Army because of his poor vision, Jim was glad he hadn't been able to join up.

Lily was still awake when he got back.

'How did it go?' she asked, coming downstairs in her dressing gown.

'It didn't, I'm afraid,' said Jim. 'A bit of a disaster. I'll tell you about it, but first, come here.' He took her in his arms and pulled her close. 'Am I glad I've got you.'

Next day Jean called round to Dora's. Sadly, Dora reported how the evening had gone.

'You see what I'm up against?' Jean shook her head. 'He's so bitter.'

'He's got a lot to be bitter about,' said Dora. 'But there is help, you know. There's ex-servicemen's charities . . . and I'm sure we could do something for him at the WVS or Red Cross if he'd only come along and see us.'

'Don't you think I've tried?' snapped Jean. 'He won't shift to help himself, that's the trouble.' Her attempts at trying harder with her nephew-by-marriage had obviously been short-lived. 'Walter's tried to talk to him about getting fitted with a new arm, a what-do-you-call-it . . . a pros-something?'

'Prosthetic?'

'That's the one. But oh, no, Kenny just stomped off to his room! I dunno what we're going to do with him.'

For once, nor did Dora.

In her dinner hour next day, Lily went down to Beryl's shop to hear what Les had made of it. Beryl leapt to her husband's defence.

'At least he got the bloke talking!' Beryl declared. 'That was a big improvement from what I heard. And then . . . well, yeah, it was unfortunate but that's my Les. He speaks — and acts, sometimes — before he thinks.'

Beryl was hand sewing some tiny beads back on a Juliet cap, and Lily's eyes drifted to the bobby-dazzler engagement ring reposing on the spike. Had Les acted before thinking when he'd acquired that?

Beryl saw Lily's look.

'I know what you're thinking,' she said. 'All of you. You think Les could never have afforded a ring like that.'

'No, I —'

'Yes, you do! Well, you're right! He didn't!' Beryl put her sewing aside, jumped up and put the ring on her finger. She came back and twirled it under Lily's nose. 'That is, he did, but only 'cos it's paste! They're rhinestones!'

Lily gaped at her.

'No!'

'Good, innit?' Beryl smirked. 'Had you fooled, any-way, and everyone else!'

'Oh Beryl. I'm so . . . ' Lily started to laugh. 'We worried he might have done something silly to get the money, something illegal even!'

'Blimey, not got much faith in him, have you? He's no Einstein, my Les, but he's not that daft!'

Daft enough to flirt with betting and black-market peaches, thought Lily, but kept quiet. Beryl extended her hand and looked lovingly at the glittering gems.

'He was getting in a right tizzy about it, bless him, sat me down all solemn and had to tell me it'd be next year before he could afford anything, what with Bobby needing shoes, and the bedroom needing papering. But I said to him, Les, I know we're solid, I don't need a fistful of diamonds to prove it!'

Lily nodded. Les was nothing like as dynamic as his flamboyant wife, but that was the point — like two poles of a compass, but the one couldn't exist without the other. Les might have his mad moments, like the peaches, but he'd encouraged Beryl to start her business and his steady wage had already seen her shop through a thin time. He was full of admiration for the way she'd turned things around; he was devoted to her as a husband and adored his son. For Beryl, who'd had a miserable childhood with a violent father and had never known security, Les was her rock.

'I was only teasing, leaving all those pictures of film stars round the house!' Beryl resumed. 'As long as it looks the part, that's all I care about. I'd already seen this little beauty in the pawnshop. Les got out what he'd saved and we snapped it up next day.'

'Beryl, you're the end, you really are!' Lily hugged her friend. 'I'm so relieved!'

'You must be barmy even thinking it was real! The insurance alone'd break us! Now let me get on with this sewing, can you? Some of us have got work to do!'

17

Lily had work to do as well, and lots of it, as September slid into October and the leaves crisped around the edges and began to fall once more.

Miss Frobisher had ordered the Christmas stock — or what she could get hold of — long ago, but with her wedding day getting closer, she was doubly busy ensuring she'd covered everything for the days she was taking off afterwards. It was left to Lily to chase deliveries, query invoices, and organise the stockroom. Miss Thomas and Miss Temple, the department's elderly part-timers, had become more elderly and more part-time as the war had gone on, so Lily had more than a full-time job. Jim was run ragged planning the arrival of Father Christmas on his sleigh (a milkman's cart decked out in crepe paper) and his installation in the grotto. This year Jim had decided that the juniors keeping the queue in order would be dressed as elves, which meant long discussions with Haberdashery, who'd have to kit them out in whatever scraps they could patch together.

A few days into October, Miss Frobisher drew Lily aside.

'It's about the 21st,' she said. This was the wedding day, a Saturday. 'We'd have very much liked you and Jim — Mr Goodridge — to be our witnesses, but it makes staffing too difficult. If both Mr Simmonds and I aren't here, then Mr Goodridge really has to be. And it's the same for you on the department.'

'Oh, but we'd never have expected it!' said Lily

155

quickly, though the thought had crossed her mind, and not just because of the extraordinary coincidence of them both getting engaged on the same day. Lily and Jim had been the first to know that their bosses were seeing one other, a confidence they'd kept to themselves until the older pair had decided it was time to broadcast the news more widely in the store.

'My neighbour — the one who looks after John for me — and an Army friend of Mr Simmonds's will do the honours,' Miss Frobisher explained. 'It's going to be a very quiet wedding and no reception, as such, but neither of us wants a fuss.'

'I hope there'll be photographs!'

Lily was dying to know what Miss Frobisher, always so poised, so elegant, would be wearing, and she knew Beryl was too.

'I can promise you that.' Miss Frobisher smiled, then switched back into professional mode. 'Now, what did you manage to get out of the manufacturer about supplies of stockinette?'

Miss Frobisher took the Friday before her big day off to get ready — she was having her hair done, and her nails. Mr Simmonds was at work and doing his best to cover his nerves in what he called his 'debriefing' with Jim, though the way his hand shook as he handed over his master keys to the tills rather gave the game away.

'I leave it all to you,' he said heartily when they'd finished, clapping Jim on the back. 'Which is fatal. I'll probably come back to find the entire first floor reorganised!'

'Only the first floor?' quipped Jim. They shook hands. 'You won't need it, because I know you'll be very happy, but — good luck!'

As she took down the blackout on Saturday morning, Lily could hardly have been more excited if it had been her own wedding day. It had rained in the night and the yard was gleaming, but already the clouds were thinning and a washy sun was trying to peep out. Jim swung her hand as they walked to work in the nip of an autumn morning.

'We're next!' he said.

It was Miss Temple's turn to work that Saturday, but when she arrived on Childrenswear, Lily was astonished to see Miss Thomas there as well. Miss Thomas explained coyly that she'd been phoned at home by Staff Office and asked to come in. Lily was frankly peeved. Miss Frobisher might have said! All right, Saturdays could be busy, but did Miss Frobisher really not trust her to cope? Downstairs, Jim was having much the same thought. He'd expected to cover both floors in Mr Simmonds's absence, but the first person he saw as he descended the stairs was the retired ground-floor supervisor, Mr Bertram.

'Asked back for the day,' Mr Bertram announced gleefully. 'A bit of extra pocket money before Christmas. The wife's delighted.'

Jim was rather less so but smiled politely. Cedric Marlow was finishing his tour of the counters, and Jim moved towards the stairs so he could be on hand when the old man's tour of the first floor began. Jim couldn't complain, of course — especially as he'd moaned before about how hard it was to manage with no cover for staff holidays or sickness — all in the name of wartime economy. But as they climbed the stairs together, his uncle turned to him.

'I know what you're thinking,' he said. 'It's not that I don't have faith in you. I know you and Miss Collins would love to have been at a certain event today, and the happy couple would have liked you there. The extra staffing — there's an additional body on Childrenswear as well — means that even if you have to miss the ceremony, you can both pop out during your dinner hour to see them emerge.'

Jim almost stumbled up the next step.

'That's very thoughtful, sir!' he said. 'Thank you! Lily — Miss Collins — will be thrilled!'

★　★　★

The ceremony was at twelve thirty, so with a bit of juggling over breaks, and swiftly arranged passes out, Jim and Lily hot-footed it to the Register Office for one o'clock.

They could see the wedding group as they approached. The sun had done its best and was shining fitfully through the coppery leaves of the beech trees. The photographer was setting up his camera with young John, spruce in a little suit and bow tie, asking questions and taking it all in. Miss Frobisher's neighbour was making polite conversation with a straight-backed chap in an Army uniform. Mr Simmonds was smart in his best suit, and his new wife complemented the autumn palette in a dress of bronze panne velvet with a fox-fur cape. They were holding hands and looking slightly dazed, as if they weren't quite sure what had just happened. Then the bride spotted Lily and Jim. She nudged Mr Simmonds who did an almost comical double take, then bounded down the Town Hall steps towards them.

'What are you doing here?' he demanded. 'If you're both here, who's minding the shop?'

Typical! thought Lily, as Jim explained Mr Marlow's subterfuge. Mr Simmonds's wedding day and his first thought was the store! But weren't they all like that, the staff at Marlows? The shop was their second home and their colleagues an extended family. Lily had met Gladys and Beryl there — and Jim of course — and she and Jim had almost been killed there. Jim always said that when he did die they'd find Marlows engraved on his heart.

'Who'd have thought Mr Marlow had such a secretive side?' Mr Simmonds marvelled.

'Or was such a romantic?' Miss Frobisher smiled. She'd always be Miss Frobisher to Lily and she'd remain so in the store — female staff were always addressed as 'Miss', married or not.

Lily looked at Jim. They knew from seeing him at Mrs Tunnicliffe's that Cedric Marlow was more than capable of keeping things close to his chest.

'I think we're ready!' the photographer called. Lily and Jim hung back as he posed the bride and groom first on their own, then with John, then with their witnesses. Then Mr Simmonds beckoned to Lily and Jim and they posed for a picture too, Lily pleased that she was wearing her blue coat and not her shapeless winter tweed. Then it was time to go — there were clothes to be changed, bags to be collected, and trains to be caught if the honeymooners were to get to the Lakes before dark.

'I'm so pleased you could come!' Miss Frobisher kissed Lily on the cheek.

'So am I,' said Lily. 'You can count on me, Miss Frobisher. I won't let you down in the next few days.

How could I when you've taught me all I know!'

Miss Frobisher smiled.

'You remind me so much of myself at your age,' she said. 'Always up for a challenge, never standing still.'

* * *

'There, there,' crooned Gladys, 'there, there.'

She was pushing the pram backwards and forwards — the big old pram that had done service for so many babies before. Beryl had used it for Bobby, and now Victor and Joy were laid end to end in it. Their tiny fists were curled up, Joy already asleep and Victor, always the harder one to settle, giving the little grunts that meant he was dropping off too. Gladys yawned. She'd have given anything to go back to bed, like her gran had with her *My Weekly*, a cup of tea, a slice of bread, and the last of the jam. It was only carrot jam, but even so . . . Did she dare to stop pushing yet? She risked it. Victor immediately opened his eyes and gave her an accusing stare. Gladys smiled at him, made a clucking noise in her throat, rocked the pram and began to hum 'Bye Baby Bunting'. It was making her feel sleepy if nothing else. But finally . . . another five minutes and Victor was off in the land of nod.

Gladys flopped into a chair. She'd changed them on the rug and the wet nappies were still in a heap, along with a towel, a soiled bit of rag, two muslins, a stray mitten, Victor's hat, and Joy's little cardigan. Gladys yawned again. The clock struck one — it couldn't be that time! But it was. Too bad . . . she had to have a sit down. She'd deal with the mess in a minute.

One o'clock . . . Miss Frobisher and Mr Simmonds would be married by now! It was a shame Lily and

Jim couldn't have gone, or any of the other staff, but Gladys knew from her time at Marlows how staff numbers had dwindled thanks to people joining up and not being replaced. Lily had known from the off that there wouldn't be anyone to cover. Still, there were bound to be photographs . . . Miss Frobisher would have looked a knockout, as usual.

Gladys looked down at her own stained skirt and trodden-down slippers. You had to laugh. It was a far cry from her own wedding day, when she'd been a vision in lace and chiffon, and Bill had, he said, been 'blown away' by her. But fifteen months and two babies later, despite the exhaustion, despite the constant round of feeding and changing and clearing up, she wouldn't have changed a thing. The joy — she'd named her daughter well — she got from the twins sometimes overwhelmed her. She wrote it all out for Bill in her letters, every detail, how much milk and how many nappies, how they got bigger and better week by week and month by month, smiling and gurgling, sounding as if they were trying to talk. In his letters back, Bill's pride in them and in her, his love and his longing to see them all surged off the page. And it couldn't be long now. It had even been in the papers that HMS *Jamaica* was coming out of service for a while. Bill was bound to be in touch soon. Even though she knew he'd have to be debriefed and deloused and medically examined as well as formally reassigned before he could even think about asking for leave, it couldn't be long.

Gladys yawned again. Just five minutes. The twins were safe, her gran was out of the way . . . she closed her eyes. Bliss.

She woke with a start. Someone was standing over

161

her, saying her name. Gladys blinked away her sleepiness and tried to focus — since that funny business with her eyes, it still sometimes took a while. A freckled face, bright-eyed, red-cheeked, was looking at her from under a sailor's cap. She was dreaming. It was Bill, but it couldn't be . . .

'Hello, my darling,' he said, dropping to his knees by her chair and pulling her close. 'Oh, Glad, I'm so happy to see you, so happy to be home! And as for this pair' — he nodded his head towards the pram — 'I've been stood here staring at them the last five minutes. I can't believe them. I can't believe I'm here and they're here — and you did it all on your own! You're wonderful!'

'Bill . . . ' Gladys finally managed to stutter. 'Oh, but I look such a mess! The place is a tip and — !'

'What are you talking about?' said Bill. He took her face in his hands; they were rough, she noticed, chapped by the Arctic winds. 'You've never looked so beautiful. I've seen a lot of the world, me — too much these past few years — but you and these two . . . trust me, you're the only world I want. Ever.'

18

Later, when Gladys had sobbed and gulped into his shoulder, gasped into it as they had their urgent but tender reunion, and then giggled into it as they lay happily together afterwards and she realised what they'd done right there on the rug, she held his face as he'd held hers.

'I can't believe we just did that! With the twins right by us as well!'

'So?' Bill grinned his crooked grin. 'How do they think they got here in the first place, eh?'

'Not to mention Gran over our heads!'

Bill pulled away slightly.

'Yeah, your gran. How is she?'

Gladys had said nothing in her letters, but Bill wasn't daft. He could tell from the way Dora's name had come up that she'd been spending a lot of time at the house.

'Oh, you know. The same, bless her.'

There was no 'bless her' about it as far as he as concerned. But Bill was in a difficult position. Her gran was Gladys's only living relative and as far as she was concerned blood was thicker than water. That was why she'd been so keen on tracking down his own mother, who'd put him in a Barnardo's home when he was a baby.

Bill's mother had been widowed young and forced to find work which meant she couldn't have Bill with her. After a time, she'd remarried, and remarried well, but her husband had turned out to be a dictatorial type with Victorian values. She'd had two daughters with him but her hope of bringing young Bill into the family as well had been quashed — she'd never even been able to confess that she had a son. She was now — bravely — divorcing her husband, but Bill knew from the few awkward meetings they'd had when he'd been home at the beginning of the year that it made little difference. There was too much time and distance between them for her to be anything to him, and certainly not now he had a family of his own. It was, unfortunately, too late for him, and he'd had to tell her so.

He knew it had saddened Gladys, who loved nothing more than a happy ending — look at the soppy films he'd sat through when they were courting! But the excitement of her pregnancy and his assurances that she was all he needed had allayed her disappointment and she'd had to accept that Bill didn't feel about blood ties the way she did. Bill had let his mother know that the twins had arrived safely, of course, and she'd sent Gladys a postal order for them, but neither of them was expecting much, if any, more contact with her. All of which meant that for Gladys's sake, Bill had to try to get along with her gran.

'She'll be banging on the floor with her stick any minute then,' grinned Bill. 'Asking where her dinner is!'

'You're right, I'd better do her something!' Gladys stood up and checked on the twins. 'They'll be good for another half hour. There's bread and dripping in the larder, if you don't mind, Bill. I'll tidy up in here, then I'll take it up to her.'

'I'll take it up,' Bill insisted. 'I'm here to look after you now, and don't you forget it!'

'I know you are. I can't believe it though. I've missed you so much.'

Bill took her in his arms again.

'Not as much as I've missed you.' It was their special saying — what they always said when they'd been apart, and he'd never meant it more than now. 'We've got a lot to catch up on. I want to hear all about it, right from the start.'

'All of it?'

'From the night you had them — a thunderstorm, wasn't it? I dunno, we don't do things by halves, do we?'

Gladys smiled and snuggled against him. How little he knew — the weather had been the least of it. She'd have to tell him the full story, the blood pressure, the problem with her sight. He'd be horrified, and he'd ask why he hadn't known before, but it didn't matter now, any of it. It was all in the past. Now Bill was home it was only their future that counted.

★ ★ ★

'You're very quiet,' said Jim as he and Lily walked home that evening. 'Not thinking about weddings, are you? Thinking 'it should have been me'?'

'Don't be daft. Can you see me in a fox-fur cape?'

'That wasn't what I meant, and you know it,' Jim swung their joined hands. 'But we can get on and set a date now. How does January 1st grab you?'

'What? We said spring!'

'I can't wait that long. And we'd never forget our anniversary.'

Lily smiled up at him. 'We can't get married till February at least,' she said. 'There's the January sale, remember. We're not allowed to take leave.'

'So we nip out and get married in our dinner hour.'

'And what about my honeymoon?' demanded Lily. 'Where would we go for a honeymoon at that time of year?'

'I don't know about you,' protested Jim, 'but I wasn't planning to spend it sightseeing. We'll have other things to do.'

To prove his point, he pulled her into a shop doorway and kissed her. She slid her hands under his jacket and held him close.

'I know we will,' she said. 'I'm not finding the waiting easy either. I do want you, Jim.'

He kissed her again, for longer this time, and she felt the shiver in her heart and the surge of heat through of the rest of her body, and his.

When they broke apart, he rested his forehead against hers.

'Let's set a date,' he said. 'Please, Lily. If I'm counting the days it might give me something else to think about, at least.'

'As soon as we get home,' she promised.

But they didn't, because when they got home, there was a surprise waiting. Who should be there, feet up, best chair, flicking through *Picturegoer* magazine, but Sid!

'Where've you been, anyway?' he demanded, when all the hugs had been done and 'what are you doing here' and 'you might have told us you were coming' had been said and he'd explained that he hadn't warned them because his leave could have been cancelled at the last minute, as had happened before. 'Mum said you're usually home just after six.'

'We, er, got a bit delayed, didn't we?' said Jim, try-

166

ing to tuck his shirt in at the back as unobtrusively as possible. 'Where is Dora?'

Sid jerked his head in the direction of the Crosbies'.

'Nipped next door. She's told me about this Kenny bloke that's landed himself on them and now Walter's got a bad head cold come on and he's making the most of it, like he would. Jean's worried Trevor's going to go down with it — she's at the end of her rag. Mum's taken round some soup and some Friar's Balsam.'

Lily shook her head.

'She never stops. You know she's been at Gladys's every day since she had the twins?'

'I'm sure she's loved every minute,' said Sid easily. 'But she can slack off there now.'

'Yes, once Bill comes home.' Jim held his hand out for Lily's coat so he could hang it up in the hall.

'He's home!' said Sid.

'What?' Lily stopped halfway through unpinning her hat.

Sid loved to be the one to deliver a headline and he made the most of this one.

'The *Jamaica* docked at Portsmouth ten days ago and the refit started last Monday. Gladys and Bill came round with the babs about four o'clock. I'd only just got here myself. Lucky I'd got a couple of beers with me so we could wet the babies' heads. Little smashers, aren't they?'

'I don't believe it,' said Lily, outraged. 'We've been here all the time, doing all the work, supporting Gladys, trying to help Jean out, you turn up like a bolt from the blue, and you're the first to know everything!'

'You haven't heard the best,' said Sid smugly.

'What?'

'Oh, no,' said Sid. 'I'm not telling the same story

twice. I've made Mum wait all afternoon, you'll have to wait till she gets back!'

'It had better be something good!' warned Lily.

'Have I ever let you down?' Sid raised his innocent blue eyes to hers, and she had to admit he hadn't. But he certainly knew how to spin things out.

To fill in the time till Dora got back, they laid the table, heated up the pilchards and cut the bread for toast. Once she was back, it was time to eat.

'Now, can we get to this exciting news of yours?' pleaded Lily as they took their seats at the table. 'And if it's just that you've got a new pencil sharpener or a bigger desk, I warn you I'm going to be highly disappointed!'

'Prepare to be amazed,' said Sid. He tilted on his chair and pulled an air letter from his pocket.

'From Reg?' asked Jim, stirring his tea as if it had sugar in it. No chance of that, the ration had been cut again.

Sid withdrew three sheets of airmail paper.

'He's got so much better at letter-writing since he's been away, even more so since he's been with Gwenda,' said Dora with satisfaction. Reg's fiancée was a spirited girl. She kept Reg up to the mark. 'Like I said, Sid, we had a nice long letter from him the other week. Dated a month ago, mind, took its time getting here, but still a nice change from an air card.'

'That's why I knew this'd be a surprise.' Sid announced smugly. 'This is dated a week ago.'

'Come on, Sid, enough's enough,' Jim chided. 'They've been very patient.'

'OK. OK. Now, do you want me to read it out or — '

'Oh, give it here!' Lily held out her hand. 'Honestly, even when you wouldn't swap your sweet cigarette cards with me, you weren't this annoying!'

She shook out the sheets of paper and began to read.

Dear Sid,
    I'm writing the same letter to Mum and Lily, don't know whose'll arrive first, but I've got some big news for you all.

'He can't have got another promotion yet,' said Dora. Reg was a sergeant. 'Maybe some commendation or something?'

'No, it's not that,' said Lily, stunned. She'd read ahead to the next line. She read out loud:

Me and Gwenda got married! I hope you all don't mind, but it could be ages yet till the both of us got home to do the deed. I got myself some leave, and we got married in Cairo.

Lily stopped there to see how everyone was taking it — well, not Sid, who already knew, or Jim, particularly, but her mum. Dora was dabbing her eyes with the corner of her apron. Lily reached out her hand.

'Oh Mum, don't cry. I'm sorry you couldn't be there.'

'It's all right, love.' Dora swallowed hard. 'I can see why they wanted to get on with it. And I'm happy for them, I really am. Think of it, our Reg . . . married!'

'And you've still got our wedding to come,' said Jim. 'You're not going to miss that!'

'Exactly, think of this as a rehearsal,' said Sid, cheerily but gently at the same time. 'Get some of the blarting . . . the emotion, I mean, out of the way

169

before Lily and Jim's big day.'

No one, of course, said anything about Sid getting married. Nothing had ever been said explicitly to Dora, but she knew her son. She knew as well as anyone that Sid was not the marrying kind. To cover any awkwardness, Lily asked quickly: 'Shall I go on?'

When Dora nodded, she continued:

Had a night at Shepheard's Hotel (dead posh, right up your street, Sid, with your high-falutin' tastes!). Photo is us in the courtyard and then the four of us — a mate of mine who was best man and Gwenda's sister, Bethan, who was her bridesmaid. The dresses were made in the bazaar in 24 hours, how's that for service? Beryl had better take note!

'There's photographs? Show us, Sid, quick!'

From the envelope, Sid produced two small black and white snaps. Dora and Lily pounced on them and Jim got up to crane over their shoulders.

There was Reg in his uniform, very smart, hair slicked down, looking pleased as punch and Gwenda on his arm, small, dark, and pretty in a long, silky dress with what looked like orange blossom in her hair. The fronds of a palm tree waved behind them and a man in a white waiter's jacket and a fez was passing with a tray of drinks.

'Never going to mistake it for Hinton, are you?' teased Sid.

In the second photo, the foursome was seated round a table of some beaten metal with drinks — possibly the same ones the waiter had been carrying — in front of them. An exotic climbing plant tumbled down a wall at their side and in the middle of the courtyard a fountain played.

Lily was quiet. It looked so glamorous, and — well, grown-up. Miss Frobisher and Mr Simmonds married, Reg and Gwenda married, Gladys and Bill reunited ... all the omens were lining up for wedding bells, marriage vows, and happy couples. Sid noticed.

'You're very quiet, Sis,' he said. 'You're pleased for our Reg, aren't you?'

'Of course!' said Lily. 'It's a bit of a shock, that's all.'

'He's beaten you to it, and you don't like it,' guessed Sid.

'Rubbish!'

'Never mind him!' Jim, still standing behind her, put his hands on Lily's shoulders. 'Remember, we're next.'

19

But with all the excitement of the evening to digest on top of the pilchards, Lily and Jim didn't, after all, get out their diaries, which had next year's calendar in the back, and pick a date.

And the next day Sid was still there, which was lovely, but meant no one had any time to themselves. While Dora went off to church, Sid wanted to hear all Lily and Jim's news while they prepared the dinner. And in the afternoon, Sid had arranged to meet up with Gladys and Bill. It was only natural he'd want to make the most of his time with his old shipmate again, and it wasn't that Lily didn't want to see Gladys and Bill, but frankly she had plenty of time to do that if Bill was going to be coming and going all winter, and what she really wanted was some time on her own with Jim.

It was not to be. The weather was fine — still warm for October — so Dora packed them some sandwiches and a flask for a picnic tea and they went to the park. Sid and Bill spread out a couple of blankets and they sprawled on the small patch of scrubby grass, almost worn away, that had been left when the rest of the park had been turned over to allotments. Gladys took the twins out of the pram and gave Joy a rattle and Victor a squeaky ball, but the twins were more fascinated by the softly stirring branches above them. They lay on the rug and waved their arms as if trying to reach them, gurgling happily.

Lily and Gladys left the men talking V1s and V2s,

height, velocity, barrage balloons, and radar and went for a stroll round the pond.

'You look like a different person since I last saw you.' Lily took her friend's arm. Gladys couldn't seem to stop smiling — at Bill, at the twins, at her friends, and at complete strangers. It reminded Lily of how she and Jim had been on the day they got engaged.

'I feel it,' said Gladys, glowing.

'Good. I know you were happy being a mum but having Bill home is going to make all the difference.'

'It already has! Apart from how wonderful it is to see him, and you know, to be . . . with him again, I hadn't realised how exhausted I was till he made the bed this morning and took out the nappy bucket and washed the pots. He's got a long leave this time, special 'cos he hadn't seen the twins, but in future, it'll probably just be overnight by the time he's got here from Portsmouth, or wherever he is.'

They strolled back to the group on the rug. Sid was explaining ('This isn't for Mum's ears, by the way') about the difficulty of intercepting the V2s. They didn't fly as straight or level as the doodlebugs so they were harder to bring down with anti-aircraft fire.

'But before you go worrying,' Sid told Lily, 'they're not aimed where I'm living or working. It's the East End that's still copping the worst of it.'

Bill looked sober — he'd been brought up in the East End, after all.

'Like it needs any more problems! But,' he added cheerily, 'now the Russkies are giving Hitler a caning in Poland, we've got free rein to bomb Germany to bits while his eye's off the ball. That'll put a spoke in his wheel.'

Jim looked uncomfortable and not just at Bill's

mangled metaphors. Lily knew his view: it was one thing when military targets were taken out, but revenge bombing of cities meant civilian casualties in huge numbers. It was all very well saying Hitler didn't have a thought for the Londoners who were being killed and if the Nazis were ever to be defeated . . . Things were pretty desperate, but 'an eye for an eye and a tooth for a tooth' just left everyone worse off, didn't it?

Lily sometimes wondered what her life over the last five years would have been like without the war. No bombs, no black market, no blackout. No worrying about Sid and Reg and Bill and all the fighting men; no rationing, no coupons, no queues. Without the war, she'd still have gone to work at Marlows just the same, met Gladys and Beryl, and met Jim. But over and above all that there had been a war, there still was, and that coloured everything.

The sun was dipping lower now; they'd eaten their picnic and Gladys had fed the twins, but it would soon be time for their bath.

'I know your mum's been a diamond, you all have, but I don't know how Glad's coped,' Bill said to Lily when Gladys was out of earshot, tucking the twins in their pram. 'And that scare with her eyesight! I can't believe none of you told me!'

'What were we going to say?' Lily defended herself. 'By the time a letter got to you, her sight could have been back. We'd have worried you for nothing, and you thousands of miles away and nothing you could do.'

'I know, but . . .' Bill looked lovingly at his wife. 'She's stronger than she looks, isn't she? I don't mean physically, but in her head. You all are who've been stuck at home, waiting it out. You'll never get a medal, like I will just for turning up, but you don't half deserve one.'

Sid went back to London next day, and Lily's week in charge of the department began.

Half-term was always busy on Childrenswear and with Miss Frobisher away, Miss Thomas and Miss Temple had agreed to do extra hours. On Tuesday, however, a flaw in the plan emerged. Miss Thomas arrived looking decidedly groggy.

'I think I'm going down with this cold that's doing the rounds,' she sniffed.

She stuck it out, but the next day phoned Staff Office to say she couldn't get out of bed. Lily phoned Miss Temple, but she couldn't come in; she was expecting a plumber it had taken her three months to get hold of.

'I'll find someone to cover your dinner,' Jim told Lily in a rushed conversation. As he was covering Miss Frobisher's supervisor role, he was pretty frantic himself. 'And Miss Temple'll be in tomorrow.'

But the plumber, in fixing one problem, had caused another: Miss Temple apologised but the water was off and she'd have to stay home again until it was reconnected.

On Friday she turned up, but her face was pale and her nose pink. The plumber had given her the infamous cold that had felled Miss Thomas, though seeing the pressure Lily was under, she struggled through.

On Saturday, though, she too called in sick. Lily had no one and no break all day. Miss Temple, her head fuzzy the day before, had made some kind of error; the coupons in the drawer didn't tally with the goods they'd sold. Lily and Jim stayed behind after closing and finally found the discrepancy: Miss Temple had snipped one coupon too many out of the customer's book for a boy's jacket. The customer was a regular one, fortunately, and Jim was sure that if the coupon was returned with a covering letter, all would be forgiven. He promised he'd see to it.

By Sunday, though, Lily was a limp rag.

'It's a miracle you haven't got this cold yourself,' Dora clucked. 'Go back to bed, I'll bring you up some toast.'

Lily had no choice but to agree. Maybe Bill was right. A medal for everyone on the Home Front was in order.

By Monday morning, though, after some rare cossetting from her mum, she was fully restored and able to greet her returning boss with a smile. Miss Frobisher looked very well, her eyes bright and her hair in its French pleat smoother and glossier than ever.

'How's it been here?' she asked.

'Fine!' bluffed Lily. 'A very good week! A few wrinkles to iron out, but we ended up twenty-two pounds over target!'

When Miss Frobisher checked with her deputy supervisor, however, Jim told her the truth. He thought she should know exactly what it had cost Lily to turn that profit.

'Wrinkles? Ironed out?' Miss Frobisher scolded when she got back to the department. 'You got through the week virtually on your own!'

Lily shrugged it away.

'It was fine,' she insisted.

'Well,' said Miss Frobisher, 'I can promise you one thing, I don't intend taking time off to get married again.' And added: 'You're next!'

That night was Bill's last in Hinton for a while. He

wanted to take Gladys out and had invited Jim and Lily along; Dora would sit with the twins.

Gladys was a bundle of nerves. She'd never left them before and though Dora was the most capable babysitter anyone could have wished for, when they got to the pub Gladys was still looking edgy.

'They'll be fine!' Bill assured her. 'They were both sound asleep, weren't they? They won't even know you're gone. Lemonade shandy for you, Glad? Same for you, Lily?'

When Bill and Jim came back with the drinks, Gladys hadn't even taken her coat off.

'Just the one, then I'll go,' she said. 'It's lovely of you, Bill, but I don't think I'm ready for this. They're too little.'

Bill put his arm round her.

'Isn't she a star? There's not one of the WRNS or WAAF or ATS doing a better job, I don't reckon.'

Before anyone could reply, a familiar figure came swaying up.

'Evening.'

It was Kenny, already well-oiled from the look and sound of him. But what could they do? Jim and Lily had spent weeks encouraging him to join them; they could hardly turn their backs on him now.

'Pull up a stool,' said Jim, and introduced him to Gladys and Bill, explaining that Kenny was a new neighbour.

It was awkward, there was no doubt about it, but at least Bill didn't go to shake Kenny's hand like Les had done. Gladys seemed transfixed by Kenny's empty sleeve — now the weather was colder, he'd had to start wearing a jacket. Somehow, they made conversation. Bill diplomatically didn't ask how Kenny had lost his arm and didn't talk about his own war service, though his discretion left Kenny free to embark on a rambling monologue and a crude joke. Gladys squirmed until Kenny, pausing for a loud belch, gave her a chance to interrupt.

'Well, this has been very nice, and very nice to meet you, Kenny, but I must be off now, if you'll excuse me. We've got two young babies.'

She kissed Bill, gave them all a little wave and hurried off, Bill assuring her he wouldn't be long. Kenny sipped his drink in morose silence and to cover it Bill produced some photos. He and Gladys had gone to a professional studio for them to mark his arrival home. There were the twins on the inevitable fur rug, and then the family group, Gladys seated with the babies on her lap, Bill standing behind like a Victorian paterfamilias.

Lily and Jim pored over them politely, but Kenny lurched to his feet.

'That's right, rub it in! First there's these two, love's young dream, headed for the altar, now it's you, married bliss and happy bloody families! I suppose you're a flaming war hero and all! And what have I got, eh? What have I got to look forward to? I've done my bit as well, joined up, served my country, and what have I got for it? Sweet FA!'

'Here — ' Bill began, but Kenny had stumbled off, glass in hand. But the barman refused to serve him again and after more expletives, Kenny reeled out.

'Nice feller,' said Bill, gathering up his photos.

'We'd better go after him,' said Jim, drinking up. 'Sorry about that, Bill, on your last night . . . '

But nothing could dent Bill's good humour.

'I'll be back soon enough,' he said. 'See if we can

178

persuade Gladys out of the house again.'

They parted outside, with hugs and 'see you soon' and Jim took Lily's arm.

'We'll try and catch Kenny up and pour him back through the letterbox, shall we? And then, as our evening's finished sooner than we thought, and there's been no chance till now with Sid and work and Bill and everything, how about we get out our diaries and pin that wedding date down?'

Lily looked up at the sky. The moon was waning among streaks of cloud. A light drizzle had started to fall. She took a deep breath. Her head felt so muzzy she'd wondered if she was coming down with the dreaded cold, then she'd wondered if it was the shandy. But she knew it was neither of those things. It was something deeper than that.

'Jim,' she said. 'I'm so sorry. But I can't . . . oh, Jim, I'm sorry but I have to say it. I can't marry you.'

20

A few weeks before, the Government had announced that they were easing the blackout. They called it the 'dim-out'. The streetlights would be illuminated again — not fully, just to the equivalent of moonlight. Like everyone, Lily had been thrilled — no more stumbling around in the pitch black by the light of a wavering torch. Now she longed for the darkness again. The pain and confusion on Jim's face — his much-loved face — was too piercing to see.

'You can't . . . can't marry me? What do you mean, can't? But why?'

Lily shook her head helplessly.

'We can't talk about it here. Please can we go home?'

Jim hesitated. Normally, naturally, he'd crook his elbow and she'd slide her arm through it, then he'd press her in close to his body. Now neither of them knew what to do. Awkwardly, they started to walk along side by side, Lily keeping her eyes on the ground, Jim looking fixedly ahead.

At home, still not speaking, but as courteous as ever, Jim helped her to take off her coat and went to hang it up in the hall. Dora had gone to bed. Lily set about making a pot of tea, which probably neither of them really wanted, but it gave her something to do. She noticed her engagement ring, reflected but distorted in the battered side of the kettle. Guiltily, she turned on the gas.

Tea made, she carried the tray through. Jim was sitting at the table. She set the tray down and sat down herself.

'Well?' said Jim. 'Tell me. What have I done?'

'Nothing!' cried Lily, then lowered her voice. The last thing she wanted was for her mum to come down. How like him, her lovely Jim, to assume it was his fault. How like him not to be angry, furious, raging, which she surely deserved, but only to want to understand. 'Nothing.'

'OK. What have I *not* done?'

'Oh Jim! It's not you, it's not you at all!' She felt her voice rise in volume again and made an effort to bring it down. 'It's me! How I feel.'

'How do you feel?'

That was a good question. She'd asked herself the same thing time and time again since the unsettling unease had started.

'I suppose the best way to put it is that I'm confused.'

'I see. Well, no, I don't. Why? Is there someone else?'

'What? No! No, no, no!'

She couldn't say 'how could you think that' because there had been a time, a couple of years ago, when she'd had her head turned by someone else's attentions. Jim had been away in the country — his mother had been ill. He hadn't been entirely straight with her about a girl there who had a crush on him either, but that was no excuse. They'd both admitted their foolishness and it had never been mentioned again — till now.

'No,' she said again, firmly. 'Absolutely not.'

'OK. But you don't love me. Or not any more. Or not enough.'

'Of course I love you! Desperately!'

'Then I really don't understand!'

181

'Let me try to explain.'

'I think you'd better.' Jim poured milk into the cups, slightly unsteadily, she noticed. Then he lifted the pot. 'I'm listening.'

'All right.' Underneath the table, Lily pleated the edge of the cloth between her fingers. She took a deep breath. 'First of all, this has got nothing to do with us having to wait all this time to get married. Or maybe it has.'

'You really are confused, aren't you?' said Jim dryly, pushing her cup across to her. 'Go on.'

'The point is that it's given me time to think. And before I get married — before we get married, I have to do something, Jim. I have to prove myself. I have to do something different. Something for the war.'

Jim lifted his eyes to the ceiling. For the first time he sounded impatient.

'Oh, not again, we've been through this! We went through it at the start of the year. All that stuff about the ATS, torn between going away and staying here. And your mum rightly pointed out that you could make a perfectly good contribution to the war effort in Hinton with the WVS, and you've been doing that. Look at what you did for those evacuee kids! And you got your promotion at work and . . . you're surely not still hankering to join up?'

Lily's chin came up, and there was that forceful set of her mouth which he knew so well.

'Yes. I'm sorry, but I am.' She tried to explain. 'The thing is Jim, I'm eighteen and I've had no experience of life. I've never really had to be tested or had to test myself. By the time Sid and Reg were my age they were in the forces, and so were most men and women.'

Jim compressed his mouth and she knew what he

182

was thinking.

'I'm sorry,' she said quickly. 'I don't mean that as a dig at you. I know you tried to join the Army but you couldn't, and I know how that rankles with you — '

'Yes, it does, of course it does, it irks me every day. But I accepted it and got on with what I could do — the ARP and fire watching.'

'I know. And that's really important work, and I know the WVS is too. But at least you had a go at joining up! And even without that, you haven't lived in the same place all your life. You've moved from your home to Hinton; you've seen a bit of the world!'

'A very small bit.'

'OK, but even so . . . ' Lily's words were tumbling out now. 'I've tried to convince myself. I know Hinton's enough for Gladys and Beryl, but seeing Sid recently, and Bill — even Kenny . . . I thought coping at work without Miss Frobisher would put it all to rest, make me feel better, that I was good at something — but it just rammed it home to me. It's not enough. I still don't feel I'm doing enough.'

'And what do you want to do? You can't think you'd be sent to the front line?'

'No, of course not, but hearing Sid and Bill talk about the Wrens, and Reg writing about him and Gwenda, her with the MTC and her sister in the WAAF . . . ' she tailed off.

Jim got up and went to the window. He tweaked a corner of the blackout which might be showing a chink of light. He turned and looked at her.

'You want the same.'

'I'm sorry,' she said lamely. 'Like I said, none of this is your fault. It's just me.'

Jim came back to the table. He placed his hands on

the back of his chair. Lily looked at the hands that had held hers, had so often comforted and caressed her. 'Lily, I knew what I was taking on with you. You're a pretty determined character and when you set your mind to something, you want to make it happen. When we first got together, we agreed, didn't we, we didn't want to be a soppy couple, only thinking about bottom drawers and babies. I said I'd never want to stand in your way — we knew we both wanted to go as far as we could at Marlows. But you've done that and now you're saying it's not enough.'

Lily held her breath. This was the tipping point. Was Jim going to say she was too demanding, expected too much, of life, and of him? Maybe that's what she deserved. She was asking a lot.

But he smiled — sadly, but still a smile.

'I can see it's not enough. In fact, the way you've been talking, it's a miracle you've hung on this long. So, if you want to join up, you should do it.'

Lily could hardly believe what she'd heard.

'Seriously?'

'Seriously, else why are we talking about it? But I don't see why you think it gets in the way of us being married.'

'Well, I just thought — '

'We simply wait. Until the war is over and you . . . you've done what you feel you have to do.'

'You really mean that?'

'What have I just said?'

Unable to speak, Lily opened her arms wide. Jim came round the table. He knelt on the floor in front of her and put his arms round her. She held his dear, thoughtful, sensitive face in her hands and kissed him.

'I don't believe you,' she said. 'I don't mean I don't

believe what you said but that you can be so good and kind and understanding and patient with me. I don't deserve it. I don't deserve you.'

'I think you mean I don't deserve you!' grinned Jim, his tone putting quite a different slant on the word 'deserve'.

'You're right there,' agreed Lily.

Jim sat back on his haunches.

'So what happens next?'

'Well,' Lily considered, 'I suppose I go along to the recruiting office.'

'That sounds like a plan,' nodded Jim. 'Any objection if I tag along?'

★ ★ ★

The nearest Auxiliary Territorial Service office was in Birmingham. Jim suggested they book leave on a Wednesday to allow a whole day for the outing.

'You don't want to run out of time,' he said. 'They might send you off for the medical straight away. Tap your knee with their little hammer, get you to walk in a straight line and look down your throat — that's what happened to me when I went to join up. And there's the eye test of course.'

That was the test that he'd failed.

Lily hadn't thought about a medical, but from then on she was careful to avoid anyone with the hint of a sniffle and to wash her hands scrupulously whenever she could. She inhaled and exhaled deeply on their walks to work and stepped out briskly, keeping pace with Jim's long legs for a change.

'Practising your marching, I see,' he noted.

Lily had decided not to tell her mum the real

185

purpose behind the trip till she knew the outcome. It was a tactic Sid had used when he'd applied for his London posting. There was no point in giving their mum something to fret about — and she would — till it was certain, he'd reckoned. So Jim and Lily had come up with a white lie about checking out the Christmas offerings in Birmingham's stores — Rackham's, Lewis's, Marshall and Snelgrove's, Grey's — there was even a big Co-op.

This wasn't a total untruth. Lewis's was of particular interest to Jim with its huge top-floor Toy department and famous Father Christmas grotto, which was already up and running.

The day they were due to go was damp and dreary, typical for the end of November, but Dora was pleased they were having some time together.

'You won't notice the weather!' she said as they set off. Lily suppressed a pang of guilt. She hated fibbing.

She'd spent ages planning her outfit: she wanted to look serious but not sober, smart but not flashy. That ruled out her plum satin blouse and matching suede shoes, but her more sensible work clothes were too well worn and too dull. Finally she settled on her grey dress with its scattering of blue and yellow flowers — the material was a bit lightweight for November but it went with her blue coat and hat — or at least didn't not go with them, which was an achievement when most of her clothes came from jumble sales. Even with her staff discount, Marlows' prices were usually too steep. Her work shoes, given a bit of spit and polish, added the sensible touch. Jim smiled at her approvingly as he helped her off the train at Snow Hill station in Birmingham.

'Very smart. I'd take you on,' he said.

'Thank you,' said Lily and they both knew she meant for more than just the compliment.

They asked directions to the recruiting office and found that their route took them past both Grey's and Lewis's. They paused to study the goods in their windows. There was some enviable stuff.

'We haven't had a radiogram that size for years,' Jim sighed at Lewis's. 'They've got much bigger buying power than us. But,' he brightened, 'they've still got the apostrophe in their name, so they're behind Marlows in that respect. They'll all catch us up in the end!'

But Lily's eyes had wandered to the slogan running across the top of Lewis's windows. 'Are You Supporting The National Effort?' it read. Well, she would be soon. She straightened her shoulders and raised her head.

'Come on,' she said to Jim, pulling on his arm. 'We can do our window-shopping afterwards.'

'You reckon?' He looked down at her, his brown eyes smiling. 'When the ATS sees what's walked through the door, you'll be whisked straight off to London in a staff car!'

21

With Lily setting the pace, it was barely twelve when they got to the office, but a woman in the khaki uniform of the ATS, a sergeant by her stripes, was locking the door.

'Excuse me!' Lily ran forward. 'We were just coming to see you! We can't be too late?'

The woman turned. She was about forty, with a quiff of brown hair poking out from under her cap and quizzical grey eyes.

'Caught in the act,' she smiled. 'I'm not closing for the day, but it's been quiet so I was sneaking off for an early lunch. But now you're here, you'd better come in.'

This was far better than Lily had expected — not a barking barrack-room sergeant but a friendly, approachable person. It had to be a good sign. The woman turned the key in the lock again and led the way into a small room, furnished with three desks, two of them with typewriters. She indicated the empty desks.

'One's off sick, the other's gone to the Post Office,' she explained. 'I expect she'll be hours, with the queuing. Have a seat.'

Or 'At ease!' thought Lily as she and Jim sat down on the two wooden chairs in front of the desk without a typewriter.

'Sergeant Matthews,' said the woman, extending her hand to them both before she sat down on her side of the desk. 'So, here you are.' Shrewdly, she looked

188

them up and down, taking in every detail, including Lily's ring. 'And this young man is your fiancé, I take it.'

'That's right,' said Jim. 'And before you ask, I'm fully supportive of what she wants to do.'

Lily looked around. The walls held the obligatory photos of the King, solemn in his dress uniform, and the Prime Minister beaming in his Homburg hat, making the 'V for Victory' sign. Various ATS posters were on show as well. There was the one of the smiling ATS girl in front of an anti-aircraft gun with the motto: 'They Can't Get On Without Us'. The more recent one was there too, stark in blood-red and black — a German soldier with his hands up in defeat. The slogan read: 'Nazi Surrender Draws Nearer Every Time A Woman Joins The ATS'.

With a happy sigh — she was in the right place! — Lily delved in her bag.

'I'd like to join up,' she said. 'I've brought my birth certificate and my National Insurance card and my identity card, of course ...'

Sergeant Matthews produced a form from a drawer. She uncapped her pen.

'Lily Margaret Collins,' said Lily, anticipating the first question. 'Date of birth — '

'Hold on. I'm not writing anything till we've had a chat,' said Sergeant Matthews. 'Don't want to waste paper, do we? So, Lily, what are you doing now?'

Lily explained her job at Marlows. She emphasised her promotion (responsible), the cash handling (trustworthy), the mental arithmetic (quick) and the need to get on with people (flexible) — she'd rehearsed it all with Jim on the train. Jim had also advised her to play up her WVS work — not just the camouflage nets and the envelope-stuffing but her efforts with the evacuees. Sergeant Matthews listened intently.

'Right,' she said. 'That all sounds splendid, and well done you. So have you any clerical experience as such? Typing, filing . . .'

'Um . . . not exactly.' Lily thought quickly. 'Though it's important to keep the stock sheets and tidy the stockroom itself, and the department in good order. I make sure of that.'

'Yes, tidy mind, good. And has Marlows been your only job? Any other experience? Factory work maybe?'

'No,' admitted Lily. 'Not yet anyway. Though if you put me to anything that required . . .' She thought quickly. What was the word? '..... any dexterity like that, er, I'm sure I'd — '

But Sergeant Matthews wasn't a time-waster, or perhaps she was thinking of the early lunch she was missing.

'Any craft experience?' she interrupted. 'Baking, perhaps? Used a sewing machine?'

Lily thought of her clumsy attempts at knitting and sewing, and the exploded house brick that had been her attempt at a loaf. She was spoilt, really, with Dora being so good at everything like that. But she wasn't mad keen to be stuck in the camp kitchen or sewing room, so a 'no' might not be a bad thing.

'No,' she admitted. 'Only hand sewing, mostly at the WVS. I help my mum with meals, and around the house, obviously.'

'I'm sure you do. Can you drive?'

Drive? That would be beyond Lily's wildest dreams! Serving in the Mechanised Transport Corps, like Gwenda? Posted abroad, even?

'No, but I'd be very keen to learn — '

190

Sergeant Matthews recapped her pen. She sat back, taking her pen with her and tapping it against her chin.

'I'm sorry,' she said, 'but I really can't take you on.'

Lily heard Jim's intake of breath. Out of the corner of her eye she saw him reach for her hand, but she waved it away.

'What?'

'You asked when we met outside if you were too late. And I'm afraid in terms of joining up, you are.'

'Too late? But I can't be — we're still fighting! The war could go on for goodness knows how long! I know you're not conscripting girls any more, but you're still taking volunteers!'

'Very few,' replied Sergeant Matthews. 'And only if they have directly relevant experience. If perhaps they can drive or have used a teleprinter. Or have foreign languages — French, German — now that's very useful.'

Lily slumped back in her chair. Sergeant Matthews hadn't even asked her about languages: she'd realised Lily wasn't of that calibre. But Lily realised something as well. She'd told Jim she'd never been tested and that was true, but she'd never been turned down for anything she'd attempted before either. Her mum had always encouraged her; her teachers had praised her. She'd been terrified of the interview for her junior's job at Marlows, but she'd still got it. She wasn't going to take this lying down.

'I'm sorry,' she said, 'I'm not saying I don't believe you but there must still be work! I know we've made progress in the last few months . . . Paris liberated, and Brussels. But a lot of Belgium's still under German control! And Holland! And what about the V2s still dropping on London — you must need people for the anti-aircraft guns? Searchlight batteries?'

Sergeant Matthews laid down her pen. She leaned across the desk, kind, concerned.

'Lily, your enthusiasm is commendable, and if you'd been of age earlier in the war we'd have snapped you up, believe me. But the ack-ack guns are manned by women who've been doing the job for years, the same with the searchlights — and barrage balloons, come to that.'

'They must have leave! Or go sick, like your typist?'

'And then they're replaced by others who are equally experienced. There's enough of them. To be honest, we're having trouble finding enough for a lot of our girls to do.' Sergeant Matthews put the form away and closed the drawer. 'Wasting a form is the least of it. I can't waste Government money by taking on someone who hasn't got relevant experience, kitting them out and spending six weeks training them at this stage in the war.'

Lily blinked. She was desperate not to give in to tears like a spoilt child who'd thought she had the chance of an adventure only to have it snatched away. Jim saved her. He spoke for the first time.

'Excuse me for butting in, I don't mean to be impolite, but 'at this stage'? How can you be so sure? As Lily says, it's not entirely going our way. And Hitler's come back at us before.'

'It's different now,' said Sergeant Matthews. 'Think about it. First the blackout was lifted. Only the other week they announced how demobilisation is going to work. Do you seriously think the Government and the Armed Forces would have done those things if they weren't confident the enemy can't hold out much longer?'

192

Lily and Jim were silent. When she put it like that . . .

'There's more,' the sergeant said gently. 'I can't tell you what, you understand why, but watch the papers and listen to the news in the next few days. There's going to be another big announcement at the weekend. And trust me, the liberation of Holland is very close. The Dutch Resistance has a superb network for information. Another week, another fortnight . . . and you'll see.'

Sergeant Matthews stood up. Lily gathered her papers and stuffed them into her bag. Clearly, the order was 'dismiss!'

'I am sorry,' Sergeant Matthews said as they shook hands again. 'I'm sure you'll do very well at whatever you set your mind to, Lily. Thank you for offering your services to us. But timing is against you.'

Lily couldn't argue against the facts. Never mind the motto above Lewis's windows, the real sign had been Sergeant Matthews locking up the office as they'd arrived. She was too late.

Jim led her away, mute and defeated. Lily felt very small. All the fuss she'd caused, the hurt and upset to Jim, had all been for nothing. She wanted to say as much to him, but she couldn't squeeze the words past the lump in her throat.

'I can't talk about it yet,' she managed. 'So please don't say anything. Let's just do what we came for, or said we did, to look at the shops and see what they've got for Christmas.'

'Don't be silly. That's not what we came for and it doesn't matter now.'

'It does matter. It's what we told Mum. She'll expect to know. So come on, let's do it. We might as well.'

'Hang on then.' Jim stopped to get his bearings,

complicated by the fact that a lot of Birmingham's landmarks had been boarded up, damaged or destroyed. 'I think Rackham's is this way.'

He led them along a street called Temple Row. They found themselves with the back of the huge store to one side and a wide-open space on the other. The city's cathedral, or what was left of it, stood in the centre. There was no roof, just a cat's cradle of blackened rafters, the result of the Blitz. Providentially, the precious Pre-Raphaelite stained-glass windows had been removed months before: some said the Bishop of Birmingham had had a vision that had inspired him to do it.

'Let's get our breath back,' said Jim.

The railings had gone, of course, and the benches, but they perched on some stone coping. Jim put his arm round her and pulled her against him. Lily burrowed into his shoulder.

'I'm sorry,' he said. 'It's tough when a dream shatters in front of you.'

'You had to go through it.' Lily's voice was muffled. 'When you got turned down, I thought I understood. I had no idea.'

'Don't be daft,' Jim replied. 'But I'm living proof, aren't I? It's not the end of the world. And look, if what Sergeant Matthews said is right, and it means the end of the war really is round the corner, well, that's the best thing that could happen, isn't it?'

Lily would normally choose honesty over tact every time, but it was too soon for her to acknowledge what Jim had said was right, or to be cheered by anything. Jim pulled away so she was forced to look at him.

'Come on, Lily, what are you saying? That you'd rather the war didn't end? Go through the Blitz again when' — he waved his arm in the direction of the cathedral — 'this kind of thing was happening? Hundreds, thousands of people killed, injured or made homeless every night? Bombs and fire and terror raining down? Let's go back to Dunkirk, shall we, have blokes like poor Kenny captured all over again? Or how things were the year after, when Italy came into the war against us? Or through everything that happened in North Africa, to Les when he was serving, and to your own brother — all that blood, sweat, and tears? You'd rather the war went on like that, just so you can 'do your bit'?'

Lily sat quiet. Jim didn't often make speeches, certainly not ones that held an element of reproach and she felt ashamed. It was selfish and stupid to want things to be different just so she could feel better, banging on about doing it for the national good, when really it was all about herself. A pigeon strutting by cocked its head and looked up at her unblinkingly, then moved on. Lily willed herself to look at Jim.

'Thank you,' she said. 'Of course I don't want us — or anyone — to go through that again, or for the war to go on a minute longer than it has to. But I needed you to tell me straight. And I needed what happened today. I needed to see that not everything works out like we want it to. It can't, and you do have to accept what you can't change and pick yourself up and get on with things.'

Jim took her hands.

'Exactly. And what's happened isn't the worst thing in the world, is it? You've got a great family and friends, a job you love — '

'Never mind that,' said Lily. 'I've got you. Lord knows why you put up with me, but you do.'

Jim grinned.

'Believe it or not, you're good for me,' he said. 'You have ideas, you've make me think, you make me laugh. In the end, we complement each other. I think we're a good team. And we're going to win through, the two of us, whatever life throws at us.'

'Or doesn't,' countered Lily, thinking about Sergeant Matthews.

'True. Though right now I could do with it throwing me something to eat!'

'Trust you, always thinking of your stomach!'

'And what's wrong with that?' countered Jim. 'We passed a Kardomah on the way here — '

'Ooh. They might even have decent coffee.' Now Lily was interested — and the relief at talking about normal, everyday things like food, was overwhelming. 'And then shall we go and look round the shops? Because now all that ATS nonsense is out of the way — '

'Oh, it's nonsense now, is it?' smiled Jim.

'Now all that ATS business is out of the way,' Lily corrected herself, 'I am properly going to look forward to Christmas. There's a party for the evacuees at the Drill Hall to organise. And Christmas at Marlows . . . We must go back to Lewis's and see their grotto.' She pulled away so she could look at him. 'But before we do, have you got your diary with you?'

'Yes.' Jim took it from his inside pocket. 'Why?'

Lily looked at his much-loved face, his high cheekbones, firm chin, his deep-set eyes behind his glasses. She had never loved him so much.

'Because there's something much more important than anything else: our wedding. I'm so sorry for what I've put you through, Jim.'

Jim gave a little shake of his head, but Lily was insistent.

'I have, I know.' And then: 'Oh, I'd get married tomorrow if we could! Wouldn't you?'

Instead of a reply, Jim swept her into his arms and kissed her. A couple of passing off-duty airmen whooped and wolf-whistled. Lily and Jim didn't hear them. The moment was purely about them and what they meant to each other, everything they'd been through and everything that lay ahead.

22

They couldn't get married 'tomorrow' — they both knew that. But . . .

'What are you doing on March 21st next year?' Lily asked Gladys and Beryl when the three of them got together the next evening for what Beryl called a 'girls' night' at her house. Bill was home again, on a forty-eight-hour pass, so he was babysitting, which meant that Gladys felt confident to leave the twins. Les had been summarily dispatched to the pub so they could have the place to themselves for a 'good old gossip' — Beryl's words again.

'Next year? How the heck do I know?' she demanded now. 'Right, I'll look in my crystal ball, shall I?'

'You don't need it, I'll tell you,' said Lily smugly. 'You'll be at our wedding, me and Jim's.'

'What?' squeaked Gladys. 'You never said!'

'We only decided yesterday, but we've set our hearts on it. We said spring, didn't we, and it's the first day of spring, so why wait any longer?'

'I need a drop more of this after that bloomin' bombshell!' Beryl lifted the bottle of elderflower wine that her mother-in-law Ivy had sent from the country, where she acted as housekeeper for Jim's invalid dad. 'Anyone else for a top-up?'

Gladys shook her head but Lily, still giddy with the ups and downs of the last twenty-four hours, recklessly held out her glass.

'Go on, tell us more!' Gladys persisted.

'There's not much more to tell yet,' smiled Lily.

'But it happens to be a Wednesday and we'll fix the register office for the afternoon, Beryl, so you won't lose a morning's trade — '

'You are joking?' Beryl, taking a sip, spluttered wine all over the table. 'What kind of friend do you take me for? Fix it for whatever time you like. It's your day, you come first!'

'Really?' said Lily. 'Oh, good because I'd like it as early as possible! Nine o'clock if we can! Less time to get nervous!'

★ ★ ★

Next day she and Jim got passes out at dinnertime to make the booking. Nine o'clock was perhaps a little early, but there was a slot at 11.15 so they opted for that.

'Sounds like a dental appointment,' said Jim as they left, pretending gloom. 'But at least the dentist is over quickly. I'm getting a life sentence!'

'Yes, and I'll make sure you suffer every day,' Lily teased. 'Far worse than having a tooth out!'

But with the date, time, and venue fixed, and applying Sid's dictum again, it was time to tell Dora.

'We've got some news for you, Mum,' said Lily as they laid the table for tea, Dora doling out the knives and forks as Lily fetched the cruet and Jim brought the water jug and glasses through from the kitchen.

'Oh yes? Is it Sunday dinner? You said you'd let me know because of setting up the Christmas grotto at work.'

'It's not about the grotto.' Jim wiped the bottom of the jug with his sleeve before setting it down on the cloth. 'It's a bit more important than that.'

199

'More important than Marlows? Now I'm interested!'

Lily caught her mum around the waist.

'I should hope you are because you're going to be mother of the bride! On March 21st next year! We booked it today!'

Dora's eyes filled with tears.

'Oh my! You never! Oh, let me sit down!' Jim quickly pulled out a chair. 'You don't half know how to give someone a heart attack! March 21st — well, that settles it, there'll be no Christmas cake for us this year! I'll have to save it for the wedding!'

Lily and Jim looked at each other and burst out laughing.

'Oh Mum, I do love you!' cried Lily. 'Straight away, all you can think about is the catering!'

But later, when she and Dora were washing up, there was one thing she wanted to check.

'You hardly ate anything, Mum,' she said. 'You are OK, aren't you, about the wedding?'

'Of course I am! Can anyone stomach snoek? Vile stuff, I never did like it.'

Lily nodded. The tinned fish from South Africa was pretty disgusting. Even though Dora rolled it in oatmeal before cooking, it was still horribly oily.

'So you don't mind it being a register office do? Only Jim and me, we're not really churchy people. And I want it to be nice, of course, for all of us, but I don't want a huge great fuss.'

Dora held up the tines of a fork for inspection before handing it to Lily to dry.

'And you think I do? I haven't got over Gladys's yet!' Gladys's big day had turned into a massive production number ('All it needs is Cecil B. de Mille,'

200

Sid had joked) which had run them all ragged.

'As long as you're sure. You do go to church, after all.'

Dora looked fondly at her daughter — her baby — taking the first real grown-up step of her life.

'Your wedding, love . . . on the first day of spring. It'll be perfect.'

Now the date was set, it didn't seem that far off, and there was plenty to keep everyone occupied in the meantime.

'Congratulations!' said Miss Frobisher warmly when Lily told her. 'How wonderful to have something to look forward to through the winter!'

'It is.' But remembering how dizzy Miss Frobisher had been in the weeks before her wedding, she added: 'But I shan't be slacking off here, Miss Frobisher, don't worry. Jim and I will be in on Sunday to set up the grotto — Father Christmas arrives on Monday, after all!'

And so he did, waving and beaming from on his milkman's cart-cum-sleigh for the *Chronicle*'s photographer. After making his way through the store, he was installed on his padded throne in the grotto, attended by his elves. Freed from their usual boring tasks, the juniors made the most of their liberation, capering mischievously around to entertain the queue of harassed mothers and over-excited children.

That wasn't the only pre-Christmas excitement: planning for the Christmas party for the evacuee children was also underway. Instead of tacking scraps of khaki rag onto camouflage nets at the next WVS meeting, Lily was put to making paper chains and Chinese lanterns out of old newspapers. The invitations had gone out and the replies received; among them, Mrs

Tunnicliffe had confirmed she'd be bringing Joe and Barbara along. The children's parents had also been invited.

'Though who knows if any of them will turn up,' Mrs Russell reflected, as she dabbed watery paint on one of Lily's completed paper chains. 'There's the cost of the fare, for a start, when most of them haven't two farthings to rub together. And with these wicked bombs still falling almost every day . . .'

Lily said nothing. It was the point she'd made to Sergeant Matthews, but she'd moved beyond that now and so had events. Within days of the trip to the recruiting office, the big announcement that Sergeant Matthews had hinted at had come.

At Brook Street, they'd been gathered round the wireless for the nine o'clock news as usual, Dora knitting, Jim and Lily playing rummy. First the chimes of Big Ben, then the gurgle and gasp of the set, and then:

'This is the BBC Home Service. Here is the news —'

'And this is Alvar Liddell reading it,' chanted Lily and Jim in unison, recognising the familiar tones of the BBC's chief announcer.

He'd been the one to break the news of the long-awaited victory at El Alamein and the country had taken him to their hearts when the professional mask had slipped for once and he'd come out with: 'Here is the news and cracking good news it is too!'

The news he delivered that December evening was almost as stunning.

'It has been announced from Downing Street that the Home Guard is being stood down. The threat of invasion is now thought to be so remote that their services are no longer required. In a statement, the Prime Minister thanked most profoundly the one and a half million men who have

202

served the country so diligently . . . '

Lily stopped listening. She turned to Jim and mouthed, 'Sergeant Matthews.'

He nodded and mouthed back, 'Stand by for the liberation of Holland.'

But first, there was the evacuees' Christmas party.

'Stand by for mayhem,' said Jim as they put up the trestle tables for the tea at one end of the Drill Hall, leaving the other end free for the party games. 'Mayhem at best. Or perhaps they'll simply kill each other.'

Lily had dragged him along to help. There were various long-suffering WVS husbands there too, including Dr Russell, who was practising having a pillow stuffed up his jumper. He'd agreed to masquerade as Father Christmas, whose arrival was to be the finale.

'That's why you're here, to keep them occupied.' Lily sucked her finger where she'd pinched it unfolding the leg of a trestle. 'Grandmother's Footsteps, Pin the Tail on the Donkey, Flap the Kipper . . . '

'I don't know why you think they'll take any notice of me.' Jim motioned to her to stand back as he upended the trestle onto its legs. '*You* never do!'

'Can I start laying up?' Dora approached from the kitchen where she'd been cutting a pile of sandwiches. Thanks to a special allocation of sugar, there'd also be cakes and jelly served with — thanks to Sam, who'd heard about the party from Dora — something called fruit cocktail. He'd sent a parcel containing six tins.

Time sped by. Suddenly it was three o'clock and the children started to arrive with their foster mothers, most of whom made a sharp exit, grateful for a couple of hours to themselves to get on with their own Christmas preparations. But there was only one foster family Lily was looking out for, and that was Mrs

Tunnicliffe, with Joe and Barbara.

Jim saw them first, out in the little hallway, Mrs Tunnicliffe helping Barbara to take off her coat and hang it up, then taking off her own coat and hat. Joe held out his hands and hung them up for her. Not only was she looking after them, it seemed she was teaching them manners.

As they came into the hall, looking around, Lily moved forward and Mrs Tunnicliffe smiled. Her hair was newly set and she had a festive sprig of holly on the lapel of her raspberry tweed suit.

'Lily! I hoped you'd be here!'

Joe gave Lily a knowing look and a fleeting grin. Barbara, her blonde hair in two tidy plaits, smiled shyly.

'You've lost a couple of teeth!' said Lily, and Joe winked.

'And the Tooth Fairy gave her a whole sixpence for each one, didn't she, Barb?'

His sister nodded and pointed across the room.

'Ah, that's Edie, her best friend from school,' said Mrs Tunnicliffe. 'Off you go then, dear, and say hello. You too, Joe, I can see your pals over there. No getting into mischief, mind.'

Barbara ran off and Joe joined a threesome who were shaking the wrapped package for Pass the Parcel to try to establish its contents.

'You seem to have them well under control.' Jim was impressed. 'I might need some tips from you later!'

'That's very kind,' Mrs Tunnicliffe replied. 'I think if children have a set routine and know the rules, they feel secure. Then they don't really have much reason to misbehave.' Mrs Tunnicliffe looked fondly across at the children and Lily marvelled at the change in her.

204

Her whole bearing was altered: she was more sure of herself again, secure in a new purpose in life. 'It took a while for them to settle down after so much disruption,' she went on, 'but I'm able to give them a lot of time, which helps of course.'

'And they're thriving on it,' said Lily. 'But you're not finding it too tiring, looking after them all on your own?' she added ingenuously.

She couldn't quite see Cedric Marlow volunteering for Blind Man's Buff or marching the animals two by two into the Noah's Ark, but she could hardly ask outright if Mrs Tunnicliffe ever had anyone around to share the load, or even to talk to about the responsibility she'd taken on.

'It's been a lifeline for me,' said Mrs Tunnicliffe warmly. 'I'm so glad you called that day. I can't remember now how the subject came up, but the idea that some of the children had been split up . . . it preyed on my mind. If that had been Violet and her brothers, well . . . '

'Lily said the same thing about her brothers.' Jim put his arm round her and Lily glanced up at him. After the way he'd ticked her off for wanting to get involved, it was tacit approval of the way she'd handled things after all. 'Joe and Barbara really struck a chord with her. We're just happy they've found a good home with you.'

'They're delightful children,' said Mrs Tunnicliffe warmly. 'Their mother's done a very good job in such difficult times. I'm simply carrying on the good work. Oh — but I must congratulate you! You're engaged, I gather, and getting married in the spring.'

'That's right!' said Lily. 'Thank you, we're very happy.'

'So you should be! Now, I should go and keep an eye on my charges.'

Mrs Tunnicliffe moved away, but Lily had her answer.

'Well, that proves it!' Her eyes gleamed. 'She might have spotted my ring, but she couldn't possibly know when we were getting married unless your uncle had told her. We haven't seen her since before we got engaged. And we've only just settled the date and told everyone at work so he's definitely seen her recently! Never mind us, you don't think there could be another wedding in the offing, do you?'

★ ★ ★

By four o'clock, the party was in full swing. The children were playing Pass the Parcel, which Jim had planned as a quiet game to calm them down before tea — some hope! To the frantic accompaniment of 'Jingle Bells' thumped out at double speed on the hall's tinny piano, it had turned into a dogfight as the children clutched the parcel to their chests while their neighbour tried to wrench it from them. Jim tried helplessly to police it as Lily helped carry plates of food and jugs of lemon squash to the tables. Then, out of the corner of her eye, she noticed a nervous-looking woman in a headscarf peer through the glass panes of the double doors. Skirting the shrieking rabble, she went out into the hallway.

'Can I help you?'

The woman looked at her. When she spoke, her voice was high and breathy and the words tumbled out, almost bumping into one other.

'It's taken me forever to get here, but I did want

to come. I'm Mrs Wilson. Mavis — Joe and Barbara's mother. I had a letter saying this was on. I've come to see them, and brought them a few bits for Christmas.' She put a lumpy string bag down on the floor.

Lily held out her hands. The woman's coat was only thin; she was thin too, her eyes huge in a pale face.

'I'm so glad you came! But you look frozen, come in and have a cup of tea — they'll be so thrilled to see you.'

'Oh, I'm not coming in!' Mrs Wilson said quickly. 'They're my life, those kids, but they've settled here now. If they see me it'll only upset them, and then I'd get upset and that'd upset them even more when I had to go and I don't want that.'

'Really? But you've come all this way — '

Mavis Wilson shook her head.

'I just wanted to see them,' she said. 'From a distance. That's enough. I've spotted Joe already; he's grown even in these few months. And filled out a bit!'

Lily glanced back through the smeared panes. Joe was taller and looked healthier, certainly.

'And have you seen Barbara? She's not playing the game, she's there, by the tea table. Red velvet dress.'

'Oh my! Look at her! Where'd she get that frock?'

Lily suspected Mrs Tunnicliffe had had her dressmaker run it up with material she already had. It was how a lot of the wealthier women managed to dress themselves and their children — they didn't have to rely on coupons. But Mrs Wilson answered her own question.

'The woman that's looking after them, I suppose she had it made. And where's she?'

Lily pointed out Mrs Tunnicliffe, who was making space on one of the tables for a plate of cakes.

'She's older than I thought.' Lily was relieved there

was no edge to Mavis Wilson's voice. She had every right to be jealous and even resentful of Mrs Tunnicliffe, who had care of her children while she didn't, but she seemed nothing but grateful. She turned to Lily. 'She has them write to me every week — well, Joe does. Barb sends a little picture sometimes, bless her, though she can write her name now real good. But that Mrs Tunnicliffe, she writes too, tells me properly how they are, what they've done, and she is good to them. There was a nasty cold going round, and she had the doctor out for Barb thinking it might go to her chest, so they caught it in time — ' She stopped abruptly. 'I'm talking too much — my husband always said I did.'

'He's away fighting, is he?'

'Burma. He tries to keep in touch.'

'It's not easy, is it,' Lily sympathised. 'And you? How are you coping? With these bombs?'

Mrs Wilson shuddered.

'It's horrible. I'm living on my nerves. I'm so glad the kids is out of the way of them. I was that scared to send them off but I'd be terrified for them if they was with me. And what you people have done for them here . . . ' She bit her lip. 'There was one young girl with the WVS Joe wrote me about. Him and Barb was split up to start with, but this young girl — Lily's her name — she wasn't having it; she knew I wanted them together. Joe's convinced she had a hand in getting them moved. I'd love to thank her.'

Lily smiled. She touched Mrs Wilson's arm.

'No need,' she said. 'As long as they're happy. But look, are you sure you won't stay?'

'No, really.' Mrs Wilson's voice wavered; her sacrifice was obviously costing her. 'It's best I don't. Don't

208

want to upset the apple cart, do I?' She indicated the offerings in the string bag. 'But will you make sure they get these few things as a surprise on Christmas Day?'

'Of course.'

Mavis Wilson's eyes filled with tears and she grabbed Lily's hands. For a moment Lily thought she was going to kiss them.

If she hadn't believed it before, she believed it now. All the Civil Defence forces — the ARP like Jim, the auxiliary firemen like Les, the now disbanded Home Guard, the WI with their jam and canning operations, the Red Cross and the WVS — they were all vital; they did a huge amount of good. The people of Britain, the ones left at home, the frightened, the bombed-out, the injured, the old, the young, the sick, rich and poor, north and south, in cities, towns and in the countryside, those volunteers had done their bit and made a difference: the nation could never have got through the war without them. It was right before her in Mrs Wilson's pathetic gratitude.

23

After that, it was a straight, speeding toboggan run towards Christmas — busy, busy days at work, and in the evenings secretly wrapping the few presents they could procure or afford, writing and delivering cards, clucking over cards received and arranging holly behind the picture frames and along the mantelpiece. Dora was busy checking her hoarded supplies. Sid would be home for a couple of days, all being well, but the daunting prospect of going without Christmas cake so it could be saved for the wedding was allayed by the arrival of a generous food parcel from Sam in Canada.

'Tinned chicken, butter — and marmalade!' Lily drooled as she and her mum unpacked the contents. 'Shortbread! Oh, Mum! And — ooh . . . ' She examined a mysterious tin. 'Maple syrup?'

Dora didn't reply. She'd uncovered a nine-inch — nine-inch! — iced Christmas cake which the accompanying letter from Sam promised was 'chock-full of Californian raisins'.

'That does it!' said Dora. 'There's your wedding cake, Lily! And there's no need to look like that, of course I'll take the robin and the holly leaves off and pipe your names on it instead! Honestly!'

'It's not that,' said Lily. 'I don't care if it's got the entire Californian raisin crop inside and a ton of royal icing on top. I don't want some factory-made cake for my wedding, thank you! I want yours, Mum, with all your love baked into it.'

'Oh, stop it!' said her mother, not a great one for displays of emotion. 'You'll set me off!'

Then it was Christmas Eve, and after a hectic day dealing with desperate last-minute customers came the traditional staff party, rum punch and mince pies in the tinsel-bedecked canteen. Mr Marlow always addressed the staff, generally a summing-up of the past year and the prospects ahead. Last year he'd gone further, announcing promotions for Mr Simmonds, Miss Frobisher, and Jim — not to mention the big move of dropping the apostrophe from the store's name.

He referred back to it again.

'My intention,' he said, 'was to make it at once less of a family concern — my family's — but at the same time more of a family concern. I wanted and want all of you to feel like one big family.' He paused and pursed his lips before going on in his dry manner, 'I didn't intend it to be taken quite so literally, but this year has of course seen the marriage of two senior staff members — Miss Frobisher has become Mrs Simmonds!'

There were cheeky 'whoohoos' and 'whayhays' from the younger salesmen who formed the backbone of the cricket and football teams, and knew Mr Simmonds well.

'Oh Lord,' Jim muttered to Lily. 'I hope next year he doesn't pick on us!'

'If he's not too busy announcing his own wedding to Mrs Tunnicliffe! Nothing would surprise me with those two!' Lily whispered back.

There was more merriment when they got home. When Lily pushed open the back door, she could hear Sid in the next room regaling Dora with one of his tall

211

tales and her mum's tuts and half-laughs of disbelief. Lily hurried in, pulling off her gloves and there he was, blond, broad-shouldered, handsome, in the best chair as usual with a glass of rum at his elbow. He'd even persuaded Dora into a small sweet sherry, having brought a bottle with him for the festivities. He abandoned his story, stood up, and opened his arms wide. Lily pressed herself into them. Her favourite brother, home for Christmas for the first time since the start of the war!

Jim and Lily had had enough to drink at the staff party, but all four of them, even Dora, sat up late roasting chestnuts in the dying fire. As the wireless played Christmas carols, they laughed and chatted and occasionally lapsed into silence as each one thought their private thoughts of others who couldn't be with them — Reg and Gwenda in North Africa, Sam in Canada, Sid's friend Jerome on his air base, and Jim's widowed dad who Lily and Jim would go and see on their next day off.

Finally, after satisfying herself that everything was ready in the kitchen for the next day, Dora announced it was time for bed. Lily kissed her mother and brother good night, then Sid and Dora tactfully melted away.

Jim had managed to cut a few sprigs of mistletoe off an old apple tree that dipped over the fence of one of the big houses on Cavendish Road and hung it from the light fitting, but they didn't need it. Being alone like this was dangerous, they both knew; it was so difficult not to get carried away. But that was one gift which Lily knew Jim would never demand of her and they both knew that by waiting, when they were finally able to be together, it would be even more precious.

'Roll on the wedding,' he whispered as they finally pulled apart. 'But first, it's gone midnight. Happy Christmas, wife-to-be!'

Dora was the first up next morning, as usual, and by the time Lily came downstairs Sid was up too and getting the fire going. They'd tried to keep off too much war talk the previous evening, but as Lily laid the table, she couldn't help wondering out loud if Sid's Christmas leave was another sign that the end was in sight. Sid, though, unusually discreet, wouldn't be drawn on military matters.

'The only important date I've got in mind is March 21st,' he declared. 'I'm waiting for my orders for that!'

He'd already heard most of their plans. Les would be Jim's best man, but Lily wasn't having a bridesmaid. Of her best friends, Gladys would have her hands full with the twins and Beryl would have hers full making sure Lily looked her best — and, it had to be said, a good advertisement for Beryl's Brides. She never missed a trick — Lily wouldn't put it past her to hand out her business cards to unwitting passers-by as the wedding group posed afterwards for photographs.

Sid fanned the fire with a folded newspaper, then held a sheet over the fireplace to draw the flames. He nodded Lily over.

'One thing you didn't mention . . . Got your dress yet?'

'Shh!' Lily scolded him. 'I couldn't say in front of Jim!' He was only in the kitchen now, making a pot of tea while Dora put the Christmas pudding on to steam. She moved closer and whispered. 'Don't panic. Beryl's on the lookout!'

By the time they'd opened their stockings and presents, it was time for Dora to get off to church, leaving the three of them to get the potatoes in the oven and the veg started. Dora got back in time to put the finishing touches to the feast and dish up.

Jim couldn't smile widely enough, but Lily was almost daunted by what was on her plate. Last year Sam had got them a few things from the Canadian NAAFI, but it had been nothing like this. Even Sid, used to more lavish meals in London, was impressed.

'Digging my own grave with my knife and fork,' he remarked gleefully. 'Any more of that chicken to go with these roasties, Mum?'

When he and Lily were tackling the washing-up afterwards, food was still on his mind.

'I know you've reserved the Drill Hall for the reception, but really, Lil . . . Instead, how about I pay for it — well, lunch, it'll be — at the White Lion? As my wedding present to you both.'

'Oh Sid!' Lily didn't know what to say. The White Lion was Hinton's smartest hotel. 'That's . . . that's too much!'

'You're only going to get married once . . . aren't you?' Sid teased. 'And,' he added in a lower voice, 'this'll be the only family wedding Mum gets. Reg has done the deed and I'm not going to oblige her, am I?'

Lily hesitated.

'The thing is, Sid . . . you don't think she'll be offended?'

'Eh?'

'That she's not doing the catering for her own daughter's wedding.'

Sid added the lid of a serving dish to the teetering pile of crocks.

'It's not that she wouldn't put on a fantastic spread, but she'd be mithering about it for weeks beforehand — and then knock herself out on the day instead of being able to sit back and enjoy it. And she's made the cake, after all, that's the main thing.'

'True,' said Lily. 'So, all right, then, I accept! It's a wonderful offer and thank you. Very much!' She stood on tiptoe and kissed him. 'But I bet you she'll find something else to worry about. You know what she's like. She's still fretting about Kenny next door since we had that awful evening with him when Bill was home.'

Sid shook his head.

'Worry's not going to help that one get better,' he remarked sagely. 'He's got to do that for himself.'

The pubs were shut on Christmas Day, but open again the next and it was clear that Kenny's idea of helping himself was still to go out and get drunk. Dora's bedroom was at the front of the house and she heard him in the street, trying and failing to get his key in the lock, cursing loudly and finally hammering on the door in frustration. She heard the sash window go up as Walter Crosbie looked out and remonstrated with him to think about the neighbours or he'd wake the whole street, which provoked Kenny into a stream of abuse. Then the window went down again and there was a pause during which Kenny was noisily ill in the gutter before the front door opened and he was ushered inside.

Dora turned over in bed with a sigh. Reg and Sid had come home a bit merry in the past, and she was sure they'd been far more than merry since they'd joined up, especially as the Forces seemed to run on alcohol — and very necessary it was too in all likelihood. But she'd never had to see her boys in a really bad way, and if they'd ever been seriously over the eight she hoped it had been in good company, not on their own, and in pursuit of high spirits rather than drowning their sorrows. Poor Kenny. He'd dug himself deep into a pit of misery — no wonder he couldn't get out of it.

Next morning, Sid commented on it too. He'd been sleeping on the sofa in the front room, so he'd heard the kerfuffle as well.

'Bet he's got a head on him today,' he observed. 'I started off feeling sorry for the bloke, but the way he's carrying on, he'll end up on the streets. Old Man Crosbie won't stand for this much longer.'

Dora, making sandwiches for his return journey to London, could only agree.

'The doctor's had to give Jean a nerve tonic,' she said. 'She's like a bit of chewed string.'

Jim and Lily were going back to work as well, and Sid gave Lily a big hug before he left.

'Bye for now, Fancy Pants,' he said — he'd always had a range of nicknames for her. 'I'm glad you've stayed home.' Sid had known about her hopes of joining up, and she'd told him about her thwarted ambitions. 'It makes me feel less bad, knowing you're around for Mum if she ever needed it. And I never did like the idea of you being an officer's comforter!'

'Sid!' Lily knew that was what some people rudely called the ATS girls — 'officer's groundsheet' was an even worse insult. 'As if I would! I know when I'm well off with Jim!' They were in the hall, her mum in the kitchen, but still she lowered her voice; there'd been no chance to ask Sid before. 'And what about your romance? Are you still seeing your American?'

Jerome was with the US Air Force, stationed out in Cambridgeshire. Even though airfields were an obvious target, he was ground crew, fortunately, which was a lot safer than him being a pilot.

'You betcha, baby!' Sid put on an exaggerated American accent.

'He doesn't talk like that, does he?'

'Nah, not really.' Sid considered. 'He's quite soft-spoken. Thoughtful. Serious.'

'Nothing like you then!'

'Well, no, but opposites attract, don't they,' Sid shot back. 'Look at you and Jim! Talking of which — I must go — but see you in March!'

First they had the winter to get through but even the weather seemed to be on their side. January started cold but dry — perfect weather for the January sales, so it was back to the old routine for Lily and Jim and it was the same for Dora. Monday was washday, Tuesday baking day, Wednesday ironing, Thursday heavy housework, Friday extra shopping for the weekend . . . all with the daily round of tidying, dusting, shopping, cooking, washing-up, putting away . . . Then there were the alterations and mending she did for Beryl's shop, and then her Knitting Circle at the WI, and her voluntary work with the Red Cross and the WVS. And there was Buddy — he still needed his morning walk, especially with the titbits that soft-hearted Sid had been feeding him.

'Yes, all right, Buddy, I know.' Buddy was whining at the door. 'It's walkies time.'

Dora clipped the lead on Buddy's collar. He might be a year older and he was certainly a little rounder, but he'd lost none of his puppyish bounce. At the park, she let him off the leash and he bounded off like a spring lamb, skittering across the path, exploring every thrilling new smell. Dora headed for her usual spot in the little rustic shelter. Buddy always came to find her in the end — he knew whose shopping bag brought the bones back from the butcher. He wasn't that daft.

It was still quite early. Dora could usually be sure of the place to herself but as she approached the shelter she could see a pair of outstretched legs — trousered, male legs. Still, she mustn't be selfish — it was understandable, the only place out of the wind. When she got closer, though, she was surprised to see that the legs belonged to someone she knew. It was Kenny, his head resting back against the rough boards, eyes closed, mouth half-open. Sleeping, drunk . . . or ill?

'Kenny? Kenny!'

He blinked and sat up.

'Eh?'

'Are you all right?'

'Why shouldn't I be?'

As gracious as ever, then.

Dora sat down. 'It's early for you to be out, that's all.'

'Free country, isn't it?'

'Oh, Kenny,' said Dora, wearily. 'Why do you have to take on so at everything? I mean, I know why, you've had a rough time. But you're not the only one.'

'Yeah, yeah, tell it to the birds.'

'I'm telling it to you,' said Dora, exasperation finally getting the better of her. 'Because it's about time someone did. We're all sorry about your arm, it's a dreadful thing to happen to a young man, and we've tried to be patient, but it's not a bottomless pit. Sympathy runs out in the end, especially when every effort to help is rebuffed.'

Kenny stared at her.

'Help? How's that then? Your Lily and her feller taking me to the pub? Meeting their mates? Pointing up that I'll never have a sweetheart or a family or even a decent night out with the lads again —'

'That's not true,' insisted Dora, 'any of it! It's your attitude that's stopping you having any of those things, that's all.'

'What would you know? You don't know how I feel!'

'So tell me.' There was a silence. 'Go on. Tell me.'

And maybe he would have done, but at that moment, Buddy came back, rushing into the little shelter with a stick he'd found. It was his favourite game and Dora knew he wouldn't take no for an answer.

'He wants to play,' she said. 'Come with us. You've got one good arm after all, and if you can lift a pint glass, you can throw a stick.'

Kenny stared at her again, then gave a short laugh.

'Go on then. Beats sitting here all morning.'

They got to their feet. Buddy had dropped the stick and Kenny picked it up. With the dog racing around them in anticipation, they moved onto the path.

'Is this what you do, then, come to the park?' asked Dora. 'I haven't seen you here before.'

They stopped. Buddy circled them crazily.

'Auntie Jean never could stand the sight of me hanging about the house. She's never said as much but I knew. So I used to lie in bed till opening time, but now, well, since Christmas, Uncle Wally says even that can't go on. So till the pubs open it's hang about here or some caff.'

'Oh, Kenny.'

He shrugged.

'I don't care.'

'I know you don't, that's the trouble!' flared Dora.

'But you should! Oh, and throw that stick, will you, that dog's making me giddy running round in circles!'

Kenny threw the stick and Buddy galloped after it. They watched him in silence.

'I had a dog,' Kenny offered suddenly. 'As a kid. A little Yorkie terrier, a stray. Rusty, I called him. Not very original. I loved that dog. He was a dog biscuit short of a pound too, just like this one. Ran out in the road after a ball, straight under the wheels of a rag-and-bone cart.'

'That's a shame.'

'I was only six. Cried my heart out. My dad said I couldn't have another — I should have kept a better eye on him.'

'You like animals, then?' Dora ventured, as Buddy brought the stick back and dropped it at her feet. She nodded to Kenny to pick it up. He did so, and hurled it away again. Kenny sniffed and pulled his muffler tighter round his neck.

'I had a pet squirrel in this one camp. In this forest, we were.' He wiped his nose with the back of his hand. 'Used to come for crumbs. But they weren't feeding us much and it was cold and one day when I was at the latrines, the other blokes killed it for meat. I come back and they've stuck it in the stove.'

Dora sighed. It was horrible but understandable. Stories were coming out about what people all over the continent — and not just the prisoners or the many others who'd been rounded up into camps — were having to eat: dogs, rats, rotten potatoes. Grass, in some cases.

Buddy was back with his stick, dropping it this time at Kenny's feet.

'There you go, boy.' Kenny threw the stick again.

220

'I tell you something, we'd all have been goners if it hadn't been for them Red Cross parcels.'

'Really?' Dora had packed thousands of them. Her local depot had had letters from headquarters from time to time thanking them and telling them where they'd been distributed, but she'd never before met anyone who'd been on the receiving end. 'That bit of tobacco . . . ' Kenny went on. 'Socks, soap — soap was like rubies out there — maybe a bit of chocolate or sweets . . . '

'I'm glad,' Dora smiled. 'I've packed plenty of those parcels.'

Kenny looked at her sidelong.

'Yeah, you're a bit of an all-round do-gooder, aren't you? That's the impression I get.'

Dora smiled again, to herself. She didn't think he meant it as a compliment and she didn't think of herself that way; she was doing her best, doing her bit, that was all. But if Kenny had observed that much, he couldn't be completely wrapped up in himself.

'I wouldn't put it like that. But I should get back to it now. I have got things to do — not good works, this time. Housework.'

'Lucky you.'

He was back to his usual laconic self.

'Buddy!' Dora called the dog. He'd met an old friend, a collie, and they were bobbing around each other while the collie's owner looked on indulgently.

'You can walk back with me if you like,' Dora added. 'You can peel off for the café. But if you want to take Buddy out any time, and save me a job, you're more than welcome.' Kenny didn't react, apart from giving another sniff. 'Oh and for goodness' sake, get yourself a handkerchief!'

221

24

Kenny didn't come round for the dog next day and he wasn't in the park either, nor the next, and Dora was disappointed. She'd thought she'd made a bit of progress — it was the first time, as far as she knew, that he'd volunteered anything apart from monosyllables or moans about his situation. But the day after that, Kenny turned up at the back gate just as she emerged with Buddy on the lead. He must have been watching from his bedroom window.

'Want me to have him?' he said, without preamble.

'Help yourself.' Dora handed over the lead. Buddy looked up briefly, then continued his studied examination of Kenny's shoes.

'Fancy a change?' asked Kenny. 'We could go down the canal.'

'Fine.' Dora tended not to go there on her own even with the dog — there could be some funny types hanging around. With Kenny there too, however, she felt safer. 'You'll have to keep him on the lead, though. If he sees a moorhen, he'll be straight in the water and I don't want a dripping dog to deal with.'

'Fair enough.'

They set off down the cinder path that ran down the back of the houses. When they got to the steps to the canal, Kenny stepped back to let her go first. She waited for him at the bottom, and even saw the ghost of a smile on his face as Buddy lived up to expectations, straining at the leash to scan the scummy water and overgrown banks for traces of bird life. The walk they took was only a short one — it was Dora's heavy housework day and she was turning out the bed-rooms — but after that, Kenny was at the back gate every day. If Dora fancied some fresh air they'd go together; otherwise, Kenny would take Buddy off for as long as an hour at a time. Whichever it was, they'd have a cup of tea afterwards. If Dora went too, it ate into her mornings, which meant she had to hurry through her tasks and rush or skip lunch to finish them or get off to her volunteering, but it was worth it to draw Kenny out and Jean declared she was eter-nally in her debt.

'The difference you and that dog's made!' she said. 'I never would have believed it! You're too good for this world, that's what you are, Dora.'

'It's hardly a transformation,' said Dora modestly. 'But maybe it's a start.'

Lily and Jim were impressed too, and Sid, when he learnt of it in letters.

'You'll get your crown in heaven, Mum,' he wrote. 'But meanwhile, Lily tells me you haven't yet got your outfit for the Wedding of the Year. I know you'll be worried about the money so I enclose a postal order — and make sure you DO spend it all at once!'

Lily was thrilled at the prospect of kitting her mother out. Dora hadn't had anything new from a proper shop since the blouse she'd bought when Sam first came to tea. The rest of her clothes, like Lily's, were from jumble sales or prime examples of 'make do and mend'. Beryl had already offered Dora the pick of her mother-of-the-bride outfits but, though Beryl would have let her have it for free, Dora had been uncomfortable, refusing to be 'gussied up' in anything too fancy.

Now, she insisted, if she was going to buy something, it would have to be an outfit she could wear
more than once. Lily could see the sense in this, and
tried to convince her mum that Sid's postal order
meant she could buy something that was really good
quality and would last — even something from Marlows. But when Lily coaxed her to come into the store
and they went round Ladies' Fashions together, Dora
nearly passed out at the prices.

'I don't care whose model it's a copy of,' she said
when Lily had persuaded the attentive saleslady to
leave them alone as they really were 'just looking'.
'What's it made of? Cloth of gold? I'm sorry, Lily,
but I could make it myself for a tenth of the price! I
wouldn't encourage them!'

Lily shook her head in despair.

'Mum, you are not making your own outfit for my
wedding!' she insisted, 'for the same reason that Sid's
treating us to a posh lunch after! It's your day as well!'

But Dora was already on her way to the lifts. Lily
followed and saw her off the premises, with Dora
promising she'd go and have a look in C&A.

Lily slipped along to Beryl's shop for another look
at her own dress. Beryl had spotted it for sale in the
classified adverts in The Lady ('So you know it's
come from a good home!') and had gone all the way
to Hereford to get it. It was pre-war, so no skimping
on fabric — a silk slip with lace overlay, a scooped
neckline and elbow-length sleeves. Lily loved it, and
she knew Jim would too. The main thing was that
though it felt luxurious, it was still simple, with no
fussy details. She knew she could wear it happily all
day and still feel like herself.

Jim had a new grey suit which he was paying for

in instalments. Gladys had lost her baby weight and was borrowing an 'occasion' dress from Beryl's stock; Beryl herself would be resplendent in a cherry red suit with a fake leopard collar. Bobby had a little sailor suit; Sid would be in his dress uniform. There was only Dora left. But Lily knew her mother; even for her daughter's wedding, old habits die hard, and Dora's of economising — and putting herself last — were very hard to break.

January slipped into February; the weather was milder and the first signs of spring began to show. Snowdrops and aconites, planted long before the war, poked up again; buds started to form on the avenue of beeches and the huge horse chestnut in the park. On some days, Dora and Kenny didn't even need to sit in the shelter. It was warm enough to sit on the low stone wall round the war memorial — to the Boer War. Its stone plinth was topped by a bronze cast of two soldiers, one standing, one crouching, with winged Victory in her chariot between them. They were the lucky ones. Below, on bronze plaques, were the names of the dead.

One day, Kenny read them out.

'Tanner, G. H. Private. Taylor, L. Private. Taylor, J. M. Armourer. Tucker, C. V. Private. Turnbull, W. Gunner . . . ' He tailed off. 'Turnbull . . . I knew a Turnbull. My mate Wilf.'

'Oh yes?' Dora kept her voice deliberately casual. She'd found it was the best way to keep Kenny talking.

Kenny sat down. He didn't look at her.

'He was right behind me at Dunkirk. We'd stuck together all the way there. Shared what we had — my last fag, his last bit of chocolate. They told us we'd be safe if we got to the beach — it was the only way to get us all out. At the same time, you could see it was plain stupid.'

'It *was* the only way, surely, to get you out?'

'That's what you know! You don't think they told you the whole truth, do you? All we hear about is the ones who got home, the miracle of the 'little ships'. They don't play up those that didn't make it, do they?'

'Well, no . . .'

'You should have been there, night and day on that beach, waiting — no shelter, nowhere to run to, nowhere to hide, sitting ducks for the Jerries.' Kenny looked up at the sky as if a German plane might appear even now. 'Dunno where the RAF were — holding them off further inland, they say — well, maybe they were, maybe they weren't. Still left us exposed. All I know is it was a living hell. I was glad to be took prisoner, I can tell you.'

Dora hesitated. Of all that Kenny had haltingly revealed to her over the weeks and months, she felt she was finally getting close to something significant.

'And Wilf? Your friend? Was he taken prisoner with you?'

Kenny didn't seem to hear her.

'We could hear the planes coming. You could tell from the sound it wasn't one of ours — we'd had enough practice. We were that tired and hungry, fed up, cold . . . you just thought 'not again'. But you ran anyway, zig-zag like, trying to dodge the bullets, heading for the dunes — not that they were any cover but you could try and burrow a bit. But the sand was spraying up in great jets with the machine gunning, you couldn't see a thing . . . we were together, me and Wilf. Then I tripped, he ran into me, and we both fell flat, him on top of me.'

Dora waited.

'I didn't realise. I thought he was just lying doggo like me. But when the planes had gone, I rolled over, and he rolled off me and I knew. There was blood coming out of his mouth. They'd got him in the back, twice. He'd saved me, saved my life. I should have got those bullets, not him.'

So it was that, was it, that had driven Kenny so low?

'Kenny,' Dora said gently. 'You can't say that. You can't blame yourself for your friend's death — it doesn't work like that. The only person to blame was the gunner up in that plane doing the firing.'

Kenny wasn't listening.

'His eyes were still open. I had to close them for him. I couldn't even give him a decent burial. It was chaos, the ships were arriving, and the little boats. They tried to herd us into them . . . I'd seen a bit of that already — the Jerries were picking men off as they waded out. I just went off on my own. No one was looking, no one cared. I hid in the dunes till the Jerries found me.'

Buddy, who'd been off in the furthest reaches of the shrubbery, returned with a stick, ready for his usual game. But after standing hopefully in front of Kenny, head on one side, stick in mouth, he seemed to realise that his playmate wasn't interested. With an almost audible sigh, he dropped the stick and lay down.

'Is that the reason, Kenny?' asked Dora. 'Why you won't do anything about your arm? Get fitted for a limb? You're punishing yourself?'

Kenny shrugged.

'It all seemed so pointless after that. The war, everything. I didn't care if we won or lost. I hadn't even

227

got the spirit to stand up to the guards, let alone try to escape. And then what happened to my arm' — he picked at his empty sleeve — 'I didn't care about that, either. On the farm, they'd told us — in German, but we knew enough by then to understand *nein* and *nicht* and all that — they told us never to touch the knife blades on the thresher. But I looked into the drum when it jammed and I just stuck my hand in. I thought . . . I dunno what I thought but I freed the straw and the knives suddenly turned and that was it, whoosh — a big slash half through my arm.' He looked at her for the first time. 'You don't feel it, you know, at the time. I feel it now, the arm and the hand that isn't there. It hurts sometimes — throbs — but I don't mind. I like it that way.'

There was no doubt in Dora's mind now. Kenny *was* punishing himself. Torturing himself, almost, over something that no right-minded person could ever have said was his fault. But who was to say what he should think, or how anyone could be right-minded who'd been through what he had — along with hundreds of thousands of others — and on both sides of the conflict. They said the end of the war was coming, and that was something everyone was hoping and praying and living for. But the realisation struck Dora all over again that while that was something to celebrate of course, the aftermath would stay with everyone who'd been through it for years to come — for some, maybe for the rest of their lives. Just as with the Great War. Nothing would ever be the same again.

She sneaked a look at her watch. It was time they got back; she had her ironing to do, and the WVS tea bar in the afternoon and somehow she sensed that Kenny had finished. He hadn't exactly answered her

228

question, but he'd said enough to convince her of what was going on in his mind and why he stubbornly resisted any practical solution to the loss of his arm. She touched his sleeve lightly.

'Shall we go?' she said. 'I'm starting to get a numb behind from sitting on this stone.'

Kenny roused himself.

'Sorry,' he said. 'I've been talking too much.'

'No, you haven't, not at all.' Dora gave a rare smile to reassure him. 'Better out than in, I always think.'

That evening, she told Lily and Jim some of what had passed between her and Kenny.

'Poor bloke,' said Jim. 'All that bottled up.'

'It explains why he's been so miserable,' said Lily. 'But now he's started to spill it out, this business with his friend . . . Well done for getting it out of him, Mum.'

As usual, Dora modestly refused to take any credit.

'It was the war memorial really,' she said. 'Once he'd started, all I did was let him talk. But now he has, perhaps he can start to pull himself together. Get that arm seen to.'

'I knew she'd make him her mission,' smiled Lily to Jim when Dora had gone off to the WI. 'He'll be invited to the wedding next!'

'You wouldn't mind, would you?'

'Not at all, as long as he doesn't drink all the champagne!' Mr Marlow always sent a bottle of champagne to any staff member getting married, so Jim and Lily were in line for two. 'But as they're such pals, maybe he can get Mum to settle on her outfit. There's only six weeks to go and I'm not having much luck!'

When Lily asked later if her mum had been into C&A again to see if their lighter-weight spring coats were in, Dora assured her she'd do it the next chance she got, but Dora knew that if Kenny came round and wanted to open up again, she'd have to let him. Six weeks to the wedding maybe, but it had taken him nearly six months to start talking and now he had, she couldn't deny him the opportunity.

25

Dora couldn't have known it, but another opportunity was about to knock next door.

'You'll never guess what's happened!'

Jean Crosbie burst into the back kitchen one morning as Dora was putting the finishing touches to a pie. It was a frequent gambit of Jean's for starting a conversation, but since it could augur anything from a juicy scandal to a blocked drain, not always one to pique interest.

'I doubt it,' said Dora mildly, who'd long since given up trying. All you could be sure of was that the revelation would be nothing to do with the last subject she and Jean had discussed and on which a sensible person might reasonably expect a follow-up.

Jean plumped down on the kitchen chair, almost fanning herself with excitement.

'Kenny's had a letter!'

Dora placed the pastry lid on her pie.

'Who from? The Labour Exchange? The Ministry of Health?'

'No! From a girl!'

Dora, who'd been holding the pie up on the flat of her hand to trim the edges, put it down carefully.

'A girl?'

'Phyllis,' said Jean in triumph. 'Seems he knew her in Liverpool!'

'Jean,' scolded Dora. 'You haven't read the letter behind his back?'

'No!' Jean looked hurt. 'He told us — he had to.

She's coming to visit!'

When Kenny came round for the dog next morning, Dora could see a change in him. He'd been looking better day by day ever since he'd started walking with her and Buddy; his face was less pasty, he held himself better, and kept himself cleaner. But this was another marked improvement. For the first time since his arrival in Hinton, he actually looked — what was the word? — chipper, and truly alive.

'I suppose Auntie Jean's told you,' he said.

'About your letter? Yes.'

Dora deliberately didn't ask who Phyllis was, as she knew Jean had, only for Kenny to clam up. As they took their regular route to the park, she waited for Kenny to tell her and when they got there and Buddy was off the lead, he did.

'We went out together, me and Phyllis,' he began. 'Oh, years ago — we were only kids — sixteen, I think. We were quite sweet on each other. But she seemed to want to get serious and my mates were ribbing me about being under the thumb, being no fun any more, so I finished it. I still saw her around, then she went nursing training, and her mum and dad moved away to the Wirral.'

'And you lost touch?'

'Yeah. But it seems she went back to Liverpool, our old haunts . . . she hadn't till then, but she was visiting her mam and dad, so I dunno why, old times' sake, look up old friends, or something . . . She saw our street had been bombed, like, and wondered what had happened to my lot. And those that were still around told her what they knew. And somehow she remembered me talking about Hinton and my aunt and uncle and tracked me down.'

'You make it sound easy. She must have been keen to find you.'

Kenny shrugged, but blushed.

'Dunno about that.'

Dora did. With all evidence of previous occupants gone and the difficulty of identifying bodies in the rubble of bombed buildings, with people's identities being mixed up, identity cards forged or stolen and sold on, and the authorities little or no help, you had to be pretty determined to find a missing person these days.

'And she's coming to see you?'

'Tomorrow. Staying over. In the parlour,' he added quickly.

'I see! Well, good. How nice. I'd better let you off Buddy duties for a couple of days.'

Kenny turned and looked at her straight. That was another thing he'd learnt to do — he'd kept his eyes downcast before, but bit by bit, he was starting to trust people again.

'I'd never have replied before,' he said. 'Let alone let her, or anyone I used to know, come and see me like this.' He tapped his empty sleeve. 'I'm not saying I feel great about it even now, but . . . I dunno. You've helped me get my head a bit straighter somehow.'

'I've done nothing,' said Dora. 'But if you're starting to feel better about things, more forward-looking, well, that's all to the good.'

'You listened,' said Kenny. 'You started me off and you listened. Thank you.'

Next day, Dora was just having five minutes' sit-down with her mending when she heard the back gate go. She was by the window, making the most of the daylight, and looked up to see Kenny coming across the yard. With him was a tallish girl, whose coppery hair gleamed beneath a pert green hat. Her brown tweed coat was both serviceable and smart and she wore sensible lace-up shoes, Dora noted with approval. So this was Phyllis.

'Anyone home?' called Kenny as Dora moved to the doorway to beckon them in and start making the inevitable pot of tea. Thank goodness there was a bit of gingerbread in the tin.

Kenny sat down on one of the dining chairs but Phyllis ranged about the room, looking at the photos on the mantelpiece and admiring Dora's antimacassars. Dora poured the tea and Phyllis finally sat down. They chatted about this and that for twenty minutes, with the women doing most of the talking. Phyllis had been nursing down south for the entire war — London, Surrey, Kent — in military and general hospitals, and in pretty horrendous conditions. Her hospitals had twice had direct hits; she'd dealt with air-raid victims and returning servicemen — burns, broken limbs, fatal injuries, the lot. She cast a lot of looks towards Kenny as she said all this, Dora noticed, but he kept his eyes down, fussing Buddy, who'd craftily slunk inside with them.

When the conversation faltered, Kenny spoke up.

'We've come to take the dog out for you.'

'Oh! Well, yes, do, that'd be a big help. Thank you,' said Dora.

'Actually, Kenny, why don't you go,' said Phyllis. 'I'll help Mrs Collins clear away. You won't be long, will you?'

'I don't have to be.'

'Good. Then you can show me the high life in Hinton,' she smiled.

234

Dismissed, Kenny fetched Buddy's lead. Phyllis waited till she'd heard the gate, then spoke directly to Dora.

'I wanted a word,' she said. 'It's lovely to meet you. Kenny's told me a lot about you.'

'Has he? There's not much to tell, is there?'

'Oh, come on, no false modesty,' said Phyllis. Dora was a bit taken aback — the girl certainly wasn't backward in coming forward. 'It wasn't just Kenny that wrote to me. His auntie sent me a letter too. Said how miserable and difficult he was when he first arrived. And she credited you — well, you and Buddy — for bringing him out of himself.'

'No, honestly — ' Dora began.

'He's an idiot!' Phyllis interrupted fondly. 'I asked him, when he came to Liverpool, why didn't he look me up, or at least my mam and dad? Or any of the old crowd? He just muttered, but I know why. He's got this fixation about his arm, or lack of it. So all right, maybe he didn't feel like seeing the old crowd, not that they'd have thought anything of it, but for goodness' sake, I'm a State Registered Nurse! Does he think I haven't seen worse than an amputation?'

Dora smiled to herself. Phyllis was a five-star plain speaker, all right; she'd even give Beryl a run for her money.

'Have you told him this?'

'Course I have. I told him as soon as he met me at the station! Told him not to be so daft. And anyway, it doesn't have to be like that! He needs to get himself sorted out.'

'I quite agree!'

'I can help with that,' Phyllis went on. 'There's charities, you know, one in particular. BLESMA it's called. Blind and Limbless Ex-Servicemen's Association. They can help.'

'We've all wondered about him getting a prosthetic — '

'I'm sure you have. He's sensitive underneath it all, Kenny is. Too sensitive. That's what finished us first time round, him caring what his mates were saying. And it's the same with his arm, telling himself that everything was hopeless and he was useless and some sort of outcast, which is rubbish.'

'His friends do seem very important to him,' mused Dora. 'Has he told you about the one he had in the Army? Wilf? The one that got killed — that's really affected him.'

'Wilf . . . yes. That all came out too.' Phyllis's voice softened. 'It sounds like they were really good pals. Look, I'm not saying Kenny hasn't had some hard times, seen some sights. But he's far better off than a lot of the patients I've nursed. And as for feeling bad about being alive — that's no way to carry on. He should be treasuring every moment.'

'We all should who've come through it,' agreed Dora.

Phyllis reached over and touched her hand.

'It's nearly over, Dora, that's what they're saying in London. Not long to go now. And I hear you've got a wedding to look forward to as well!'

★ ★ ★

Phyllis didn't stay just one night, she stayed three. She and Kenny didn't come for the dog again, but Dora saw them going off into town and coming back with parcels and one day, a large box of Kunzle cakes.

236

Jean was over the moon.

'The difference in him!' she exclaimed, bringing over a custard slice for Dora to have with her tea. 'Splashing his money around — and not on drink! And she's sprucing him up all right! New shirt, jacket — and a tie!'

'She's a force of nature, that one,' said Dora, cutting her cake into three to save a morsel each for Lily and Jim. Ersatz filling or not, shop-bought cakes were an exceptional luxury.

Dora saw the difference in Kenny for herself when he brought Phyllis round on her last day to say goodbye. She'd taken him to the barber's and he had a new haircut, thick and glossy with Brylcreem. He'd also had a professional shave — something that was obviously difficult with only one hand. His face and neck were often pocked with tufts of beard and little cuts.

'We brought you a present,' he said shyly, handing over a package.

'What? You shouldn't have . . . '

Tutting, Dora unwrapped a small bottle of lavender water and some handkerchiefs embroidered with her initial. Handkerchiefs were even harder to come by than fancy cakes — either Phyllis had sacrificed her own coupons for them, or they were (whisper it) black market, but the pair of them waved away Dora's thanks.

'For the wedding,' Phyllis smiled. 'If I'm not mistaken, you'll be shedding a tear, so they might come in handy.'

'That's very sweet of you,' said Dora, moved. 'I hope we'll be seeing you again.'

'That's up to Kenny,' replied Phyllis coyly, though Dora doubted he'd have much say in the matter.

Phyllis really was a case and a half, thought Dora. She'd obviously been carrying a torch for Kenny all these years, and now she'd found him again it was burning more strongly than ever.

She kissed them both and wished them well. Somehow she thought she'd be getting news of another wedding before the year was out.

Hope was on the horizon whichever way you looked. The Allies had finally won through in their campaign in the Ardennes and after Holland, the whole of Belgium had been liberated. At home, the Auxiliary Fire Service was stood down, another sign that the Government was feeling optimistic.

'At this rate, the war might be over before we're married!' Lily exulted to Jim.

Sergeant Matthews now seemed more like her saviour than her nemesis and she almost felt like going back to Birmingham and thanking her, though she suspected that the recruiting office itself might be closed by now.

By the beginning of March, there was even success in the question of Dora's outfit. In Paige Gowns she found a smart navy suit with corded piping on the collar and cuffs and in C&A, a pale-blue blouse with pintucks.

'Honestly, Sid,' Lily told him over the phone. 'She looks lovely. So smart — like . . . like Greer Garson in Mrs Miniver!'

'Steady on! And she actually spent all the money?'

'Not quite,' admitted Lily. 'She made the shop knock some off because the hem on the skirt was coming down slightly at the back. And the blouse was on special offer.' Sid chortled and Lily went on. 'So there's enough left over for a hat.'

And that Lily was determined Marlows' Millinery department would provide. When clothes rationing had come in, the Government had decreed that hats didn't need coupons. There was method in their madness — if women couldn't have many new clothes, they reasoned, a new hat would cheer them and their outfit up. They'd been right, too.

Sensing that her dinner hour wouldn't be nearly long enough for such an important transaction, though, Lily booked a couple of hours off one morning and she and her mum set off from Brook Street together arm in arm.

As they passed the various houses, Dora detailed which neighbours had given her their sugar coupons — it had become the tradition throughout the war in most neighbourhoods when a wedding was in the offing. Dora had done it herself when other people had had a wedding in the family. As a result, she was hopeful that Lily's cake would at least be top-iced.

At Marlows, Lily enjoyed the novelty of walking in through the swing doors as a customer and up the carpeted main staircase. As they did so, she looked down on the ground floor. Last spring, she'd been working down there and again the Accessories department was a kaleidoscope of colours. On Small Leathers, Rita was rearranging her wallets and purses while the infamous Betty Simkins surreptitiously fluffed up her hair in her reflection on the countertop. Lily smiled. There were plenty of shoppers — the store was definitely busier and cheerier with every week that passed as the country became convinced the end was in sight.

Lily had already briefed Miss Burrows, the first sales on Millinery, that she'd be bringing her mother in.

'A difficult customer if ever there was one!' she'd warned. 'That is, she's lovely, but she'll dither and take ages, so if there's another customer waiting, please see to them first. But I shan't let her leave without buying something!'

Miss Burrows seated them on velvet stools at a table with a triple mirror and Dora produced her suit jacket, which she'd brought with her for a colour match. Miss Burrows bore it away and returned in triumph with seven hats for Dora to try.

'All a true navy,' she said, laying out five differently shaped felt, feathered, and veiled confections. 'And I brought a couple of others — a lighter blue and a saxe blue — in case you favour something tonal. Now I'll leave you alone for a while to see if you can whittle them down to a couple of favourites.'

With a sly wink at Lily, she was gone.

To Lily's enormous surprise, her mother bypassed the sensible felt-with-a-brim and reached straight for a fitted navy velour with a feather. She anchored it on her head with the hatpin provided and looked at her reflection this way and that.

'Can you show me the back with the hand mirror?' she asked, and Lily jumped to her feet.

'This is the one,' said Dora.

Lily blinked. She hadn't even looked at the price. 'You're sure?'

'Not too plain, not too fussy, it'll go with my blue coat and my grey jacket and skirt. And I can change the feather or take it off altogether if I want to. Versatile, you'd call it.' She reached for her bag and handed over her purse. 'Go and settle up, Lily, will you? I think I might keep it on!'

You could have knocked Lily down with the feather

on the hat, but she did as she was asked. Everything was going right.

26

Time was galloping on. Soon, unbelievably, the wedding was only a week away. March had come in more like a lamb than the proverbial lion — so far, the month had been mild, settled and dry and the auguries looked good for the first official day of spring.

Everything was in place — dresses, hats, shoes, flowers. Lily and Jim, in consultation with Dora and with Sid, the sophisticate of the family, had chosen the menu for the private room at the White Lion — soup, duck with redcurrant sauce, and (the luxury!) trifle. Drinks would be ordered from the bar and there'd be Mr Marlow's champagne to have with Dora's cake, which she was about to ice. Sid would be arriving the night before and Bill, who'd been posted to HMS Birnbeck at Weston-super-Mare, had put in for a twelve-hour pass. Beryl, in her own finery, would come to Lily's to help her dress, Sid having by then got Jim out of the way. Jean and Kenny, plus a handful of other neighbours and WI and WVS friends of Lily and Dora were going to come to the register office to see them emerge. So would Miss Frobisher and Mr Simmonds, singly or even together, they promised, if they could both get away. Jim was being mysterious about the night away he'd booked for them, and with a flutter in her heart, Lily was practising signing her name as 'Lily Goodridge'.

In the meantime, life went on. Lily and Jim went to work and Dora's daily round continued, including Kenny calling round for the dog.

She was pegging washing out when he arrived, Buddy getting under her feet.

'He won't leave me alone these past few days,' she complained. 'Sticking to me like glue, he is. I hope he's not sickening for something.'

Sam had opened a Post Office account to pay for Buddy's board and lodging, but a vet's bill would put a proper dent in it.

Kenny bent down and fussed the dog.

'Bright eyes, pink tongue,' he said. 'Not much wrong with him.'

'Well, take him off my hands for a bit, then, if he'll go without me,' said Dora. Then, she thought to herself, I might even sit down for five minutes. She reached down to the basket for Jim's shirt. 'You know where his lead is — Ooh . . . aah . . . aah.'

She doubled up with a hand to her stomach.

Buddy whined as Kenny put out his good arm to support her.

'Dora?'

But Dora didn't reply; instead she gave little whimpers of pain. She was as white as the shirt that had fallen from her hand and was trailing on the bricks underfoot.

Alarmed, Kenny looked around.

'Let's get you inside,' he said. 'A bit of a sit down, that should see you right.'

Dora was beyond making a reply, but as Kenny tried to walk her towards the back door, Buddy still whining in concern, her knees buckled and she slumped against him.

'Hell . . . ' Kenny muttered under his breath. He thought quickly. His uncle was at work, Trevor at school, and Jean had gone to the shops. He knew the

243

neighbours on the other side were out all day. It was no use calling for help. He tried again.

'Dora, come on now, can you walk a bit? It's only a few steps. I'll help you.'

Again, all Dora could do was to make indeterminate noises of pain. Kenny could see it was hopeless. As gently as he could he eased her to the ground next to the privy and the coal shed. It was hardly ideal. The ground was cold and hard but he shrugged off his coat and tore off his jumper, rolling it into a pillow and using his coat as a blanket over her. Her face was a chalky white, her lips blueish and clamped in pain as she clutched her stomach. Buddy tried to lick her face.

'You stay, Buddy, eh? Keep her warm, boy.'

Almost keening, Buddy lay down close by Dora's side.

And to Dora, if she could hear him, Kenny said, 'I'm going for help. I'll be as quick as I can. You hang in there. For me.'

* * *

Lily was dealing with a difficult customer. Well, not difficult, exactly, but it was an awkward situation. She and Miss Temple had seen the woman approaching across the sales floor — a new customer, not anyone that either of them recognised. When the woman reached the counter, Lily stepped forward with a smile.

'Good morning, madam. May I help you?'

It turned out she wanted almost a complete wardrobe of boy's clothes. It was unusual, but it did happen — maybe the child was being sent away to

244

relatives. Together Lily and Miss Temple had begun assembling the pile on the counter, but when the woman came to pay and produced her book of coupons, things started to look fishy. The coupon book was grubby and crumpled. It looked as though it had passed through many hands — thieving hands perhaps; there was an active market in stolen coupons. Up close, too, the customer wasn't the usual Marlows breed. Her fur coat was a mangy thing, almost bald in places, and her shoes were down at heel. There was nothing wrong with that in itself — some of the poshest people in the district, the gentry almost, had fallen on hard times since the start of the war. Their houses had been taken over by the military or for hospitals and they'd been reduced to living in the lodge or the old keeper's cottage. Their tweeds were shabby, their fur coats moth-eaten, but their shoes were always polished to a shine — one had standards, after all — and they kept their air of refinement in the way they held themselves and the way they spoke. This woman had none of that. She seemed shifty and nervous. Lily had the nasty feeling she'd been put up to it by someone. She was about to call Miss Frobisher when she saw her approaching anyhow. Lily excused herself and went to intercept her, to explain the situation out of the customer's hearing.

'Miss Frobisher, I'm glad you're here. Could you possibly — '

'You need to go, Miss Collins,' said Miss Frobisher abruptly.

'I'm sorry?'

'We've had a telephone call. Your mother's been taken ill.'

'Mum? Ill?'

Lily was astounded. Dora was never ill. A cold, a sore throat, a bit of indigestion . . . honey and lemon, glycerin and thymol and a bottle of soda mints were the only medicines she ever kept in the house.

'I don't know the details,' said Miss Frobisher, 'but they've taken her to hospital.'

Lily's eyes widened and she almost swayed.

'Hospital?'

'Off you go. I'll take over with your customer.'

'Th-thank you,' stuttered Lily. 'Yes. Er . . . thank you.'

The mangy coat and the tatty book of coupons went right out of her head. Lily was in such a state that she even started in the wrong direction, towards the main staircase that she'd climbed with her mum just the other week. It was only when she passed Lingerie that she realised where she was. She quickly backtracked, almost stumbling towards the double doors to the back stairs used by staff. From then on, she took everything at a run, scrabbling her things out of her locker, completely forgetting to sign out at the timekeeper's office, and realising only as she ran towards the hospital — she couldn't have stood the wait for a bus — that she hadn't told Jim. Maybe Miss Frobisher would. Maybe, maybe . . . but Dora ill? What sort of ill? What could it be?

At the hospital she flung herself through another set of double doors, almost colliding with a nurse pushing a wheelchair, gabbling to the girl on the reception desk that her mother had been admitted, and where could she find her? As the girl checked interminable lists and made a phone call, Lily almost hopped up and down in frustration. Where had it happened? Who had telephoned? How had they known who to

246

contact? Had Dora managed to tell them?

Finally the girl had an answer for her. Mrs D. Collins was 'in theatre', that's why she'd been hard to track down. She directed Lily to the Surgical Ward, where, she said, Dora would be taken after her operation.

An operation . . . Dora, who'd never been near a doctor for years, let alone been in hospital!

Lily charged up two flights of stairs. At the top she followed the signs until, on a chair in the corridor, she saw Jean Crosbie.

'Jean!'

Jean stood up at once.

'Oh hello, love, I'm glad you're here. Kenny got through then, to the shop.'

'Kenny?'

Lily seemed unable to do anything except repeat what people had said. It was as if her brain had completely stopped working.

'He was with her when it happened. Collapsed in the yard, she did. He was the one who called the ambulance.'

'Collapsed?'

She was at it again.

'It's all right. By the time the ambulance got there, I was back from my shopping. I came in with her. She wasn't on her own.'

'No . . . good. Have they said what it is?'

'Appendix, they think.'

Lily struggled not to repeat 'appendix' too.

'I see . . . well, that's not too serious, is it?'

'Doesn't have to be, no,' said Jean, but something in her voice made Lily suspicious.

'But . . . ?'

'To take her like that, sudden, in awful pain she was, Kenny said . . . well, I'm sorry, love, but it sounds like it might have gone bad, you see. Burst.'

Lily was beginning to feel rather sick herself. 'That's not good, is it?'

'I'm sure she's in good hands.'

Lily put her own hand out to the wall to support herself. Her legs weren't working too well either.

'Oh Jean,' she said. 'Mum . . . so ill . . . I can't take it in.'

Jean patted her on the shoulder. She wasn't the motherly sort, but her worn face was kinder than Lily had ever seen it.

'Now, Lily, you mustn't take on so. Your mum'll need you to be strong.'

Lily bit her lip, but she nodded and straightened her shoulders.

At that moment, the lift door at the end of the corridor opened and a porter emerged, pushing a bed. A nurse was walking beside it holding up a drip. In the bed was a pale white figure, lying very still.

Lily ran towards them.

'Mum!'

But the nurse frowned and motioned her to stand back as the little party passed them and went through into the ward.

'I'll be off now,' said Jean, with rare tact. She touched Lily's arm. 'I'm sure she'll be all right, love. She's in the best place.'

Lily nodded mutely, then pushed through the doors into the ward.

They were positioning Dora's bed in the corner nearest the door, close to the nurses' little office. The ward sister, supervising the procedure, gave Lily a stern look.

'No visitors until two,' she said crisply. 'Who are you? Who have you come to see?'

'I'm her daughter . . . ' said Lily faintly. 'Mrs Collins's daughter. I've just arrived. Please can you tell me what's going on?'

'One moment.'

The sister satisfied herself that the bed was at an exact right angle to the back wall and that the locker was dead straight against it. She checked the drip on the stand and took Dora's pulse, writing it on the chart at the end of the bed. Then she signalled to Lily to step into the office.

'Peritonitis,' she said, without preamble. 'It should never have got to that stage. Has she been complaining of stomach pains? Any bouts of sickness?'

'No . . . ' said Lily, then she thought. It hadn't just been that time with that horrible oily fish — the snoek. Dora had often been eating a bit less at mealtimes, passing her leftovers to Jim. Lily had caught her a few times swallowing a couple of soda mints or a spoonful of bicarb. 'That is . . . maybe. I think she thought it was indigestion.'

'Grumbling appendix, more like,' said the sister. 'And this is what happens if it's ignored. Severe pain, and an emergency operation.'

Lily's legs felt weak and she felt for the chair behind her.

'Emergency? It's serious then?'

'She's not well,' the sister said plainly. 'We caught it in time, the doctor says, just about, but I'm afraid I can't pretend her condition isn't serious. It's all going to depend on the next few days.' She stopped and looked at Lily. 'Are you her only family?'

'Er, no, but . . . ' Her voice shook. 'The only one that's here. In Hinton, I mean.'

'I see. Well, we won't be able to tell you much more today. She'll be very groggy when she comes round and she needs complete rest. You can telephone in the morning.'

'I can't leave her!'

'There's nothing you can do for her,' said the sister, sounding a little kinder. 'You've had a shock, dear. Go home and get yourself a cup of tea. You need it.'

Bemused, Lily let herself be ushered away; her last sight of her mother was of Dora's still, white face against the snowy pillow.

Outside in the corridor she sagged against the wall. She had to get a grip. She had to tell Sid . . . He'd want to know; he might be able to come up. But should she tell Reg or wait until there was better news? Assuming it would be better . . . There was nothing he could do, anyway. Nothing any of them could do. Dora, her recovery — her life maybe — was in the hands of the doctors now.

Steeling herself, Lily walked towards the stairs; her legs were so jelly-like she didn't trust herself not to fall. In the little glass porthole of the door, she caught a glimpse of her reflection and an image flashed into her mind of her mother in Marlows, trying on her new hat, so proud and pretty, Lily holding up the mirror for the back view, her mother's face reflected three ways. Oh dear Lord, the wedding! They couldn't have it now!

27

Lily went home. What else could she do? She had to collect herself before she went to the telephone box to try to get a message to Sid, but as she put her key in the lock — it saved time to use the front door for once — it opened and there was Kenny in the hall.

'I didn't like to leave the place unlocked with no one in, and I didn't know if you had a key, seeing as the back door's always open,' he explained as Lily followed him numbly through to the back room.

She sank into a chair. All her mother's things were there — her sewing machine, her basket of mending, her knitting, her *Woman's Weekly*, open at a recipe she'd told Lily she was going to try, her coat and scarf on the back of the chair, ready, no doubt, for the tiresome daily trip to the shops. Lily closed her eyes. She couldn't give in to tears.

'You were with her,' she said to Kenny. 'You called the ambulance and got her to hospital. Thank you.'

'She's going to be all right, you know.' Kenny dropped to his knees beside her chair and briefly put his hand, his only hand, on hers. Lily looked at him. He had nice eyes when you looked at them properly. Greenish and grey at the same time.

She nodded. She knew they were both thinking the same thing, though for different reasons. Dora had to be all right. For Lily because she was her mum, and for Kenny because of his friend, the one who had died.

'I'll put the kettle on, shall I?' he asked, but before

Lily could reply, the back door crashed open, there were footsteps in the kitchen, and there was Jim.

Kenny got to his feet.

'Hello, Jim. I'll leave you to it.'

Lily stood up and Jim folded her in his arms. Neither of them heard or saw Kenny go as he closed the back door quietly behind him and stopped to pat Buddy in the yard.

Later, after she'd cried and cried, Jim went to telephone Sid at the Admiralty. Sid wasn't at his desk. 'On a training course' they said, but they promised to get a message to him. Jim also phoned the hospital again, even though they'd been told not to, only to hear that there was 'no change' in Dora's condition.

'That's good,' he tried to reassure Lily when he got back. 'She's not taken a turn for the worse.'

Lily put the heel of her hand to her head. It ached.

'You do realise, Jim . . . ' she began.

'The wedding's off,' he said. 'I'll cancel everything.'

'It's not off,' said Lily quickly. 'But we'll have to postpone it.'

'Of course.' Jim moved her gently out of the armchair so he could sit in it, and pulled her onto his knee.

'I'm so sorry.'

'Don't be daft. We'll wait till your mum's better. Fully better, I mean. So that she — and we — can all enjoy it properly.'

Lily sniffed.

'She has to get better, Jim, she has to! And I feel so bad. I've been so wrapped up in us — in myself — for months that I ignored the signs!'

'No, you didn't,' said Jim. 'And if you did we all did, your mum included. She didn't let us see.'

252

'That's because she puts everyone else first, you know what she's like.'

'I do. She must like it that way.'

Lily shook her head.

'If anything happens to her I'll never forgive myself. But it can't . . . I can't imagine life without her.'

'You won't have to.'

'She's just . . . she's always been there, always been . . . just Mum. I thought she always would be. I took it all for granted. I tell you, Jim, I'm going to appreciate her better in future if I get the chance!'

'And you will. Get the chance I mean.'

Lily sighed. Jim's own mother had died back in 1942, but she'd been ill for a while after a stroke and their relationship had been nothing like Lily's with Dora. And it wasn't just mother and son versus mother and daughter. Sid's, even Reg's, relationship with their mum was far closer than Jim's had been with the embittered woman who'd resented her only son's move to the town, had never taken to Lily, and had made both of those things plain.

By now, the whole day had passed and it was getting dark. Jim made them something to eat and forced Lily to swallow it — not that she could taste anything. She realised she'd never asked how he'd come to be at home in the middle of the day, but Jim said Miss Frobisher had told him he could go.

'I'll go in tomorrow but she said she doesn't expect to see you for the next couple of days,' he explained. 'So we'll phone the hospital in the morning and you should be able to visit in the afternoon. You ought to be here, anyway. If the Admiralty's as efficient as I hope they are — else how have we got this far in the war — then Sid will probably send a wire. Or he may even turn up!'

Lily nodded. She was so wrung out she couldn't form any more words, not even of thanks to Miss Frobisher for Jim to relay.

'You're exhausted,' he said. 'Let's go to bed.'

There was something in the way he said it that made Lily look up.

'Yes,' he said. 'I'm going to get in your bed tonight and sleep with you. Next to you.'

'You mean . . .'

Jim took her face in his hands.

'We should have been married in less than a week, Lily, so it's hardly a carnal sin. But we won't do anything. I just want to be with you. I'll hold you till you fall asleep, OK?'

Lily fell against him. 'Oh Jim. I do love you!'

'I know,' he said. 'I know.'

★ ★ ★

'It'll all look better in the morning' was one of Dora's favourite sayings. She was so often right, and she was right this time as well — to a degree.

When Lily woke she couldn't at first work out what was going on. There was an unaccustomed weight pressing on her ribcage and she was warm, much warmer than she usually was in the chill of the early mornings at this time of year. Then she realised that the weight was Jim's arm and the warmth was coming from his body. She even smiled to herself before she remembered why he was there and yesterday's terror gripped her again.

She wriggled out of his arm and sat up. Jim rolled onto his back and opened his eyes.

'Good morning,' he said.

'Hello,' said Lily shyly.

It had been a squash and a squeeze, the two of them in her single bed, but fitting themselves in with a degree of comfort had made them both laugh — something Lily had thought she'd never do again. It wasn't how they'd planned to spend their first-ever night together. That should have been on honeymoon, during which their double bed would arrive and be installed in Lily's room. As Furniture department supremo, Jim knew that newlyweds, or about to be, qualified for first dibs on Utility furniture, and how to go about getting a permit from the Ministry for Fuel and Power. They'd chosen light oak with slatted ends so that Jim, being tall, could stick his feet through the gaps. They'd been approved and the bedstead and mattress had duly arrived in Marlows' warehouse. Now that was something else that Jim would have to put on hold.

Jim squinted at his watch.

'Time for a cuddle?' he said.

It was barely seven o'clock. She couldn't phone the hospital yet. Lily snuggled down again.

It was a risk. She knew how much Jim wanted her — she wanted him too, badly, and they'd come close on a couple of occasions. But at the same time — and they'd talked about this — they both wanted to hold off till they were married. Now it would mean an even longer wait.

Jim wrapped his arms round her again and she stroked his chest where the springy hairs poked up out of his pyjama jacket. He kissed her forehead and then the top of her head and gave a little sigh. Lily kissed the hollow at the base of his throat.

'I'm sorry, Jim,' she said. 'We can't. It wouldn't feel

255

right. Not while I'm thinking about —'

'Shh,' he said. 'It's OK.'

They lay there for a while, then Jim said he should get up if he was going to get to work, and Lily slipped out of bed and down to the privy, leaving Jim to get up and get dressed in private. They were both cleaning their teeth together at the kitchen sink when there was a tremendous knocking at the front door. Could it be Sid already?

It wasn't, but it was the next best thing — a telegram.

ARRIVE 2.30. SEE YOU AT HOSPITAL. CHIN UP. SID

The cavalry was on its way.

Lily left the house with Jim when he set off for work. He squashed in the telephone box with her while she called the hospital to hear that her mother was 'stable' — again, he said, a good sign. Then he kissed her and rushed off to Marlows while Lily made her way back home, to wash up the breakfast things and make the bed, take the swill bucket down to the pig bin and bring in the washing which was stiff on the line from yesterday — a pitiful reminder of the interruption to Dora's routine. As she dropped it into the basket, shivering in the chilly March air, Lily realised she'd have to do some ironing. Jim would need his shirt in the morning, and she'd better walk poor Buddy, and go to the shops — they were almost out of bread . . .

If the reason for her new domestic duties hadn't been what it was, she might almost have laughed. Lily Collins, housewife — there was a role she felt totally unsuited for! A good job that was something else she and Jim had talked about, she thought, as she shrugged on her coat — she certainly intended to keep working after they were married. It was true that some of the Marlows staff who'd gone off to do war work might want their jobs back — the men, almost certainly, though Jim was senior enough now not to be under threat. As for the female staff — well, some would have married and be happy to give up work, some would be mothers, while others might have got a taste for a different way of life and find Hinton too much of a backwater, so Lily hoped her job would be safe too. But that was all for the future. For now, she had more pressing problems — like getting enough food in to feed Sid's legendary appetite, and without the help of his ration book, which wouldn't arrive till he did.

The shopping and the housework occupied her all morning and by ten to two, she was at the hospital with a clean nightdress and Dora's toothbrush, soap, and flannel, pacing the corridor outside the Surgical Ward with the other impatient visitors.

At two o'clock exactly a nurse propped open the swing doors and they all pressed in. Lily was shocked to see her mother still lying there with her eyes closed, a drip still taped to her hand and a sign saying 'NIL BY MOUTH' above the bed.

Lily gently pressed Dora's free hand.

'Mum,' she said softly. 'It's Lily. I'm here.'

'Lily . . . ' With what seemed like a monumental effort, Dora opened her eyes. She turned her head on the pillow and smiled. 'Hello, love.'

'Oh, Mum.'

Lily was so relieved to hear her speak, she couldn't manage anything more. As it was, her voice was almost as weak as Dora's.

'I'm sorry about this, love. And your wedding . . .'

'Mum, that's the least of my worries!' It wasn't entirely true but it was certainly second on the list. 'And you don't have to say sorry! Except for ignoring the signs!' Lily drew up the hard chair and sat down by the bedside. 'I think you had had signs, hadn't you?'

Dora closed her eyes and shook her head. Lily changed tack. It was no use lecturing. What was done was done.

'How are you feeling anyway?' she asked. 'Pretty sore, I expect.'

Lily could well imagine it — remember it, rather. When she and Jim had been caught in the bomb blast, they'd been trapped under three floors of shattered masonry. Lily had been bruised and battered all over. She'd felt as if she'd been run over by a tank and at this moment she suspected that her mother might well be feeling the same.

Dora licked her lips, which were dry. There was a glass of water on the locker with a sort of lolly stick in it, wrapped round with lint. Lily remembered those. She pressed the swab against the side of the glass to squeeze out some of the liquid, then touched it to her mother's mouth.

'Nice,' said Dora gratefully.

'Good. We don't have to talk,' she said. 'You have a rest, that's what you need. And Sid's coming. He'll be here soon.'

Her mother nodded. The usual Dora would have protested that he shouldn't have; that she was being such a nuisance; that she didn't want to put anyone out. That she didn't was a sign of how far removed she was from her usual self.

They sat there quietly, Lily holding and stroking her mother's hand, Dora responding with a feeble squeeze of her own, until there was a kerfuffle in the doorway. It was Sid, of course, incapable of doing anything without a bit of a fanfare. He was in his uniform, looking more striking than ever, blond hair slicked down, blue eyes scanning the beds. At his elbow was a fluffy-haired probationer who must have shown him the way to the ward and was clearly angling to get to know him better. But he politely ditched her as Lily waved and jumped up to give him a hug. She noticed his raised eyebrows when he approached the bed — in Sid always a sign of concern — but when he spoke, he did a brilliant job of hiding it.

'Hello, you,' he said, bending to kiss his mother's forehead. 'What have you been doing to yourself, eh, putting us to all this trouble?'

Lily remembered he'd used exactly the same tone with her when she'd been in hospital with her injuries.

A lump rose in her throat. Thank goodness for Sid!

28

Visiting ended at three; ten minutes before that a nurse came round ringing a bell. Dora had become a little more animated when Sid arrived — there wasn't much choice with his personality — but she was still visibly weak, pale and clammy, and talking tired her. As they stood up to go, Sid and Lily assured her they'd be back at seven for evening visiting, but once they were outside, Lily turned a worried face to her brother.

'Oh, Sid. She doesn't seem very bright.'

Sid didn't patronise her by brushing off her fears. Now they were out of sight and earshot of their mum, he was more serious too, but he smiled and said, 'It's a big op, Sis. Come on, let's get out of here.'

He led the way to the stairs. When they got outside, Sid lit up a cigarette.

'You can't expect miracles,' he said. 'It's only been twenty-four hours. And Mum . . . well, she's not got a lot of resources, has she? None of us has — everyone's worn thin since the start of the war, and we're all tired out, frankly. Especially people like Mum who've been doing more than ever for the past five and a half years.'

'I suppose so.'

Again Lily felt guilty. So much had changed for her over the course of the war, and in a good way — starting work, meeting Jim, making new friends, doing new things. There'd been tough times, anxious times, lots of them, but she still had so much to look forward to — the rest of her life. But for older people, of her mother's age and over, the war had brought only hardships, really — managing a home with rationing and shortages while 'doing their bit' as well. They'd been through four years of the Great War in their youth and had seen that snatched away — now they'd had to endure more years of worry and weariness.

'She'll buck up.' Sid linked her arm through his. 'Give her time. Now come on, what do you say to tea and buns at the ABC tearoom? We've got to keep our strength up, anyway.'

It made such a difference having Sid there — you couldn't help but be reassured by him. Over their tea and buns — very welcome — he told her about life in London and asked about goings-on at the store. He'd realised straight away that plans for the wedding would have to be put on ice. Lily explained that Jim had taken on the sorry task of unscrambling the arrangements and uninviting their guests.

'It's a big disappointment for you, Sis. Can you fix another date?'

'No,' Lily replied firmly. 'It's all off till Mum's properly better. Jim and I have already decided.'

Sid nodded.

'That's my girl. We can nip into the White Lion on our way home; I'm sure they'll return my deposit. Or hold onto it if we promise them another date.'

'Thank you, Sid. It was such a kind thought.'

'Well, the offer still stands when you name the day. Take Two as they say in the movies!'

Sid had always been a film fan — one of the many attractions of his American friend Jerome, Lily was sure, was that he'd worked on film sets before joining up.

But first and above all else, their mum had to get better. Till then, life itself was on hold.

★ ★ ★

They went back to the hospital in the evening, armed with flowers, magazines, and, at Jean's recommendation, arrowroot biscuits which Lily had scoured Hinton to find. At seven o'clock precisely, the same ritual was enacted: the doors were pinned back and the visitors surged forwards. But the curtains were drawn round Dora's bed.

Sid was unperturbed.

'They'll be dolling her up for us,' he said. 'Getting her in her own nightie, brushing her hair, I expect.'

Then the curtains parted and the ward sister — the same one Lily had met the day before — bustled out.

'Ah, it's you,' she said in her usual brusque manner. 'Doctor's with her.'

'There's nothing wrong, is there?' Lily was immediately on alert. It seemed rather late for the doctor to be doing his rounds.

'If you wouldn't mind waiting in the corridor, he won't be long.'

At that moment the curtains parted again and the doctor appeared. He was young — even younger than the one who'd attended Gladys. Were they getting them straight from medical school? The sister smiled at him, softening like wax in a flame.

'This is Dr Lee,' she explained. And to the doctor — Dr Mark Lee, it said on his badge — she said, 'Mrs Collins's son and daughter.'

'Ah, pleased to meet you.' Dr Lee shook Sid and Lily by the hand, almost breaking her wrist with his

262

grip. 'Nurse is just making your mother comfortable. Shall we have a word outside?'

Lily glanced at Sid, who shrugged. Dr Lee bounced off briskly, the pair of them following, Lily's heart in her mouth. But when they got there, Dr Lee turned round, frowning, but at the same time looking almost excited.

'A very interesting case,' he said. 'I gather from your mother she'd been having stomach pains and ignored them. Very silly, giving herself peritonitis like that, but that's mothers for you, isn't it? Mine's the same, whiff of burning martyr! A proper mess she presented us with, the surgeon said, bits of appendix all over the shop!'

Lily wished he'd stop sounding quite so pleased about it. He was practically rubbing his hands.

'And?' frowned Sid.

'What's happened is what usually happens — the chance of a nasty infection. Bits of gunk end up where they shouldn't, you see, and then — '

'Then what?'

'Septicaemia!' said Dr Lee, almost triumphantly. 'So you have to leap in PDQ.' He leaned in conspiratorially. 'I've only been here six months' — that fitted with Lily's medical student assumption — 'but to be honest,' he went on, 'they can be a bit slow on the uptake. I've come from London and the minute her temperature started going up over the afternoon, I suggested sulphonamides — '

'Hang on, hang on,' said Sid. 'That's what they use on the troops, isn't it?'

The doctor brightened even more, if that were possible.

'That's right! Are you a medic? Army? Navy? RAF?

Or civvy street?'

'Navy,' said Sid. 'And no, I'm not. But you pick things up, don't you?'

'They're amazing drugs,' enthused Dr Lee. 'Apparently, at Tobruk — '

'Yeah, that's where I first heard they used them,' Sid agreed. 'And Monte Cassino — '

Lily interrupted.

'Before this turns into a Pathé newsreel, could someone please explain to me, whose medical knowledge stops at aspirin, what you're on about? What are these . . . sulphonamides?'

Dr Lee turned his puppyish enthusiasm on her.

'Antibacterial, antimicrobial, they act as competitive inhibitors, you see — '

'They stop an infection in its tracks,' Sid intervened helpfully. 'Ideally before it's really taken hold.'

'There you are. In a nutshell,' said Dr Lee. He beckoned them into a huddle again. 'You remember when the Prime Minister disappeared for a while in the winter of '43? They said he had a heavy cold?' He shook his head and rolled his eyes. 'Pneumonia. It was sulphonamides that pulled him through.' He stood back to let the full import of this revelation sink in. 'So they've been tested on about the most important guinea pig in the country! Your mum's lucky to get them. And she will get better on them. She's picking up already — give it another twenty-four hours and you'll see a real difference.'

He seemed happy to carry on chatting, but Sister, seemingly jealous of the time away from her, came and called him to her office with some story about paperwork. Lily and Sid followed them into the ward.

264

The curtains round Dora's bed had been drawn back. After that build-up, Lily almost expected to see her out of bed and executing a tap dance. She wasn't, of course, but she was propped up, hair brushed and in her own nightie, as Sid had predicted. She was still clearly unwell, but thanks to Dr Lee's wonder drugs, did look a little brighter. And she now had the energy to say all the things Lily had expected earlier in the day.

'I'm being such a nuisance to everyone,' she said feebly. 'And your wedding, Lily . . . '

'I've told you, you're not to worry about that!'

'But I do. You and Jim must still get married, you really must. Everything's in place.'

'Everything except you!' Lily shot back. 'What kind of wedding would that be? Tell her, Sid!'

Sid backed Lily up.

'Nothing is happening in this family till you're on your feet again. And fully better.'

Dora sighed.

'I hope it won't be long. I just want to get home.'

Lily leant forward and gave her a careful hug.

'And I can't wait to have you back! Look at my washday hands already!'

But the other thing Dr Lee had impressed on them was that Dora's recovery would take time and when she came home she was to have complete rest — bed rest at first. She was not to exert herself, or in any way put pressure on the scar.

Lily resolved one thing: she wasn't going to take Dora, and everything she did, for granted again.

★ ★ ★

True to Dr Lee's word, the miraculous sulphonamides did their work and Dora made steady progress. First they got her out of bed and sitting in a chair; then, she reported proudly, she'd taken a few steps, leaning on a nurse. Gradually her world expanded. She walked up and down the ward with the nurse, then with Lily, and finally by herself, first from bed-end to bed-end, and eventually, slowly, without any support. But she was still stooped and her hand often went to the site of the operation as if for reassurance that the scar was still closed and the dressing in place. Dora was always resolutely cheerful, but it was hard for Lily to see her mother, usually so fit and able, reduced like this.

In the meantime, of course, the first day of spring — the day of the wedding — had been and gone.

'I'm so sorry,' Dora said on the day she came home to Brook Street, as Lily settled her in her own bed. Her new blouse was still hanging up on the back of the bedroom door, so it didn't get creased in the tiny wardrobe. 'Your day all in ruins because of me!'

'Mum, you didn't plan it!' said Lily. 'And it's fine. Did you see the weather on the 21st? Pouring! We had a lucky escape!'

'You don't mean that.'

'Maybe not, but we're not in any rush to rebook. I want to know that you're properly better before we pick another date.'

'We want to know.' Jim spoke from the doorway where he was hovering with a tray of tea.

'Oh, Jim!'

'Enough. We're not even going to think about it for a couple of months, are we, Lily?'

'No. You're the priority now.'

Pale from the exertion of the journey from hospital and the stairs, trapped in bed and helpless for the first time in her life, Dora had no option but to agree.

★ ★ ★

Neither of them was quite as chipper as that, of course, and neither were their guests. When Lily and Jim had told everyone about Dora, after concern and sympathy for her, everyone had been desperately sorry for them and their abandoned plans. Gladys had actually cried — but then Gladys cried at anything — a greeting in a birthday card, pictures of kittens, someone's painful chilblains — while Beryl had flown into a panic that her leopard-collared suit would be 'too wintry' for the late spring or summer wedding which looked most likely now. Miss Frobisher had been sorry, too, when Lily went back to work.

'You must be so disappointed,' she sympathised.

'Worse things happen at sea,' said Lily gamely, quoting Sid.

But when Jim held her close she often thought of the night they'd spent together, how lovely it had been to have him near her, and longed for the time when it could be lovelier still. But for now it was best foot forward, shoulder to the wheel, and all the rest of it.

She'd been back at work since the third day of Dora's hospital stay, but now her mum was home, she had weightier responsibilities. She'd never realised before quite how much her mother did, and she marvelled that she managed it all. Of course, Dora didn't have a full-time job, but she had all her voluntary work, which took up almost as much time. Jim helped a bit, doing the washing-up, taking out the

267

ashes and the slop pail, but Lily was exhausted. She was getting up early to do odd bits of washing before she left for work, ironing in the evenings after trying to cook tasty and nutritious invalid meals, and all the time trying not to let her mother see how frazzled she was. Jean and Gladys were doing the food shopping and checking on Dora in the day when they could manage it, but as Dora gradually improved enough to get dressed and come downstairs, Lily had even more concerns.

By now it was early April, but full recovery would take at least six weeks Dr Lee had said — and she knew her mother. There was no chance of Dora Collins sitting around waiting for people to do things for her; stuck at home without supervision, Lily knew she'd find endless jobs to do, clearing out drawers, taking everything out of the larder and wiping down the shelves, even cleaning the windows. And she was proved right.

One day, knowing Jean was at the WVS tea bar and Gladys at the baby clinic, Lily got a pass out at dinner-time and went home to make her mum some lunch. She found her with a pile of scrunched-up newspapers and a bottle of vinegar at the ready.

'What are we going to do with you?' Lily demanded. 'Sit down!'

'As if I can sit here and look at that!' Dora indicated the window overlooking the yard. 'Now the sun's shining, it shows up every smear!'

'You're supposed to be taking it easy!'

'Tch,' said Dora. 'I've never been so idle. Or bored! It doesn't suit me!'

'Well, get used to it,' Lily replied. 'I'm getting good practice in housewifery — is that a word? — for when me and Jim get a home of our own.' Then she added, 'Mind you, so is he, and he'll need it with my efforts, poor man!'

She cleaned the offending window herself under Dora's critical eye ('You've missed a bit in the corner!') then heated them both up some soup and quickly washed up their dishes and the pan. On her way back to work, she called next door and asked Kenny to go in and sit with Dora.

'And don't let her out of your sight!' she ordered.

Like a prison guard, she thought, though she obviously didn't use that phrase to him.

Dora, meanwhile, was still in the armchair where Lily had positioned her with her Mills and Boon from the library, but her eye had already wandered to the shelf with Jim's books on it — what dust-gatherers they were! Surely dusting a few books couldn't do her any harm ...

'Anyone home?'

'Kenny!' she called. 'In here! But boots off, please!'

'I know!' he chanted back.

'This is nice,' said Dora as he came through in his socks. 'I'd offer you a cup of tea but you'll have to make it yourself. I'm under strict instructions from my daughter not to move.'

'She can be very fierce, your Lily,' reflected Kenny, thinking of how Lily had just laid down the law to him. 'Mind you, you've told me a few home truths yourself.'

'Not as many as Phyllis, I don't think!' smiled Dora. 'When's she coming up again? Or are you going to see her?'

There'd been a lot of coming and going between Hinton and London for the two of them since the girl's first visit.

'Funny you should ask . . . ' Kenny bit his lip, bashful. 'I'm going down to see her this weekend, as it happens. And . . . I'm staying in London, Dora. For good.'

'Oh! I see!'

'There's more facilities and better treatment down there,' Kenny explained. 'More expertise in fitting limbs and that.'

'Right,' Dora mused, but couldn't stop herself from adding, 'and is that the only reason?'

Kenny looked even more bashful.

'No, maybe not,' he admitted. 'Meeting up with her again, well . . . I've realised maybe I was a fool to let her go the first time.'

'Hindsight's a wonderful thing,' said Dora. 'But to get a second chance is even more wonderful.'

She was thinking of Sam. He'd been devastated to hear she'd been taken ill, wiring Lily the money to buy 'the biggest bunch of flowers you can' for her return home.

'That's what it feels like to me,' Kenny enthused. 'About everything. Phyllis has already been in touch with some people who can help me. And fixed me up some appointments.'

'That's very good news, Kenny,' said Dora warmly.

'I'll let you know my address,' said Kenny. 'I'll be in lodgings — Phyllis is finding me somewhere. She's in the nurses' home, you see.'

She'd run him like a greyhound, Dora thought, smiling. Still, he needed it.

'You must keep in touch,' she said. 'Let us know how you're getting on.'

She looked down at her library book: *With All My*

Worldly Goods by Mary Burchell. On the cover, a radiant bride and groom were cutting their wedding cake. Kenny and Phyllis . . . Well, why not?

29

The staff entrance to Marlows was round the back in Brewer Street. Made late by her detour to enlist Kenny, Lily was taking it at a gallop when who should she see ahead of her but Jim.

'Where've you been?' she panted, catching him up. 'You never said you were going out at dinner-time — secrets already, huh?'

'Not even married and my time's not my own,' Jim sighed dramatically, opening the entrance door for her. 'I've been to the register office as it happens.'

'Oh, Lord.' Lily signed back in in the timekeeper's ledger. 'Has Mum been nagging you as well?'

As they'd been drinking their soup, Dora had again pressed Lily to name another date.

'I don't need nagging, I went of my own accord,' said Jim with dignity, taking the pencil from her. 'I've brought you a selection from the end of April through to the middle of May. The doc will definitely have signed your mum off by then.'

Lily checked there was no one from management behind them, then stood on tiptoe and gave him a kiss.

'I do love you,' she said. 'Tonight, we'll decide.'

* * *

When Lily got back to the sales floor, things were quiet — so quiet that Miss Frobisher had strayed over to the Toy department. She beckoned Lily to join her.

272

'Which do you think?' She indicated a selection of board games, newly arrived. 'Submarine Hunt, Sky Battle, or Ocean War?'

John was coming up to six in the summer, Lily knew.

'They're a good price,' she said. At 2/- each they were very reasonable. 'But if the war ends as soon as we hope, they could be reduced before John's birthday!'

The end was looking more and more likely. Since the start of the year, the Allies had reportedly taken over a million German prisoners on the Western Front and many more as they swept up through Italy. On the Eastern Front, where Russian forces were pressing steadily westwards, almost another million had surrendered. Hamburg, Nuremberg, and of course Berlin were still holding on but the Allies had scented victory and they were not going to let up now.

Miss Frobisher's hand hovered over Ocean War.

'I could have one put by,' she mused. 'I think he'd like this one best.'

Just then, Mr Simmonds approached with Jim at his heels. Mr Simmonds was looking very smug, and Jim had his Cheshire Cat grin on again — a Cheshire cat who'd lapped up a whole churn of cream.

Miss Frobisher returned Ocean War to the display.

'Ah, you've heard!' she said.

'Yes!' answered Mr Simmonds. 'And we're on! Or rather, these two are!'

Lily looked from one to another like a spectator at a tennis tournament. Were they talking about the wedding? Her wedding? After all that, had Jim settled on the date by himself and shared it with Mr Simmonds? Thanks very much!

273

'Erm . . .' she hazarded.

Jim looked at Mr Simmonds. 'May I? he said.

Mr Simmonds nodded and Jim turned to Lily.

'What do you say to two weeks in London? All expenses paid. On a management training course! Both of us!'

Confusion, then disbelief, then delight, chased each other across Lily's face.

'What? You . . . and me?' She turned to Miss Frobisher. 'That's . . . Jim — Mr Goodridge — I can understand, but why me?

'Now, Miss Collins,' said Miss Frobisher sternly. 'Don't go fishing for compliments. It demeans you.'

'I wasn't fishing. I mean it!' protested Lily.

'You don't see what others see, Miss Collins,' said Mr Simmonds. 'Why you deserve it. How you've matured since you started here.'

Lily looked at Miss Frobisher for confirmation.

'Let me remind you,' she said. 'Back in '42 when your brother went missing, you went to pieces, so distracted I could only use you in the stockroom. Your mother's just been gravely ill, but apart from a couple of days off at the beginning, you've been here every day, out front, dealing with customers perfectly normally, no matter what extra responsibilities and worry you've been carrying at home. Do you start to see what I mean?'

'Well . . .'

'Must I go on? You and Mr Goodridge were nearly killed in that bomb here. Plenty of members of staff would never have been able to set foot through the doors again, but you came back. And just last year when I was away — '

'Yes, all right,' said Lily, embarrassed at this parade

of her virtues. 'Thank you. But none of it felt like anything special to me. I was only doing my job.'

'And we think you could do an even bigger job in due course,' said Mr Simmonds. 'Especially when things get back to normal after the war. Junior buyer on one of the larger departments, perhaps.'

Junior buyer! What would her mum say?

'There is just one thing,' said Jim. His smile had faded. 'I did explain to Mr Simmonds. This course, it's at the end of April and the beginning of May.'

Lily burst out laughing.

'Here we go again — another postponement! It had better be third time lucky!'

* * *

Within days, Lily and Jim had their acceptance on the course confirmed, and a whole load of bumf about it arrived.

'The course will take place at the offices of the Retail Services Training Board, Tottenham Court Road, London,' Lily read. She and Jim were up on the roof of the store with sandwiches; on warmer days it offered the chance of some fresh air at dinnertime without the bother of a pass out. 'Please report to the Reception desk at 9.30 a.m. on Monday 30th April. Your employer will supply you with a rail warrant for travel the day before. Hostel accommodation will be provided at YMCA and YWCA hostels as required. Please bring your ration book with you — '

'Blah, blah,' said Jim. 'Have a look at what they'll teach us.'

Lily rifled through the booklet.

'You will be guided through every stage of the retail

275

process,' she read again, 'from the importance of making the right buying decisions, through supply chain management, merchandising, understanding customer behaviour, and a strategy for — Jim, I don't even understand half these words!'

Jim took the booklet from her and put it to one side.

'It's blah, blah again. You'll be fine. It's all long words and high-falutin' talk for what you do every day without thinking. Buying decisions — that's what you know sells well, plus ten to fifteen per cent of new lines as a try-out and dropping stuff that's sticking. Supply chain management — all that means is chasing manufacturers, cutting out as many middlemen as you can. Merchandising — in plain English, that's — '

'Oh, stop it! It's all right for you, you've got your School Certificate. I left at fourteen!'

'Only because your mum couldn't afford for you to stay on! You're a natural learner, Lily. Once you're back in a classroom, you'll be teacher's pet before the end of the first day. You could probably teach the course if you put your mind to it. It's a good job I don't feel threatened by being married to a career woman!'

'When we finally get married!'

Their much-postponed wedding had become almost a standing joke.

'I know. Call me superstitious,' said Jim, 'but I'm not going back to that register office till we've been to London. After the last few months, who knows what might get in the way this time?'

★ ★ ★

They might not have a new wedding date, but with Dora duly signed off by the doctors, the daffodil trumpets blowing merrily in the wind, and the news from Europe getting more encouraging by the day, Lily and Jim were in good spirits when they set off for London.

It was exciting to be having an adventure — not as exciting as embarking on married life, perhaps, but at least they'd be spending all day, every day, together, and evenings as well, even if not whole nights. There'd be no ARP duties for Jim, no WVS for Lily. They'd be free to enjoy themselves, with all that the capital had to offer, and among those things was Sid.

But when Lily had asked if they could meet up, Sid had been unusually reticent. 'Operational matters' were keeping the Admiralty busy and he was reluctant to make an arrangement only to let her down. He took the telephone number of the hostel and said he'd let her know. It was disappointing, but Lily could understand — if Sid being busy meant a quicker end to the war, she was happy to wait.

Their train clanked into Euston only forty-five minutes late. Emerging through the station's magnificent classical arch, they paused to take stock. It was a lovely sunny Sunday.

'Let's walk,' said Jim, map in hand. 'The hostel's not that far. I'll carry your case.'

Lily had visited London once before and they'd both seen the newsreels, but to see the scale of the destruction they passed was still a jolt. Between stretches of dust and rubble, even the intact buildings were battle-scarred. The roads were pitted and potholed, the pavements cracked or missing entirely. It was sad to see, but there were still signs of hope. The war couldn't stop the seasons of the year: the plane trees were a vivid green and the wings of starlings were iridescent as they caught the sun. A barrow boy passed, singing the rude words about Hitler that someone had made up to the tune of 'Colonel Bogey'. Other words came to Lily's mind — those of the Prime Minister five years ago after the retreat from Dunkirk. 'We shall not flag or fail . . . we shall go on to the end . . . we shall never surrender . . . ' Tears came to her eyes. They hadn't, and now things really were almost at an end.

As Jim had promised, their hostels weren't far, and they discovered they were side by side. They parted to dump their things, agreeing to meet again in twenty minutes. But when Lily stuck her head out of the window of her dormitory, a familiar head was poking out of the window next door. Jim!

'Where's your bed?' she asked.

'Two up from the window,' he replied.

'Mine too!' cried Lily. 'We can knock on the wall!'

'If only I'd brought a pickaxe!' mourned Jim.

Next day, they presented themselves as requested, and with twenty others were shown straight to their classroom. Their tutor, Mr Robson, was a tall, bald man with a bow tie and a brisk manner. After a cursory good morning and a brief introduction, he launched straight in.

'Notebooks out, pencils at the ready,' he said, turning to the blackboard. 'So, who can tell me, what is a shop for exactly?'

It went on like that all day. Mr Robson had an unnerving habit of balancing on the balls of his feet, rocking forwards till Lily felt sure he'd topple over, which hardly made it more relaxing. Thank goodness, thought Lily, she and Jim had opted for safe seats in the middle of the class, not the front row. All in all, by the time they were let out at five thirty, her brain felt like one of the jumbled messages which, it was emerging, British boffins had managed to unscramble, giving the Allies early warning of the enemy's planned attacks. As much as anything, this breakthrough had hastened the end of the war — and there was no doubt it was speeding towards them now. Newsboys were shouting themselves hoarse and their placards competed for the most attention-grabbing headline. There were almost too many to choose from. Lily didn't know which way to look.

MILAN, GENOA, VENICE AND MUNICH TAKEN

SOVIET TROOPS PIN DOWN NAZIS IN BERLIN

MUSSOLINI DEAD — MOB TRAMPLES BODY

'It's the end,' said Jim, eyes shining. 'It has to be.'

30

There was a peculiar atmosphere in the classroom next day. Everyone, including Mr Robson, tried to give the course their full attention, but at dinnertime everyone stampeded for the newsstands to devour the latest developments. But it was another full day before the news that everyone had been waiting for came.

'Have you heard?' As they collected the meagre breakfast provided by the hostel, one of Lily's classmates broke the news. 'Hitler's dead!'

Lily bolted her toast and gulped down her tea, then raced out to the nearest newsstand. Jim had beaten her to it, and met her halfway, waving the paper. With solemn music and drum rolls, it had been announced on German radio last night. Hitler, apparently, had fallen 'fighting the forces of Bolshevism'.

'Fallen, indeed!' scorned Jim. 'Trying to make out he was some kind of hero defending the citadel? We all know he's been holed up in his bunker for weeks!'

Lily was scanning the paper.

'What do you think happened? Did he kill himself?'

'Either that or one of his henchmen that's still got a slight grip on reality saw him off. He's finished, whatever.'

'It's finished. It's over now, Jim, surely.'

There was an even more peculiar atmosphere in the classroom in the days after that. Everyone was keyed up somehow; everything felt unreal. The war in the Far East raged on, but all eyes were on Europe. Hitler had supposedly handed power to Admiral Dönitz who was fighting on with the rump of the Nazi army, but with the Red Army laying waste to Berlin, it was a hopeless cause.

Lily waited for a message from Sid but there was no word from him, and not much more from the powers that be, either. The papers reported plans for a celebratory 'Victory in Europe' day, with extended licensing hours for pubs and dance halls, and bonfires allowed for the first time since 1939 (with non-salvageable wood, of course). But the days dragged on and there was no indication of when that day would be, just a sort of limbo. It was hard to concentrate sitting in a classroom, far from home.

'Miss Collins? If I could have your attention?' Lily had been gazing out of the grimy window, wondering what Dora would have to say about it when she replied to Lily's excited postcard home. 'What steps could you take to increase interest in a promotion that doesn't seem to be working?'

Lily dragged her attention back to the imaginary store and imaginary footwear department where a promotion of slippers hadn't yielded the hoped-for boost to sales. So much for teacher's pet!

Finally, the announcement came. At 2.40 in the morning on May 7th, Germany surrendered unconditionally on all fronts. There would be two days of public holiday, with the first, May 8th, to be called Victory in Europe Day. VE Day had arrived!

There was a long queue for the telephone booth at the hostel, and even longer ones outside every phone box, but Lily was determined.

'I don't care how far we walk, I've got to make contact with Sid, and I have to try and get a message to Mum!' she said, dragging Jim in her wake as they

281

pressed through the crowd. Londoners had started celebrating early. They were spilling onto the pavements from the pubs, music was blaring from gramophones in the flats above shops and people were dancing in the streets. 'I never imagined I wouldn't be with her on the day the war ended!'

'I know. It'll be fun being here, though.' Jim had caught her up and steered her round a puddle of spilt beer.

'There was talk of a party in Brook Street when it finally came,' said Lily.

'Well, your mum'll be at the centre of organising that! She won't have a chance to miss you,' said Jim consolingly.

Eventually they came across an empty phone box in a quiet square near Regent's Park. Lily tried Sid first, but at his lodgings his landlady said he wasn't back yet. Lily left a message asking him to call the hostel and suggest a place for them to meet up next day. Then she dialled Beryl's number — it was the only way to get a message to her mum.

'Hinton 353?'

Lily pressed her pennies into the slot.

'Beryl? It's me, Lily!'

'Lily!' shrieked Beryl. 'Oh, isn't it wonderful! It's all over! And you're in London for it! What's it like there? Les has gone down the pub — there'll be some sore heads in the morning!' Just as Lily was wondering if she'd ever get a word in, Beryl turned from the mouthpiece and hollered. 'Dora! It's your daughter on the phone!'

Then there was a crash and a wail from Bobby. Beryl dropped the receiver to see to him and Lily turned to Jim, who'd squashed in the box with her.

'Mum's there!'

Bobby was soothed, the receiver was picked up again, and Lily heard her mum's voice.

'Hello! How are you getting on? How's your course going?'

'Never mind that, what do you think? Isn't it marvellous about the war? I'm sorry I'm not there with you.'

'Oh, I knew you'd start worrying about that! I shan't be on my own! There's not much doing in their street, so Beryl and Les are coming over to the Brook Street party, and so's Gladys and the twins, because Bill can't get home. No one'll mind as long as they bring a contribution for the food.'

'Oh, good!' Lily felt a surge of relief. 'What's it like in Hinton? It's chaos here.'

'It's the same. The bunting's up already in most places, and the flags, and Bobby's got his little Union Jack to wave. You've just caught me, I'm off to the WI in a minute to make paper crowns for the children.'

Lily sighed happily. Her mum was busily occupied; she might not have her family around her but she was among friends. That was the next best thing.

'The pips are about to go, Mum,' she said. 'I'm trying to contact Sid, to meet up tomorrow. I love you, I'll see you soon!'

'Bye, love — enjoy yourselves!'

Lily replaced the receiver. Jim put his arms round her.

'There's no one waiting for the phone,' he said. 'Let's have our own private celebration.'

They parted reluctantly outside their respective hostels. They'd walked back through even more exuberant crowds, but they had to be in by ten or they'd be locked out, even on a night like this. Inside, the message Lily had hoped for was pinned up on the noticeboard.

MEET YOU 2.30 P.M. VICTORIA
MONUMENT IN FRONT OF THE
PALACE. I'LL MAKE SURE YOU CAN
SEE ME. SID.

'Have you seen this?' Beryl waved the *Daily Mirror*. 'They've given us a weather forecast!'

'What's it say?' Gladys looked up from the production line in Dora's kitchen. Dora was slicing bread; Gladys was spreading a smear of meat paste for the filling.

'Rain,' said Beryl in disgust and read, 'The warm snap of yesterday will not continue.'

'If that's the best they can do they needn't bother!' exclaimed Dora. 'After six years without a forecast I'm better off looking out of the window. It's set fair for the day!'

'Any tea on the go?' Les came in from the back room looking bleary. 'I feel like a slug in a salt mine.'

'We know whose fault that is! And have you left those children on their own in there?' Beryl tutted and scuttled off, not listening to Les's protest that Bobby was listening to a *Toytown* story on the wireless while Joy and Victor were safe in the playpen.

'Family life,' sighed Gladys happily. It wouldn't be long before Bill was home for good, she knew; he'd been told he'd be among the first to be demobbed.

Across town, another little family were savouring their first day of freedom. In Albany Road, where Peter Simmonds had moved into Eileen Frobisher's

284

flat, a street party was in preparation too. But Peter seemed subdued.

'What is it?' Eileen and Peter were helping to set up trestle tables and chairs down the length of the road. Neighbours were starting to bring out plates of sandwiches and hastily made cakes, jugs of squash, and pots of tea.

Peter tucked a chair into place.

'I'm all for celebrating,' he said. 'We deserve to. God knows it's been a long time coming. But you have to give a moment's pause for all the lives that have been lost, and the injured, fighting men and civilians. And then there's the prisoners. And the refugees. Millions of them. And as for those camps they've discovered . . . '

Horrific pictures and newsreels had begun coming out, about the so-called labour camps. Auschwitz, Belsen, Dachau. Names to strike terror into your heart; scenes of unimaginable cruelty. Millions exterminated, and the survivors barely alive.

Eileen touched his arm. As a former soldier, he felt it deeply.

'I do,' she said. 'Give pause, that is. Some people have paid such a heavy price. But I thank God for that silly injury that got you out of it, and gave us the chance to meet.'

'I do too, believe me! It's all part of life's lottery isn't it?' He smiled, and paused. 'I've never told you this, but before I had to leave the Army I was due to be posted to the Far East. Burma. I'd have been there through all of it, the Irrawaddy, the push for Rangoon . . . We mustn't forget the war out there isn't over. And the Nazis've got nothing on the Japanese. It's going to take something pretty special to make them lay down their arms.'

John ran up, wearing a paper crown.

'When can we have tea? I'm hungry!'

★ ★ ★

Daphne Tunnicliffe was in the garden. The wisteria on the terrace was coming out; the lilac was in flower, the ferns were uncurling and the hardy geraniums showing their colours. The garden was coming to life again, and she could take real pleasure in that for the first time in years, though even over the winter it had seemed more alive, thanks to having children in the house once more.

The last of Hitler's dreadful rockets had fallen on London at the end of March: after Easter, Joe and Barbara had gone home. It had been a painful parting for her as she'd handed them over to the chaperones at the station. The children were excited at the prospect, of course, Barbara proud in the new coat Daphne had had made for her out of one of Violet's, Joe bright-eyed, his socks round his ankles as usual. Barbara had hugged her and given her a kiss; even Joe had let himself be hugged. He'd promised to write, and he had, bless him — a few lines to say they'd arrived safely. Daphne doubted she'd hear any more — he was a ten-year-old boy, for goodness' sake. He'd be too busy playing on bombsites to sit and write letters! Daphne had told them they'd be welcome to come and stay any time, but she doubted that would happen, either. She missed them, but she was grateful to have had them. If she'd helped them, they'd helped her more — to see that life had to go on. There would always be another generation coming through, new lives to nurture. A future.

The telephone shrilled inside the house and she went to answer it. It was Cedric.

'I wondered . . . ' he began, 'today seems to have come upon us so suddenly in the end, it's rather taken me by surprise. Are you doing anything special? Seeing anyone? Joining in with anything?'

'No,' she replied. 'I was in the garden. Just thinking.'

'Oh, you don't want to do too much of that! Especially not today. Perhaps then,' he hazarded, 'unless you'd rather be on your own . . . would you like some company?'

'I'd like that very much.'

'Oh, good.' He sounded relieved. He was always so tentative with her, never wanting to presume. 'You see, the military have given me my car back. It came last week. Rather battered, and painted an unattractive khaki.'

'Oh dear!'

'But on the other hand, there is a small residue of petrol in the tank. I could come over and we could take a short drive. Out into the country, perhaps. Take a look at this England, the one we've been fighting for.'

'Oh, that would be lovely!' exclaimed Daphne. 'Thank you! I'll pack us a picnic, shall I?'

'Excellent! Shall we say three o'clock?'

'That will be perfect,' she smiled. 'Thank you, Cedric. I can't think of any better way to spend the rest of the day.' She hesitated. Oh, why not say it? It was the truth, she realised. 'Or anyone I'd rather spend it with.'

★ ★ ★

In Brook Street, the party was well underway. Everyone had eaten and drunk their fill and someone had wheeled out their old upright piano for a sing-song. First the old songs from Dora's youth, from the music hall and the First War: 'My Old Man Said Follow the Van', 'Pack Up Your Troubles', and 'Tipperary'. Then the newer ones — the ones, they said, that had won the war: 'Roll Out the Barrel', 'We'll Meet Again', and the one they were singing now, 'There'll Always Be an England'.

Gladys was holding the twins on her lap, encouraging them to clap along, Beryl was giving it her all, and Les had revived and was singing lustily. Bobby, worn out with the excitement and full of food, had fallen asleep under the table, his head resting on Buddy, who was similarly replete. Dora got up and slipped quietly inside.

She poured herself a glass of water and went through to the back room where so much had happened in the last six years — so much anxiety, fear, and tears, but so much love and laughter too. She looked at the photographs on the mantelpiece — her faded wedding picture, Arthur by her side; the three children when they were young; Sid in his uniform; Reg and Gwenda on their wedding day. She took a letter from behind the clock. It was from Canada, dated the end of April. She smoothed it out and read it again.

Dear Dora,

Thank you for your last letter and all your news. I'm so glad to hear you've been discharged by the hospital — that was a scare we could all have done without. I hope you are continuing to take care and rest well — I know what a busy person you usually are and like to be. But you must take good care of yourself. I hope Lily and Jim can soon set another date for their big day but it's great they have the opportunity of this training course. I always thought those two would go far.

Well, it seems things are moving to a conclusion in Europe at least — and I have to tell you, Dora, also over here. In addition to her other problems, the doctors at the sanatorium have informed me that Grace has a tumour. It seems it's quite advanced and there is no cure. I've known about it for some weeks, but obviously didn't say anything before, when you were unwell yourself. The end is not going to be pretty, but I gather will not be too long drawn out, which is something. All in all, it's maybe a mercy. Poor Grace has had no life since our son was killed and it affected her so badly.

I hope I'm not being premature, Dora, in saying that when the end has come for her, and the war itself is over, and things open up again, I hope to come back to England someday and look you up. Let's hold that thought for now.

God bless you.

Sincerest good wishes as ever to you and the family,

Your friend,

Sam

Dora folded the letter and put it in her pocket. She often handed Sam's letters to Lily to read, but maybe she wouldn't do that with this one.

★ ★ ★

'We're never going to find him in this crush! What was Sid thinking?'

It was half past two and Lily and Jim were trying to make their way across the Mall to the monument, but the crowds were pressed so tightly together it was impossible to make any headway.

'We'll find him all right!' Jim, who with his height was head and shoulders above most of the crowd, had spotted something. 'Look!'

He grabbed Lily round the waist and lifted her off her feet so she could see too.

Sid was at the monument itself. He was sitting on one of the bronze lions which surrounded the marble Queen Victoria, and holding above his head a banner on two sticks. It read:

LILY COLLINS! OVER HERE!

'Trust you! I'm not a bit embarrassed!' she teased when, thanks to Sid's semaphore, they finally reached him and embraced.

'I thought it was genius.' Sid was trying to roll up his banner as best he could in the confines of the crowd when it was promptly seized on and carried off by a couple of revellers, for no reason at all.

'Why are we here, though?' asked Jim. 'Do you know something we don't?'

'The King,' said Sid cryptically. 'They're going to do a balcony appearance, the whole family. Let's get ourselves in pole position. I won't be happy till we're right up front, practically hanging off the gates.'

And that's where they were when at three o'clock, sure enough, the King and Queen and the two prin-cesses appeared on the balcony. If the noise of the crowd had been loud before, now it became deafening. The royal party smiled and waved, and smiled and waved again, and again. The crowd waved back. They gave three cheers, several times, then burst into the national anthem and 'Land of Hope and Glory'. Lily looked up at the King and Queen, then down and around, this way and that, marvelling that she was there. The crowd — men and women, old and young, serviceman and civilians — surged and moved. Some were laughing, some dabbing their eyes; others, complete strangers, were hugging ecstatically. Jim was shaking his head in wonderment, Sid cheering. Lily knew she'd never forget it.

Finally, the royal family went back inside, but Lily felt sure it wouldn't be their last appearance of the day.

'What now?' she asked Sid.

'Something to drink!' he said. 'If we can find a pub that hasn't run out of beer. Maybe something to eat as well, a bit of a rest, and a catch-up. And then . . . there's someone I'd like you to meet.'

Lily turned to him, excited.

'Jerome?'

Sid shrugged, almost shy for once.

'Seemed like a good day to cement Anglo-American relations, don't you think?'

They walked and walked. There was so much to see and it was impossible to find anywhere to sit and rest anyhow; in a lot of places they were carried along by the crowds, drunk and sober, singing and dancing. It was difficult to stay together and after Lily had twice been pounced on by drunks and Jim had been dragged into an impromptu conga, they formed a human chain, holding hands, with Lily in the middle.

291

As darkness fell, London lit up. Sid brought them in a winding way round to Whitehall, where all the Government buildings were floodlit, filling the streets with warm yellow light; so were the Houses of Parliament and Big Ben, whose bells had been stilled for the duration of the war. Now, like the church bells, they could ring again. Along the Embankment, strings of lights were on, reflected like diamonds in the water; tugs on the river chugged up and down and hooted for joy. It was a London that no one had seen for six years.

When they'd taken it all in, Sid steered them in the other direction, towards Piccadilly Circus, where the neon sign advertising Gordon's Gin, which Lily knew well from pre-war newsreels, had been replaced with one reading simply 'Peace in Europe'. The famous statue of Eros had been removed at the start of the war and the site boarded over — now everything like that could be restored.

'There he is!' Sid dragged Lily and Jim behind him, forcing their way across the packed pavement. In the doorway of a tobacconists stood a man in the uniform of the American Air Force.

He was tall, dark and handsome; of course he was. She would have expected no less. Her brother made the introductions. Jerome swept off his cap, took Lily's hand, and bent over it in a formal, old-fashioned way.

'I'm happy to meet you at last,' he said. His voice was warm and friendly with a soft American accent, certainly not a drawl. And then, almost teasingly, 'I've heard a lot about you.'

I wish I could say the same about you, thought Lily, trying not stare too hard. His hair was so dark it was almost black, as sleek as sable. He had olive skin, a small moustache and laughing eyes, like Sid's own. She liked him; she knew that straight away.

'I dread to think what!' she replied.

Sid was watching her, smiling, but she sensed his tension. She knew she'd be the only one of the family ever to meet his chosen partner; her approval meant everything to him.

'It's very nice to meet you too,' said Lily. And for Sid, she added, 'I mean it. Sid means a lot to me.'

'No wonder,' Jerome grinned. 'He's a great guy.' A look passed between him and her brother, who gave a bashful grin. Jerome turned to Jim. 'And you must be Jim.' The men shook hands. 'You two are taking the plunge, I hear.'

'Yes,' said Jim emphatically. 'As soon as we get home, we're setting the date for the wedding and we're not moving it again!'

'Let's drink to that!'

Jerome had brought cans of American beer from the base. He opened them deftly and handed them out. Lily sneezed and spluttered as the fizz and a taste she wasn't used to hit the back of her throat. Sid thumped her between the shoulder blades while Jerome apologised.

'An acquired taste, maybe?' he said. 'You'll get used to it.'

Crowds flowed past them still cheering and shouting, as they stood in a huddle, drinking and chatting. Jerome told them about the exuberant scenes that had been relayed from the States, ticker-tape parades in New York, a presidential address in Washington, jubilation in every state.

'So, what are we doing now?' he asked after a while.

'I think this is where we part,' said Sid. 'These two

lovebirds have been stuck with me all afternoon. I think they probably want to be on their own.'

It was a tactful way of saying that he and Jerome would like their own private celebration too. Lily knew that the Trocadero, a club which had a men-only bar — and where Sid and Jerome had met — was nearby. She suspected they'd be heading there.

The men shook hands again and Lily kissed her brother goodbye.

'He seems lovely,' she whispered. 'But you will be careful, won't you, Sid?'

The danger in her brother's chosen lifestyle would always be a worry to her. There was so much prejudice against his sort.

'Oh, come on, Sis,' grinned Sid. 'Love conquers all, you know. If we don't believe in that, what can we believe in?'

He winked at his sister and lifted a hand as he and Jerome walked away.

* * *

Lily and Jim let them go. They lingered in the doorway, dazed by the constant swirl of people, dazzled by the lights, their ears buzzing from the thrum of the crowd. Then Jim took her hand and led her out onto the pavement again. Wandering on, they found themselves in St James's Park. It was hardly empty, but the crowds were thinner, people seated in groups or collapsed on the ground, sleeping or passed out. They found themselves a space as far away from anyone else as they could. Jim spread his jacket on the ground and they lay back on it, looking up at the sky.

'My feet are stinging!' said Lily. 'You only realise

when you stop.'

'We've walked miles,' Jim replied. 'All in a huge, big loop. But I wouldn't have missed it. Would you?'

Lily snuggled closer.

'No. I'm glad now that we were here. Just us two. And I'm thinking . . . '

'What?'

'That maybe it was meant to be . . . that we didn't manage to get married before the war was over. Now, when we do, there'll be nothing hanging over us.'

'Except the sky and the stars.' It was a clear night, and away from the newly lit streets, they seemed incredibly bright. 'Just think, they've been up there all the time. Looking down on us, thinking 'what do those crazy humans think they're doing to each other now? Will they never learn?"

'And they'll still be up there when we're gone,' said Lily dreamily. 'Long gone.'

Jim turned on his side to face her.

'Yes. But before then, Lily, we've got a lot of living to do, you and me. We've had to live a half-life till now, but this is our real start. All our future together. And it's going to be bright just like the stars, I know it.'

He took her in his arms and kissed her, and Lily knew it too.

Author's Note

It's no secret that coronavirus has devastated traditional shops. 2021 finally saw the collapse of Debenhams, the last remaining department store in many towns and cities, though the name remains — bought, inevitably, by an online retailer. There's no doubt shopping has changed for good, which only makes me feel even more nostalgic and affectionate as I step through the doors of Marlows, which now feels like pure social history.

The Victory Girls was written, edited and produced in and between the various lockdowns of 2020/2021. That it's in your hands at all is down to the tenacity and dedication of the HarperCollins team, led by my editor, Lynne Drew, and supported by Lara Stevenson, Jennifer Harlow, Jeannelle Brew, Isobel Coburn and Sarah Munro. I would be remiss not to thank Lydia Mason, who copyedited the manuscript and helped to polish up the details. Claire Ward and her colleagues produced another brilliant cover for the HarperCollins edition — my thanks to them all. Thanks also to my agent, Broo Doherty, who's been on the end of the phone at all times for virtual tea and pep talks.

I needed a lot of medical advice for this book — not for me personally, thankfully — but for the characters. Dr Mostafa El-Dessouki and Dr Mark Crooks very generously helped me in their areas of expertise. Any mistakes are mine alone.

Step forward, too, the usual cast of friends, in particular Mary Cutler, Claire MacRorie and Debbie Crooks, and my family — Livi and Ash, Clara, Cressie and my husband, John — all of whom allow me to witter on and work things through.

If there's one good thing about coronavirus it's that it seems to have sparked a return to reading — specifically books about the war years, which had their own very real dramas, hardships and losses. It's a comfort, I think, to read about the past and to know we've been through worse — and also to read books which reinforce how much good kindness, calm, common sense and caring can do. I hope *The Victory Girls* does just that.

So finally, my biggest thank you is to you, the readers who've warmed to Lily, Gladys, Beryl and their world and tell me so on Facebook or Twitter. Tapping away at the keyboard on my own all day, it's so encouraging to hear that you love the characters as much as I do. If you can help other readers to find and enjoy the books by posting a review on Amazon or GoodReads and by spreading the word, that would be great too. And do look out for the next Victory Girls book, due in spring 2022.

Jo
March 2021